UNTIMELY RIPPED

UNTIMELY RIPPED

Revised Edition

Joel Weinsheimer

Authors Choice Press

San Jose New York Lincoln Shanghai

Untimely Ripped
Revised Edition

Authors Choice Press
an imprint of iUniverse.com, Inc.

For information address:
iUniverse.com, Inc.
5220 S 16th, Ste. 200
Lincoln, NE 68512
www.iuniverse.com

ISBN: 0-595-19956-9

Printed in the United States of America

For Joyce, with love

Epigraph

Macbeth. I bear a charmèd life, which must not yield
To one of woman born.
Macduff.   Despair thy charm,
And let the angel whom thou still hast served
Tell thee, Macduff was from his mother's womb
Untimely ripped.

Chapter 1

That warm July evening when my life began—or began to end, I don't know which—I left Libby singing to the last dishes in the sink and drove slowly into Pequot Lakes for a copy of the *Star Tribune*. That's what I'd done every night since the *STrib* fired me. Not that I cared what was in it after spending nine months of self-imposed exile in my mother's cabin at the lake. I'd been writing part-time for the *Lakes Area Sentinel* ("Pets Blessed in Second Annual Ceremony: Five cats, nine dogs, and two gerbils baptized in lake water"—actually they were just sprinkled because of concerns about full immersion). All this had pretty much cured me of any curiosity about the Cities, the latest sales numbers for Jesse Ventura action figures, the umpteenth referendum to build an outdoor Twins stadium, or whatever happened to be the crisis du jour.

So it was not the news that drew me irresistibly to greater metropolitan Pequot Lakes for my paper that evening and every evening. It was the bylines. That's really all I ever wrote for when I was with the paper—the byline proclaiming the identity of Evan Wade to the entire literate world. So now, by way of this night's penance for the stupidity that got me fired, I forced myself to look once again at the place where, with a little less self-assurance, my name should have been displayed. Once again I forced myself to read the names of Anne Chisolm and Ben Drake, who had been working my beat, writing my stories, and stealing my byline, while I sat cooling my heels for nine months in a lake of self-pity.

But what I read under Ben Drake's byline that evening jerked me out so hard that I would never be the same: "Prominent Doctor Slain. Dr. Marian Barclay was found dead in her Lakewood home on Saturday evening....No signs of forced entry. No suspects apprehended in the case...." No nothing.

Back at the cabin, my head still reeling, I told Libby I was going down to the dock to sit for a while. "I'll come down in a minute," she hollered back, as I reached the steeply banked stairs that descended down into the darkness and the memorable past.

I knew Marian Barclay from way back, long before Libby, before the *STrib*, before college even. We were hardly more than kids. So long ago, but I still remember everything—her lush, auburn hair, multi-layered in the glare of summer sun, hair the color of bright gold on the surface but in the depths almost black. I remember the anklet chain with the little heart on it that caught droplets of water that glistened there, liquid silver, in the moonlight.

But most of all I remember her eyes. Marian was not what I would call a pretty girl. She had nothing of what I and a million other guys were panting for at that age, the bouncing boobs that raise a young man's fancy, the artful squeals and giggles that promise a lively game of beach blanket bingo. The guys around the lake preferred the Nordic types, and she was not pretty that way. Marian Barclay was beautiful. She radiated beauty from within, the special kind of beauty that can make a grown man weep. It was a solemn, almost sad beauty that makes a man want to embrace, and protect, and cleave to a woman forever.

But, truth is, that summer I was still a boy mostly, older than Marian by a few months, but years younger in every other way. I was ready for any bump and tickle that offered itself, of course. But I was not ready for her. For Marian's solemn beauty communicated a silent reprimand to boyish jokes and games. She left me ill at ease, at a loss for what I was supposed to do exactly. I felt as if her gaze were making some nameless demand I could not fathom or posing some invisible threat I could not avoid. She almost never laughed, smiled rarely, and then only with her eyes.

Those eyes. I would do something simple and thoughtful—she loved the water lilies I'd wade out to pick for her—and my sole reward would be her sober, smiling eyes, slowly rising to meet mine. I would say something childish—"don't let the eels get in your swimsuit!"—and Marian would turn to me, just letting her silent reproof wash over me with those wide, fearsomely deep eyes. Midnight blue eyes, just short of black. Bottomless eyes, the color of the lake on moonless nights. A man looking into such eyes too long, too deep, would surely drown.

Those eyes were now closed. I didn't have time just then to wonder what happened to her, because for me, Marian was not yet gone—at least no more so than she had been for the last twenty years. I hadn't thought much about her after we had words and parted ways that fall. A whole lifetime, it seemed, had intervened since then. She went on to Carleton and Med School. I struggled through my sophomore year at the U before starting to hang around the *STrib*. But now, sitting wordlessly on the dock bench, just like we did so many nights that summer, I listened to the quiet shlup of ripples feebly protesting against the shore, and a tidal wave of memories flooded over me.

By the time of ice-out that spring, the whole lake knew somebody had bought the mansion on the point. You couldn't call it a cabin, Mom said, even if it was on a lake. We lived in a cabin, a real cabin, the same one her parents built and rebuilt and raised her in. That was long before the green river of 3M and Honeywell profits started flowing north, transporting replicas of the trophy homes in Kenwood to Greater Minnesota. The Lake Country had finally become a suburb for Minneapolis, the City of Lakes. Bought and sold three times in the ten years since it was built, the mansion on the point was too big for our modest lake, a massive, three-story edifice, puffing its ostentatious chest out from the steep bank, as if to say, "I've got it, and you don't."

None of us locals had ever been inside. The only way you could get in was to take the "cabin tour," originally conducted by the Historical Society to celebrate our log cabin heritage, though most of the stops now were not at "real cabins" but half-log monuments to capitalism, like this one. You could see its glories from the outside, though. It was built to be looked upon. Every weekend evening in the summer, a long flotilla of pontoon boats carrying lobster-red pilgrims from the Cities circled the lake in ritual procession. As they passed the shrine on the hill, its richly varnished cedar catching the last gold of sunset, androgynous men with budding breasts and great bellies, pointed the hand that did not hold the Bud toward the object of their silent envy and vocal contempt.

I suppose whoever was in the house could have heard the comments shouted above the roar of outboards. You can hear everything on a lake. But nobody tried to whisper because we had never seen anybody there. So one night, after the procession had ended, when I swung our little fishing boat with the souped up six-horse Merc toward the point and cut the engine, I was a little surprised to see a dark profile on the dock bench.

"Sorry, I didn't know anybody was here," I called out in apology for being a little too close. There aren't any property markers on a lake, but civility prescribes a certain distance.

"Nobody here but me." The quarter moon emerged from behind a cloud to reveal a girl who looked eighteen or so. She was just sitting there looking out over the black water. Her hunched shoulders made her wet swimsuit gap a little. She shivered now and then from the chill night breeze but seemed reluctant to go back inside. Her long, smooth legs stretched out to the full. Her toes pointed out, just touching at the tips. A silver anklet chain caught the moon.

"Been swimming?"

"Yes," she said without glancing in my direction. "You?"

"Not me. I'm not much of a swimmer."

"What are you doing out here, then?"

"Well…fishing." I was sitting in a fishing boat after all. And I didn't want to say I was tooling around the lake with a six-horse Merc because I had nothing better to do with my life.

"Where's your pole?"

"Oh. Yeah. Guess I forgot it."

"Then you can't be much of a fisherman either."

The male ego is a fragile thing, like a mosquito, bloodthirsty but easily crushed. No hint of a laugh could be detected in her flat voice, and she hadn't even looked at me, though the boat floated only a few feet away. The black water held her eyes. She was mesmerized by it, the way others are mesmerized by fire, gazing unblinkingly at something I couldn't see.

"Good," she said suddenly standing up, as if having come to a decision. "I hate guys who go out trolling. It's so superficial." She turned delicate features framed by long dark hair away from the lake until her eyes caught mine. "They think a big pole is enough."

"Absolutely," I replied. "Quite true."

"I'm Marian. Want to come in for a Coke?"

"Sure! I'm Evan Wade."

Yesss! I thought. Victory snatched from the jaws of the deep. I had landed a live one! I jumped out of the boat, tied it to the dock, and followed Marian to a little elevator thing that carried people back up the hill to the house.

"Cool," I said in genuine admiration of the device. I had climbed the seventy-two stairs that separated our cabin from the lake so many times that I had buns of steel. She went on without reply to open the front door and turn on the light. What a place! The whole works. Oak floors, a fireplace of lake stones rising three stories to a beamed cathedral ceiling, and all of it decorated like the centerfold of *Northern Living* magazine.

She seemed to notice none of it.

"I really love your home," I said with more than polite enthusiasm.

Now, for the first time, Marian let her disdain wash over me, her deep eyes flashing.

"This isn't a home. It's a tourist attraction. Nobody actually lives here. They just visit for a while. My father and Francine bought it fully furnished last spring. They'll sell it in a year or two and never think twice about it. When my mother was alive, it all used to be different. We lived in a home that really belonged to us, and wasn't just something we bought." Gazing through the vast picture window that looked onto the invisible lake, Marian had left the mansion on the point far behind, not to mention the young man in it.

"Everything in our house showed the touch of my mother's hand," she mused. "The doorframe with pencil marks, where she put a ruler on my head, and said, 'Look how big you're getting, Marian!' The lilacs she planted and cried when the deer ate them. I cried, too, right along with her, and she caught me up close to her with a sob and a laugh. That house was like a book that told the story of our lives." Marian paid so little attention to me, I began to wonder whether she remembered I was there.

"That's why Dad sold it right after she died. Mom was still there in everything, he said, and he couldn't bear it. To me it was like he sold a photo album, worthless to everybody else but priceless to me. It's been almost eight years since we moved out, but I still haven't forgiven him. I miss our house. I miss Mom, and every year I lose a little bit more of her, because I have no place to hang my memories. No home."

"I know, I know," she snapped before I could get a word in. "The homeless girl in the mansion!"

I was about to protest that I was thinking no such thing, but then stopped. I seemed to be doing all right by keeping my mouth shut. She wasn't really talking to me anyway. At least, she never looked at me. Her little home movie was an extension of a private reverie that had begun on the dock bench below and hadn't ended yet. The habits of loneliness don't suddenly stop just because you're in company, and Marian was lonely, all right. Lonely and distant and gorgeous.

I was a goner.

I remember seeing a short once in one of these artsy movie houses. No dialogue. It opens with a man fishing from the shore of some gulf or ocean. He would bait his hook, cast out far, and reel in one gleaming fish after another. After a while he gets hungry from all the work and spies a bag lying on the shore. He takes out a fat sandwich from the bag, and as he is bolting it down, a hook emerges through his cheek. The screen darkens as he is helplessly dragged out into the deep.

Marian had done nothing to bait the hook but tell me a sad story about an eighteen-year-old who still missed her mother. If I had been less silenced by where I was and with whom, I might easily have altered my whole life and hers with a simple observation: from my experience, living with your mother in the family home doesn't quite live up to the nostalgia-filled reruns of "I Remember Mama" that Marian had summoned up. I realized that, in sober fact, living in the home of my mother and my mother's mother actually meant little more than drinking out of ancestral jelly glasses. I was not quite so quick as Marian to dismiss what money really can buy.

For Mom and me, a penny more or less made all the difference. She never had a job that paid much above minimum, and so we had to make do. I was grateful and all. But just a few more worldly goods, as Mom called them, would have made my life a lot saner. When I was sixteen, I lusted for a leather bomber jacket I saw in the Daytons window during our annual trip to the Cities. Silly, I know, but for months I yearned for that jacket with the heart's true yearning, as other men yearn for purity or power. We weren't really poor, but a life of unrelieved renunciation deluded both of us about the importance of things we didn't have, inflating them with exaggerated desire in my case and contempt in hers.

The money made a difference between Mom and me, too. She thought that abstinence, which made her scrape Land'o'Lakes wrappers for the last bit of butter, was putting stars in her crown. As far as I was concerned, it was pointless or, worse, self-indulgent, even miserly. We were sitting on a pot of gold. Though the cabin wasn't much of anything, the land was worth a fortune—ten acres of pine and birch and red oak, with a quarter mile of prime shoreline. Selling it, we'd have enough to buy a decent house in town or the country or anywhere so long as it was off the lake. Developers were always coming round and salivating, and I kept telling Mom to take the money and run. I never cared about the lake anyway. I never cared much about anything, except that leather jacket.

Headlights swept through the Great Room. "Looks like they're back from the Club," Marian said, and soon a high female voice gave out with a singsong "We're home! Sorry we're so late, Marian darling. I hope you got something for yourself to….Oh, and hello to you too, young man," the woman gushed in surprise. As I rose shyly to greet her, I couldn't help feeling the visceral teenage guilt of being detected in flagrante by The Parents. Other than being alone, without adult supervision, we were doing nothing to be ashamed of in the slightest, of course, but perhaps in some obscure way sexual guilt is always justified.

"Marian, won't you introduce me to your friend?" Francine Barclay was really quite attractive, even elegant in her way. And if you've got it, flaunt it, I guess. Her golf blouse was open one button too many, or too few, tempting you to sneak a peek at the amplitudes cradled therein, but actually revealing nothing. Her saffron shorts were made of a silky material that is somehow formal and casual at once, as most befits the game of golf and a few of the people who play it. But they fit her all right. Francine Barclay had a waist and narrow hips at an age when most women have lost them from childbirth—or child-rearing.

"Francine, this is Evan, Evan…."

"Wade. Evan Wade," I chimed in, sounding a little too close for comfort to "Bond. James Bond." Mom and I knew everybody around here, and so I didn't get much practice with formal introductions. "Glad to meet you. I was just going by in the boat and I happened to…"

"Well, we're so pleased you stopped in." Francine didn't shake my outstretched hand; she clasped it tenderly as if we were dear friends, and didn't let go.

"Marian doesn't know many young people at the lake, do you, honey? I keep telling her, You've got to be friends to make friends. Don't you think so too, Evan? Will you be going to college next year? Marian's going to Carleton and then to Med School. Aren't you, dear?

"I'm considering it, Francine, but I really think I should get started in college before I decide what comes afterward."

"Oh, Med School for sure. A doctor's the only thing these days for a young woman of intelligence and means. Don't you agree, Evan? Why, when I was young, we had only three choices, teacher, nurse, and secretary. Besides being a mother, of course. It was so lucky, when Buddy's first wife passed away, that I was already working right there by his side to help him through that terrible time. Oh, and here's Buddy now." She led me, my hand still manacled in hers, toward the portly but distinguished-looking man who had just made a somewhat stumbling entrance into the kitchen, tossing car keys on the table.

"Buddy, this is Evan Wade, Marian's new friend. Evan, this is my husband—my cara sposa, as they say in Italian." I would have had more confidence that Francine knew a third word of that language, if she hadn't called it Eyetalian.

"Hey." Marian's father grunted this warm salutation with unaffected ease. "Want something to drink?" He sauntered over to the wet bar whose gleaming taps and crystal decanters beckoned invitingly. "How 'bout a beer? Or maybe you'd prefer the company of Mr. Daniels or Mr. Beam. Jack and Jim, to their friends. Ever notice that the finest liquor bears men's names? Now, Francine—the only gentleman she allows down her throat is Johnny Walker." He chortled deeply at his wit, since nobody else was.

"I was just getting Evan a Coke when you came in," Marian interjected, trying to conceal her father's vulgarity and her own embarrassment. Marian's dark eyes flashed daggers to which he had long since become invulnerable.

"You're old enough for more than Coke, aren't you?" Buddy inquired, one eyebrow raised. They weren't his eyes she inherited.

"Only in Wisconsin," I had to admit. That was back when the states set their own drinking ages, and many a Wisconsin carry-out battened itself on the greenbacks of Minnesota teenagers.

"Yes, dear, you just get Evan a Coke." Francine seemed inexplicably unaffected by the whole exchange, as if she were hard of hearing. But I imagine Buddy Boor gave her ample opportunity to develop a facility for oblivion.

"You run along to the kitchen, Marian. Evan and I are going to sit down together on the divan here and get to know each other." Francine pulled me down very close to her, though the couch must have been eight feet long. "Who are you, Evan Wade, and where did you come from? Who are your people? I'm absolutely fascinated by families and things. Now, Evan…Wade. Let me see. The Edina Wades, of course! Didn't I meet your parents at the Hillstroms' coming out party for their daughter Tina?"

"No, ma'am, I don't believe so," I replied, hoping she'd leave well enough alone.

"Then it must have been at the fund raiser that Solomon Arcante threw at the IDS Tower when the Guthrie Theatre was having all that terrible money trouble. Wasn't that your father who had us all in stitches when he introduced Sol, who everybody knows is fey, as the Guthrie's fairy godfather?"

"I doubt it, ma'am, but I can't be sure."

"Can't be sure?"

"No, ma'am. Wade is my mother's name."

"Francine…" Less drunk than his wife was opaque, Buddy sounded a warning note from behind the wet bar.

"Oh, how fascinating!" Francine exclaimed. "Your mother's name! Was that the fashion at the time, like hyphenated names is now?"

"Quite unfashionable, I'd say. I never knew my father. He left before he had a chance to marry my mother, but she was a good Catholic girl, one way at least, and so here I am. Evan, the natural son of Evelyn Wade."

"God damn it, Francine!" Buddy exploded. "Why do you have to go sticking your nose in where it's got no fucking business! If you were so goddamn interested in 'families and things,' why didn't you just go and have one of your own? Now, why don't you just leave this poor boy and his mother alone?"

Whether it was Buddy's outburst or my explanation that had managed to penetrate Francine's porcelain consciousness I can't say, but at this point her wonderful opacity apparently failed her. She just stared at me, open-mouthed, with the same look on her face as everybody gets when they realized they've stepped in it, real good.

"Oh, I see…so sorry" was all she could manage.

"No problem," I said, which really was the truth. She had embarrassed herself more than me. I didn't have a problem with my illegitimacy, though nobody likes being called a bastard, especially if they are one. And nobody ever did call me that who died with all his natural teeth.

Sitting there speechless and distracted, Francine had finally liberated my hand, and so I took the opportunity to make my escape.

"I'd really better be going now," I said, standing up.

"Yea, sure, well. See you, then." Buddy uttered his valediction with predictable cordiality and eloquence.

It was when I was leaving that I noticed Marian, undelivered Coke in hand, standing motionless in the dim kitchen, her auburn hair illuminated by a single recessed light from above. Head slightly bowed, she was looking full at me for the first time, really wanting to see who was before her, looking intently, inquiringly, compassionately on this fatherless waif—giving me, in precious compensation for all that had passed, her eyes.

From another world, I heard distant strains of "Come with me, to the sea, to the sea of love." It was Libby plopping down the dark stairs and onto the dock. She had her suit on and a towel slung around her neck. I couldn't tell her about Marian. Nothing but the bare essentials, anyway.

Libby and I were still on slippery ground with each other, though we'd been living together for a while. No need to stir up trouble. Some things other people just wouldn't understand. Some things you're not sure you understand yourself.

"Whatcha doing, big guy?" she asked, flicking her towel at me.

"Just thinking," I said, still gazing out at the lake. (Eyes dark as deep pools rose slowly to meet mine.)

"Yeah, I bet you're thinking how smart you were to stick me with all those dishes."

"Right."

"Well, don't congratulate yourself quite yet, Mr. Thinker. I left the casserole soaking in the sink, and I can hear it calling your name. 'Evan, Evan, will you scrub my back?' Hear it? Hey, I've got an idea! Come on in for a swim with me, and I'll wash the thing myself. Come with me, to the sea! You don't need a suit this time of night."

"Thanks, I really don't feel like it right now." Fact is, I never felt like swimming, even on the doggiest dog days of summer.

Libby sidled up close to me, whispering, "I might even be persuaded to take off my suit, too. Though a nice girl has to watch out for lake eels these days!" (Unsmiling disdain washed over me.)

"Not tonight."

"No swim, huh? Well, ok, Mister, how about a shower then?" At that, Libby cannonballed herself off the dock, creating a giant mushroom of water that drenched me.

"Hey, Evan," she shouted laughing as she came up. "You're the only guy I know who's all wet without ever getting in the lake!"

Chapter 2

"Unto Almighty God we commend the soul of our sister departed, and we commit her body to the ground; earth to earth, ashes to ashes, dust to dust."

The ancient, enfeebled preacher seemed deeply moved by the occasion, though I don't think he'd ever laid eyes on Marian alive. He didn't seem to know much about her. His grief didn't seem forced or artificial, though, just not personal. I suppose he'd buried enough people over enough years that he no longer needed to ask for whom the bell tolls.

"Man, that is born of a woman, hath but a short time to live, and is full of misery. He cometh up, and is cut down, like a flower. In the midst of life we are in death. Amen. Friends, on this sad day, as we lay to rest the mortal remains of Marian Barclay, let us think not only of her tragic and savage death. Rather, let her passionate commitment to life inspire us by example. Life itself was her great vocation. Her life at the hospital was dedicated to bringing life into the world.

"How many mothers' thanks are due to Dr. Barclay. How many babies owe their safe passage to this generous, caring woman who did not receive the blessing of motherhood herself. Think of these babes, crying, laughing, growing into adolescence, maturing into adulthood. Truly, they are her children, the living memorials of her commitment to life. Oh, Death, where is thy victory?

"Jesus said, Let not your heart be troubled. In my Father's house are many mansions: if it were not so, I would have told you. Amen. As we say our last farewells, let us take to our hearts the lesson of her life and be comforted in the certain knowledge that Marian Barclay is not merely at rest. She is truly at home in the mansion of her Heavenly Father."

And so, offering a belated goodbye at the graveside, I hoped finally to conclude the long unfinished story between Marian and me. But the effect was just the opposite. I began to think of her far more often, and more vividly, than I had for many years.

Occasionally I had anxiety dreams about her. Sometimes, I would dream of her body lying motionless on the living room floor where her husband found her. Suddenly the eyes of the corpse would open upon me, full of hurt and accusation. Sometimes, I would thrash around in the bed, flailing my arms and legs, choking and coughing.

Libby didn't know what to do. "Just nightmares," I said. I had hoped that attending the funeral would put an end to my insomnia and Libby's inquisitiveness. No such luck.

It was a beautiful day for a funeral, or a wedding, for that matter. Summer in full bloom, birds dancing in air, and squirrels in trees cavorting for sheer joy of life. On such a day, even the mourners could not help but throw their shoulders back and breathe deeply the breath of life.

I didn't know most of the small inner circle of the grieving, though I scanned them out of journalist's habit. Two men flanked Buddy and Francine. The older one—Simeon Landreau—was sobbing audibly; the younger, Marian's husband, stood bowed, away from Buddy, with one arm around Francine.

A somewhat larger number of people attended the supposedly private ceremony uninvited. The motorcycle cops who led the procession kept the gawkers and well-wishers at a distance. I noticed a couple of glowing young women who were soon to receive the "blessing of motherhood" and a couple of harried, sallow women who already had. A fat boy, too old for Marian to have delivered, slouched half-hidden behind them. There were several other men, workers from the maternity ward, or the cemetery, perhaps. I saw an anorexic-looking girl with very long flaxen hair holding up a pro-life sign, and there was also a certain newspaper reporter whom I had no desire to talk to. I nodded to Ben Drake in a curt way that said, "I recognize you and have nothing to say."

The Barclays had given me permission to pay my respects. Apparently, I had made quite an impression on Francine way back when, because when I phoned, she didn't need to be reminded who I was. Now, seeing her again, after the passage of so many years, she seemed to me untouched by time. Silver hair had replaced gold, to be sure, but she looked all the more elegant, long and lean, hardened by years of insult and forbearance. Buddy, on the other hand, had the gummy, bleary eyes of a man much older than he was, and he was pretty old. He looked shrunken and eviscerated, like an empty bag of skin. Jim Beam had been no friend to Buddy Barclay over the years. He carried a cane, and with each step hammered it into the ground, as if punishing the earth for taking his daughter, as it had taken his first wife, years before.

Buddy had finished receiving condolences from the immediate family when I made my way over to him. "I'm so sorry for your loss. Thank you for allowing me to come," I mumbled, as I shook his hand.

"You!" he exclaimed in surprise, withdrawing his hand as if snakebit. "I never...What the hell are you doing here? I want you out of here! Who invited you?" All heads turned, as his shouts echoed among the gravestones. The police sauntered over. The impertinent fat boy peered between them to get a glimpse of the spat.

Wonderful, I thought, a squabble at the cemetery. I had no idea what brought this on, but it was just great. Maybe the grieving father and I could jump in the grave and duke it out. I was sure Ben Drake wasn't missing any of it.

"Why, Buddy," Francine interjected. "I told Evan he could come. When people called, I just, well,...and you had so much on your mind. Now, honey, it's all right if he wants to..."

"No, it's not all right!" he shouted, brandishing the cane above his head. "What's the deal after twenty years? Do you go to all your old girl-friends' funerals? Or are we going to read about this tomorrow morning in the *Star Tribune*, from you and your scumbag buddies? She gets murdered, and up pops the devil! Here you are, out of the blue! You're no old family friend, come to hold my hand and say how sorry you are. I want to know just what the hell you think you're doing here."

"Buddy, please...." I was grateful for Francine's attempts to intervene, however ineffectual, partly because I had no desire to make a scene but partly also because I didn't know how I would have answered Buddy's questions. I didn't know why I had come. What was it that had drawn me out of exile, back to the Cities? Maybe I was nothing but a curiosity seeker, no more connected to Marian than the others strewn among the trees. "I'll leave, if you like. I didn't mean to...."

"Out! Right now! Wait a minute! What was it with you and Marian, anyway?" Buddy shouted, his feeble frame shaking with rage and frustra-tion. "She wouldn't tell us anything. She pined for you like a mooncalf that fall, and then when she had pined it all out, she just withdrew even further. After a while, she wasn't angry, or sad, or anything—just empty. What the hell happened?"

"I'm sorry, Buddy, I don't know. Marian and I liked each other a great deal, but...."

"Liked each other? You poor blind idiot! Marian didn't **like** you!" Suddenly Buddy softened, as a cloud passed over the glaring, summer sun.

"Oh, the hell with you. The hell with everything. Maybe it was me. I know I wasn't the father I should have been to Marian after her mother died. I missed Sara so much. She kept me straight, she knew what was real. I miss her now...and here," Buddy broke off, staring at the casket already in the ground.

Tears welled up in his eyes, as his face contorted in pain. "Every time I looked at Marian, I saw my Sara gazing back at me, and so I stopped look-ing. I threw myself into the business, so I wouldn't have to be home much.

I threw myself into the bottle. You know, I was actually glad when Marian left? That is what's ripping me up inside, now that I can't have her back. I was actually glad when she left! I couldn't stand their eyes upon me, either of them. And now they're both lying here together. It'll be my turn before long."

Francine could be still no longer. "Oh, now Buddy, you're still strong. Strong as a blue ox. But when our time comes, we'll be over in Hillside, won't we, dear? Just the two of us."

"Yes, Francine. Hillside. Not here. I couldn't bear their eyes."

She led him off on unsteady feet toward the black Cadillac which had brought them from the funeral home that day, the same car in which Francine would ride once more, widowed three weeks to the day thereafter.

"What are you doing here?" asked a voice from behind me. That question would not go away.

I knew who it was without turning around, and I decided that I better say something to him about keeping the little graveside scene he just witnessed out of the paper. "I might ask you the same, Ben. What brings you here? The dog woman demote you from metro to the obits?" (The guys at the *STrib* had little affection for their boss, Sheila Hund, and had taken to calling her the "dog woman," after she had heard the B-word once too often and declared using it to be a firing offense.) "Bit of a comedown, isn't it?"

"Now, Evan, mustn't be vindictive. Ms. Hund was miraculously transformed from a pit bull to a chihuahua, once she extracted a certain thorn from her flesh. All of us down at the office are truly grateful for your demise. Did you get our Thank You card? We weren't sure it would be properly delivered when we addressed it to Evan Wade, The Boonies." He punctuated the line with a little tug on the ends of his hand-tied bowtie. Contrary to type, Ben Drake was one reporter who prided himself on being a natty dresser: every day (as far as I could tell) he displayed a new tie and every day new braces to match.

"By the way," he continued, rocking back on his heels and placing his thumbs behind his suspenders in case I hadn't noticed them, "we loved your lead story on animal baptism. Sheila posted it on the bulletin board as a model for Anne and me and all of us reporters to contemplate—if we want to remain gainfully employed, that is. Very impressive, I'm sure, but maybe I could farm you out an obit once in a while, for auld lang syne. You know, just in case you wanted to try your teeth on something a little meatier."

"Thanks, I'm a vegetarian now. Striking bowtie, by the way. We don't see them much up north. You still moonlighting at K-Mart?"

"Why thank you, Evan! Great things, these bowties. You might try one yourself. Oh, but you've always been afraid to tie the knot, no? Yes, I think that's the way Anne put it after the two of you separated. Yes indeed. 'Afraid to tie the knot,' she said."

"Your tact and sensitivity never cease to amaze, Ben. And congratulations on your promotion. Glad to see you don't mind driving your Beamer over the bones of the dead." We sauntered between the headstones toward the few remaining cars, among them a brilliantly waxed BMW Z3 roadster, gleaming in the afternoon sun. I knew it was his, because he insisted on driving nothing else. But this was a new one—bought with my salary, no doubt—forest green, leather interior soft as a bomber jacket, well appointed, convertible top down.

"You know me. I always enjoy driving, Evan, especially in a cemetery. Something so life-affirming about it, don't you think? Speaking of the dead—not you, this time, but Dr. Barclay—I'm still doing follow-ups on the original story I wrote and..."

"Oh, you wrote that? I hadn't noticed." I propped my butt on his car, centering it precisely over the logo.

"Right. Sure, Mr. Evan 'get-the-headline-for-the-byline' Wade," he replied, as he sidled me away and wiped off each little blue and white square with his monogrammed handkerchief. "With your connections down at the Bureau, we both know very well that the dog woman would have assigned you the Barclay story if you hadn't...and just exactly what did you do to get yourself summarily canned? A story on canine roadkill?"

"Something like that."

"Ms. Hund was a little close-mouthed about the precise circumstances of your termination. You might say she was tight-lipped, except that dogs have no lips. Did you ever reflect on that fact, Evan? It's true. That's why dogs can't kiss. Suck, yes! But kiss? Not anatomically possible! That's Sheila for you."

"Not for me anymore."

"Anyway, I assume your interest here is professional, not personal? The case is still wide open as far as I can tell. Queenie and his pals down at the BCA are interrogating—correction: they're holding 'formal discussions' with—some rabid Pro-Lifers downtown."

"Pro-Lifers? What is Queenie thinking of? Marian Barclay was an Ob-Gyn at Riverside!"

"Yes, yes, but the fact remains that the wackos were stalking her for the last couple weeks, after they saw her going in the Overdale Women's Clinic. Sort of gives a little twist to the parson's lovely eulogy, doesn't it? 'Think of these babes, smiling, crying, laughing.' At Overdale, they're not babes at all, just 'products of conception.' In the midst of life we are in death, all right."

"I don't believe it for a second," I said, disgusted and angry.

"So you knew Dr. Barclay, then? I wondered about that. I didn't think the *Lake Country Sentinel* would send a reporter down to cover a local story like this, but from what I can tell, you're obviously not here as a friend of the Barclay family."

"Friend enough to ask you to keep a lid on the old man's outburst."

"Why, Evan, you're asking me to abrogate my sworn duty to report the truth, the whole truth, and such juicy truth, at that. The story writes itself! 'Funereal Fracas: Solemn Interment of Dr. Marian Barclay Marred by Secretive Squabble!' Everyone will want to read about it."

"Right. Inquiring minds want to know. Ben, this is no news. Bad enough that old man Barclay thinks I'm still one of the scumbags who work for the *STrib*. You've obviously been squeezing a lot of juice out of this story already. Can't you just leave it alone? As a favor to me?

"Of course, Evan. We've always been close, you and I."

"It's just a family matter of no interest to anyone else."

"So you're a family member?"

"No," I admitted.

"Not here as a reporter. Not a family member. So, what are you doing here then?"

Chapter 3

"What are you doing here, Marian?"

For two weeks the Barclay family had not been spied anywhere around the lake. At least that's what our neighbor Hilda Hillstrom said. Nothing escaped Hilda's hundred-power binoculars, which swept the lake tirelessly from dawn to dusk . She was the one who reported Werner Omdahl to the DNR for peeing off his dock that summer. "He kept it zipped after that, you betcha," Hilda confided to us smugly. No doubt she had been scanning tirelessly to observe any repetition of the offense.

At any rate, the Barclays had disappeared back into the Cities as unexpectedly as they had appeared, and I assumed I would never see Marian again. 'The big one that got away' was how I had begun thinking of her, conveniently forgetting that I was the one who was hooked. So when I descended the seventy-two steps down to the water that night, I was startled to find Marian dripping wet on our dock bench, profiled against the moon-lit ripples of the lake.

"Don't you love it, Evan?" Marian gazed out into the darkness. "Don't you love the lake at night? During the day it's not really a lake, just a water park. Seven Flags over Pequot. Teenagers on jetskiis and their sun-baked fathers, floating like red bobbers at the end of ski ropes, yelling 'Hit it!' to some guy in a two-hundred horse runaround."

"That's runabout," I reminded her. Spellbound by the scene, Marian ignored my pedantry, ignored the wet bathing suit that made her hunch her shoulders and shiver slightly.

"At night, after sunset and after the parade of boats is finally over, the lake comes back. That's the time she returns in her mystery. In her majesty. But you know all this, don't you, Evan?"

"Sure," I agreed. "The lake's real nice at night."

"During the day, it's all surface. At night, that's the only time you sense how deep it is. Some nights I wish I could take our elevator down the hillside, past the dock, down through the looking-glass surface into the other world below. That's what I was thinking about when you came over the other night. I saw myself walking all alone in a deep underwater valley, through waving fields of seaweed stirred by a liquid wind. A pair of loons flew overhead. Not in the air. That's not their element. I saw them flying underwater, spiraling down together, two by two, into the depths. Then you were there."

What do you say to someone who has just invited you into their secret garden? "Hmmm," I replied noncommittally. "Sorry I interrupted your day dream, or night dream, or whatever it was."

"You didn't interrupt it, Evan. You became part of it. Don't you ever dream of things like that?"

There she had done it: she had tagged me, and now it was my turn to share with her something deep and private that I hid from everyone else. Truth is, I've never been very good at sharing, not popsicles or toothbrushes or fantasies. The holy sacrament of confession irritated me so much I almost turned Protestant (until I heard of testimony meetings). Some things are God's business and nobody else's. But Marian wouldn't let go. "I know you have dreams like mine," she insisted.

"Well, sort of…" I couldn't tell her that she had in fact already become part of my night-time fantasy life—a vivid part. But no man can ever be that honest with a woman. So I dredged up something completely different, hoping it would satisfy her.

It did.

"Once when I was a kid, my mom took me for vacation to Mammoth Cave, and I haven't been able to get it out of my head ever since. All of us going through the tunnels had to stay together on a narrow path with only a guide rope to hang onto. It seemed like the further in we went, the darker and wetter the cave got. The walls dripped with seepage and condensation, forming dark pools that gathered along the walkway.

"After the guide had talked himself out about -tites and -mites, he brought the group to a halt and pointed toward a large jet-black pool that receded far into the blackness. 'Ladies and gentlemen,' he intoned sternly, 'at this point in our tour, I must ask you to be very careful. Watch your step and keep your balance at all times. We at Mammoth Cave have never yet lost any of our guests, and we do not intend to begin today. But the pool before you is unimaginably deep, so deep that it has never been fathomed, though for many years geologists have tried to do so. Anyone falling into this pool would in all probability be lost forever.'

"And, sure enough, right then, somebody gave out a whoop and fell over the guide rope into the water! Everyone shouted and screamed and ran to help. Then they all gasped in surprise as the guy, who had been flailing around and choking, suddenly stood up, shook himself off, and walked back to the group. The water was only a couple feet deep! Everybody started laughing at the joke that had been played on them, but I clung to the rope all the tighter. It was no joke to me. To drown in the unfathomable pool, to be lost forever in the Mammoth Cave—that, for me, is the scariest thing of all."

All I wanted in response to my little confession was a noncommittal "Hmmm," but instead Marian turned toward me for a moment without saying a word. Silently laying the fingertips of her right hand on my cheek, she closed her eyes and brought her lips to mine. Softly, very briefly, she kissed me, more in comfort and reassurance than in passion. I didn't realize until then how much I needed reassurance. I never felt quite safe with Marian—then, or at any other time. She was a dangerous woman somehow.

"Hold me, Evan," she whispered pleadingly, tearfully, without opening her eyes. "I don't have anyone. I need you. I need you to hold me, and be with me, and stay with me." As she drew me tightly to her, I felt myself falling, falling, unable to stop. I kissed her lips and cheeks and forehead. Her very need was dangerous, so deep it was, and I was so young. Marian shuddered in my arms and wept quietly. I kissed her closed eyelids to keep them closed. They tasted wet and salty like the unplumbed sea. I prayed she wouldn't open them, for I knew if I looked too long and deep into those dark pools, I would be lost irredeemably.

I gazed out over the lake at some distant light that gleamed along the shore. We didn't talk. We kissed once in a while, and I held her close for what seemed like forever.

Then, as my arm was beginning to cramp up and go numb, she suddenly stood up and asked, "Is your mother home?

"Yes," I said. "But don't worry. She won't come down here."

"No, no. I meant I'd like to go up and meet her."

What kind of an idea was that? Let's stop necking so I can meet your mother? It wasn't natural. But Marian's mind was always making weird little leaps that no one else could follow. So I just said, "Sure. You can meet her if you want."

Actually, I wasn't sure. I didn't know how Marian would react, or how my mother would. Usually I picked my dates up at their houses. I'd never brought a girl home before.

As we reached the top of the stairs, I hollered, "Mom, we've got company!" so that she could make herself as presentable as possible. My mother emerged through the screen door, wiping her hands on her apron, as she slipped it off the shoulders of her print dress. That was all the preparation that visitors needed or got around our house.

"Mom, this is Marian Barclay. Her folks own the place on the point."

"Why, hello, Marian. Welcome to our home! My, what a lovely girl you are. Won't you come in? I didn't hear any boat pull up to the dock. Don't tell me you swam all the way from the point!" Marian's wet swimsuit was still dripping.

"Evan, can't you see that Marian is shivering? You run get her one of my cotton robes from the back closet."

"I'm really fine, Mrs. Wade. I don't want to be any trouble."

"Nonsense. It's a wonderful warm night—when I was your age, I used to enjoy taking a dip on nights like this, too—but nobody likes to sit around in a wet suit. Now, here, Evan, give that to me. You just hold this around you, Marian. It's not much to look at, but it'll take those shivers out."

The simple white robe was indeed not much to look at. But like home-spun magic it turned Marian's tanned legs a rich golden olive and made her long wet hair look black, not multi-shaded auburn like it was in the noonday sun but jet black, as if sculptured in obsidian or figured on a Grecian urn. I mean she was more than pretty.

"Good. Now that's better," Mom said, admiring her creation. "I was just out in the kitchen cutting up some things for tuna salad tomorrow. I know! I just made some fresh sun tea this morning. You two have a seat and I'll fetch some."

"I don't want to get your couch wet," Marian objected.

"Oh, that old couch won't mind a bit of lake water." Mom paused to laugh her large, big hearted laugh. "Why, once when Evan was a little baby, and I was changing his diaper on that very couch, he sprayed…"

"Mom!" I shouted. "You don't have to tell Marian all that stuff."

"Well, all right, if you're so embarrassed!" she scowled at me in mock annoyance. "Anyway, furniture that can't stand getting a little damp has got no business being at the lake. It's got no business being in a family. Now, make yourself at home, Marian, and let's hear no more about it."

"Thank you, Mrs. Wade. You're very kind." I didn't bother correcting Marian about the "Mrs. Wade" thing. My mother let everybody call her that, rather than be all the time explaining what everybody knew and was nobody's business.

"I'll just leave you two kids in here, and get back to my kitchen. That celery won't cut itself up, you know! Let me get that iced tea now."

Here come the ancestral jelly glasses, I thought in my embarrassment. But Marian saved my pride.

"Iced tea would be nice. But...," Marian stopped short in a moment of indecision before going on. "You know what I'd really like, Mrs. Wade? I probably shouldn't ask but...could I give you a hand with the salad? I don't get much of a chance at home. We eat out most of the time. I'm sure you don't like people getting in your way in the kitchen, but I'd really enjoy it, if you wouldn't mind very much."

This weird little leap of Marian's surprised even my mother. She certainly had never heard me offer to "dice one-third cup of celery," unless I needed gas for the Merc. But she recovered quicker than I did.

"Why, of course, dear. That's so nice of you! Many hands make light work, they say, and I'd be glad for the company. Evan isn't always Mr. Congeniality around here. And," she added over her shoulder as they left for the kitchen, "men always have their important man things to do." I took it that my presence in the kitchen was not required.

A little miffed, I plopped down heavily on the couch and sat there for a moment. But then I had to do it. I had to put my face and nose down to the seat cushion, sniffing here and there. I could detect no scent remaining from my youthful offense. But—and maybe this was just my imagination—I thought that that old living room couch smelled of our whole family history: talcum powder and Kool-Aid and Swedish meatballs and chianti, the 3-in-1 oil I used on my HO-guage train, the Walleye we ate every Friday, a cheap cigar Uncle Karl had the audacity to light up indoors until Mom got the broom after him.

I wished Uncle Karl was my father.

Snippets of conversation and laughter drifted out of kitchen over the tap-tap, tap-tap of twin pairing knives.

"Recipe? Oh, no dear, it's just something my mother taught me."

"Carleton College, I guess. That's what my dad and Francine…"

"…easier to wash the celery **before** you cut it."

"She died eight years ago now."

"My, yes, plenty of onion. Too much. Any more and we won't be able to taste the tuna!"

Marian came running out of the kitchen laughing aloud and rubbing her eyes, tears streaming down her face. When I saw that over the white robe she was wearing a tiny green apron with red Christmas trees, I started laughing too, and my mother came in, and we all laughed together and had a good time.

After that evening, I never saw Marian laugh again.

"Thank you, Evan," she said as we returned down the stairs to the lake. "It's been a long time since I've been so happy. Thank you."

"No problem."

"You're so lucky! I don't think you know how lucky you are."

"What do you mean?"

"Your home. Your mother.

"Oh. Yeah. Lucky."

"Francine will never be my mother. Doesn't even try to be, really. She's always on my case when dad isn't around, and when he is around, he's on the bottle. I feel like an orphan. I've lost both my parents. At least you've got one, and your mother is so wonderful."

"I see what you mean." I started to untie the wimpy little boat from the dock, hoping I was "lucky" enough to have the gas to get her home.

"You don't need to do that, Evan. You've been so great to me tonight. Just hold me again, before we say good night." Raising her deep eyes to mine, she opened the white robe and gathered me into it, along with her, gathered me to the holiness of her body, and I held her there, pulling her close to me, a young woman, firm and mature, in all her glory. Then, as I began to grow erect, she shed the robe and dove silently into the dark water without a splash.

I stood there watching as long even strokes made dark legs and arms seem one with the water. Marian was in her element again. Maid Marian. The Lady of the Lake. So effortlessly she swam, it seemed she could go on forever. Out and out into the dimness. Soon, I could see only silver limbs flashing in the moonlight, and then nothing but water.

Chapter 4

"Wake up, Evan! Wake up!" Libby was propped up on one elbow, shouting and shaking my shoulder, beside herself with fear. "You're having another nightmare! Wake up, dammit!"

"Ok, ok! I'm awake now," I reassured her, half opening my eyes. The sun had not yet come up over the lake. The bedroom seemed colorless in the twilight, like an old black and white photograph. Only a dim red glow in the east gave promise of the dawn.

It was in the early morning that Libby was most beautiful. For me, her strawberry blond hair and freckles were the image of freshness and spring and what made it worthwhile to get out of bed in the morning. Raised on a horse farm near Breezy Point, Libby was anything but prissy. She had the farm girl's carelessness of body that made her sexier in overalls than in an evening gown. She didn't need to flaunt it. You couldn't miss it, even in the business suits she wore to work. Libby's hair was so curly and wayward that it would not stay fenced in a clasp or roped in a ponytail. It was always escaping out the sides, so that even on calm days she looked like the Girl from Breezy. You had to take delight in disorder to find Libby beautiful. I called her Strawberry Delight.

But she was not happy at the moment.

"You're scaring me, Evan." Libby turned away from me in a fret, but I curled up spoonwise behind her. She brought my hand to her breast and pressed it to her, scrunching up inside my arms, trying to make herself feel small and safe. "You're scaring me. At night you're gone somewhere that I can't go."

"I'm right here with you, Libby."

"Sometimes I can't wake you up," Libby said, talking to the wall in front of her. "You don't know how long I've been shaking you just now. It scares me. It's like you're down so deep, I can't bring you up out of it. It scares me. You're flailing your arms and moaning, and I try to bring you out of it, but you just pull away. It's like you're terrified, but you still don't want to wake up! I get so scared and lonely. More lonely than when you're away, because you're right here but still a million miles away."

I brushed her strawberry locks aside and, saying nothing, kissed her neck in reassurance.

"I missed you, hon, when you were in the Cities," she went on. "When you were gone, I had nothing to cuddle with but the pillow, and the pillow's missing certain essentials for serious cuddling."

"I'm back now, and"—I said, with a little thrust for emphasis—"so are the essentials." I circled my arms around her and pulled her in tight. We lay there for a long time watching the sun disperse the last blue of night, spreading the red glow all around, until it suffused the whole sky and lake. The sunlight painted our walls crimson, and still we watched on, each enveloped in our own thoughts. We snuggled as close as our bodies could get, but the mind is its own place, and my mind was in another time, with another woman.

"Red sky at morning," Libby said, as she pulled away from me and rolled out of bed and stood looking out the window. "You're still somewhere else. Where are you, Evan?"

"I can't get that funeral out of my mind. That's all. You know, 'Man, that is born of a woman, hath but a short time to live. He cometh up, and is cut down, like a flower.' Simple stuff, powerful stuff. You can't shake it so easy. Why do they have to do that to people? And they haven't caught the sicko that killed Dr. Barclay. That's got my nose twitching, too, like ragweed. But as for you! You don't need to worry about me!" I said jokingly, trying to lighten things up a little. "I'm fine! Right here, right now, with you."

"I know, Evan. And this is ok for now. But I want us to be going somewhere. Together." Libby slipped on an old white bathrobe. I couldn't stay focused on what she was saying. "We've been together in your mother's place—what is it now? Five months? Where is this going? Where are we going?"

"We're going to work," I said with a smile. It was so unlike Libby to be glum that I was sure she'd forget about all this in a minute if I gave her half a chance. Basically a happy person with a song and a laugh on her lips, Libby didn't get into these funks very often, and when she did, the subject was always the same.

"Don't try to put me off, Evan. You know damn well what I mean. I'm thirty-one years old. What we have with each other right now is great. But if we don't have a future together, then it's nothing. Just an illusion that has us suspended in limbo, a bad dream that's keeping us from having real lives, and we both ought to snap out of it, right quick. Will you think about it, Evan? Promise me you'll think about whether we have a future. Or else shake me hard and wake me up, so I can get on with my life." Libby gave me that direct, serious look that demands a direct, serious answer.

"Ok," I said. "I promise."

In the shower I began fulfilling my promise, but not the way she hoped. I wondered how much time Libby and I still had left together. I was wondering only because she was wondering about it, and she was wondering because she knew that until that moment I hadn't given a second thought to "our future together." She was afraid that that meant we weren't going to have any future; and if she kept pushing me to write blank checks on tomorrow, we certainly would not. I'd had enough of that kind of pushing before. Seemed like my whole life was some woman pushing me. I could easily have gone on with Libby just as we were, one day after the other, for a very long time, just so long as I didn't have to formal-ize it, legalize it, and swear to it.

What is it with women?

Different sense of time, I guess. Seize the day is a man's philosophy, but for women, today isn't enough. They make you swear what's going to hap-pen from this day forward, as if each day is complete not in itself but only in what it leads to, as if the present is realized only in the future, not right away. Maybe the psychobabble has it right: two forms of civilization, one for each gender. Men—the hunter-gatherers who kill it and eat it. Right now. Women—the planters who sow it, and harvest it. Long after. For them, it's germination and gestation, nurturing and culturing.

And suddenly I understood what Libby and I had been arguing about, without ever mentioning the matter at all: I knew Libby wanted a baby just as much as I did not. Attachments, obligations, ties, complications. Babies are the worst. A wife you can divorce. A child is yours, for better or for worse, till death do you part.

"Are you going to visit your mother this week?" Libby asked at the breakfast table, innocently spooning down her Cheerios while delivering a swift kick to my groin. She couldn't have known what I'd been thinking. But if I was right about her hopes, why was it so impossible she could read my fears about having to visit my mother?

"Sure, if I have a chance."

"Make a chance," Libby urged. "Sacred Heart may be the best nursing home around here, but it's no real home at all, and you've got to make an extra effort to get over there. It's the only thing that makes her happy any-more."

"If she recognizes me," I added, remembering that the last two times I went to see her, she greeted me like a stranger. The Alzheimer's left her a few good days, of course. But I was almost more afraid to find her lucid than blank. The good days were her worst, and mine too, because then she knew where she was, and the pain she felt I felt too, as keenly as if she and

I were still one flesh. Birth is the beginning of the tie, not the end. The umbilical is never really severed, except by death.

Libby left for Family Services in the county courthouse, and I was off to the *Sentinel*. But my epiphany continued to occupy my thoughts as I drove down Highway 371 that morning. I thought about the mother-child bond that could not be severed by any alienation, whether physical or emotional. I thought about the pressure that adoptees feel, the irresistible drive to find their birth mother. I thought about Roy Macklin, my father. A man with a name but no face, except the one I could see in the mirror. I wondered who he was. I wondered who killed Marian. I was doing entirely too much wondering these days.

Sherman was standing at the open door of the *Sentinel* building when I pulled into the parking lot.

"Glad to have you back from the Cities, Evan. Ready to put your hand to the plow again?"

"Well, to the keyboard, anyway. Good to be back, Sherm." The fact is that Sherman Helmholz had never plowed an acre of land in his life, and certainly not with any hand-held plow. However, as editor of the *Lakes Area Sentinel*, Sherm felt it incumbent upon him to affect a certain earthiness. He didn't let it be generally known that he had graduated from the U's School of Journalism, the same school Eric Sevareid attended and didn't graduate from. Sherm would rather be thought a hayseed than have it known he was an expert in HTML, who set up the *Sentinel*'s sophisticated website entirely by himself.

Sherman Helmholz knew his business and he knew his readers' tastes all right, just like the dog woman at the *STrib*. So, not being totally incapable of learning from experience, I paid him the respect he was due and found that he paid me in the same currency. Knowing that I had been raised in the Lake Country he loved and served made it easier for Sherm to hire me on the rebound. But he still suspected that my journalistic sensibilities had become so jaded by time served in the Twin Cities of Sodom and Gomorrah that I could only write about scandal and sensationalism. I think my "Pets Blessed" story had somewhat allayed his fears, though. It was sort of a princess-and-the-pea test, and only a genuine country mouse like me could have passed it. So I was pleased but not surprised when he assigned me another lead story.

"Yessir, I came up with the idea yesterday evening when the little lady and I were sitting on the porch swing, watching the world go by, and suddenly she turned to me and said, 'Sherman, you need a haircut.' That's all the inspiration I needed," he said, beaming with pleasure. "I want you to write me a nice story on Charlie Weaver."

"The barber of Brainerd?"

"That's right. Charlie Weaver. He's been down there for years."

"What's new at Weaver's?"

"Nothing I know of."

"So, what's the story?"

"Why, that **is** the story! Nothing whatever is new. Have you ever heard of anything like it? Everybody in Crow Wing County knows Charlie. Every man, I should say. He doesn't do women. Women's hair, I mean!" Sherm exclaimed, giving me a wink and an elbow in the ribs. "You know, other than St. John's College, Charlie's is the only bastion of male privilege left in the state. Charlie's is the last vestige of real country."

"Vestige?" I said, catching him with his thesaurus open.

"Why, yes. You surprised that us outstate folks know words like 'vestige'? As I was saying, the cracker barrel is long gone and the barbershop replaced it as a primary site for apophantic discourse."

"Ok, you got me. What is apophantic discourse?"

"Why it's shooting the breeze!" he replied with a big laugh. "But soon barbershops like Charlie's will be bulldozed out of existence by chains with names like Shear Pleasure and Mane Street. There won't be any barbers left anymore, just hair stylists. So you get your citified ass down to Brainerd before Charlie's disappears, and take your camera along to record it for posterity. We'll do a nice spread, and everybody will read it and say, 'Yup. That Charlie. A good man! We used to have a lot of his kind around here once, but lookit here now. A man can't even get a decent haircut without coming out smelling like he just got a perm.' And everybody will say, 'Damn right! You're sure right about that, all right. A damn permanet.' And they'll be damn right!"

You had to love Sherm. So I picked up my pocket PC and digital Nikon that could feed pictures directly into the mainframe, and I headed off to capture in word and image the Barbershop Where Time Stood Still.

The square cement-block shop, adorned only by a revolving barber-pole, stood out like a white wart on the roadside edge of the blacktopped parking lot. Further in from the street was the mall, or what went by that name in Brainerd. Japanese and Florideans flew into Minneapolis by the planeload to worship and tithe at the Mall of America. This, however, was more like a plaza. Yet even by comparison to the bygone era of plazas, Charlie's place was pretty antiquated. Not one generation out of date, but two. Isolated and lonely, like an aged and forgotten grandparent, it persisted, unmoved by the ceaseless flood of innovation.

"Morning, young fella," Charlie greeted me. Opening the front door was like walking into a Rockwell painting. "Have a seat and I'll be right with you." He pointed his scissors toward the row of wooden chairs where three men were seated, choir-like, hands on knees, all staring at me like I was from Mars—or suburban Kenwood. Charlie returned to vigorously clacking away at the few wisps of hair remaining to the balding man in the chair.

"Hello, Mr. Weaver," I said. "My name's Wade. Evan Wade. I'm not here for a haircut."

"Evan Wade," he mused. "Evan Wade? Sure enough! Didn't your mother use to bring you in sometimes when she came into town to do the shopping?"

My name was passed down the row of waiting customers. ("What?" "He's Evan Wade, he says." "Of course, it's the Wade boy.") I felt like a celebrity.

"Yes, she did bring me in a few times, sir. You have a remarkable memory. That was a long time ago. Thirty years or more." I looked around, trying to square past and present, but I remembered nothing of those ancient times except the sneezing. Charlie never did believe in wetting your hair before cutting it, and so snippets of hair circulated through the shop like motes of dust. They sprayed around eyes and into nose, while little hands were cruelly prevented from itching them by the barber cloth. I sneezed out of anger and frustration. I sneezed out of revenge. Great full-lung, open-mouth sneezes, with a spray that cleared the chairs in front of me, and prompted my mother to exclaim, "Evan! My goodness!" and to laugh her big-hearted laugh.

"How is that fine woman, your mother?" Charlie inquired.

"She's fine, thanks. Been over at Sacred Heart for about a year," I explained, hurriedly adding, "I'm with the *Sentinel* now, and Sherm Helmholz sent me down to do a story on your shop."

Charlie stopped clipping and looked squarely at me. "She can't be too good if she's at Sacred Heart. You give her my regards, Evan, first chance you get. To raise you all by herself like she did....You give her my respects."

Not wanting to go down that road any further, I said, "Glad to" and proceeded: "I would have called first before I came over, but I couldn't find your number."

"Would have been a real surprise if you did, Evan. There's no phone here."

"No phone?" I spied an unused radio in the corner, so he wasn't a total Luddite.

"How do your customers make appointments, then?" I asked, hoping to generate a little controversy to spice up this non-story.

"Don't need any," volunteered the old coot in the barber chair.

"That's right," Charlie said. "Everybody's welcome to come when they like. I get to them just as soon as I can. The fellas come in and sit a spell, and chat until it's their turn. Nope, no appointments. Appointments are for folks in a hurry. Nobody's in a hurry who comes in here. We're not going anywhere, at least not in a hurry." ("That's right," repeated the choir. "No hurry. We're not going anywhere. Nope.")

"Sure. We're fine just where we are," Charlie continued. "Just take every day as it comes one day at a time. That's the best way. The future'll take care of itself. Every passing fad and fashion can just pass right on by, for all I'm concerned."

"No fashion magazines here, I take it," I said, scanning the hairy copies of *Popular Mechanics* lying scattered about.

"That's for sure," Charlie said. "Fashions and fashion cuts and fashion magazines, that's fine for the ladies, you know, but the ladies only come in here when they're bringing in their little tykes. Like you, Evan." ("No new fashions here," affirmed the choir. "One day at a time." "Things just the way they are!")

"Yup. If they want fashion," Charlie said, pointing his scissors out the window, "they'll have to go to that new women's store they're putting in across the street."

"Now, Charlie, didn't you hear?" said the man in the chair standing up, completely shorn. "That's not a women's store. That's going to be a clinic, my Shirley tells me. A women's clinic, and folks around these parts are none too happy about it. This ain't the Cities. No, sir. What're they thinking of? We are God-fearing people up here. If our women have women problems, they can go to St. Josephs and get the best care money can buy. If they need anything else, they're not going to get it around here! Or anywhere else, if we can help it!"

I could smell it. Real news, and no human interest story. Real, honest to goodness news falling out of the sky right into my lap.

"My Shirley says her and her lady friends, including Reverend Bergdahl's wife, you know, they had a meeting last night and called in the cavalry. They're going make darn sure this so-called clinic never opens its doors."

"How they going to manage that?" the barber asked, peering out the window.

"Why, Charlie, see those folks over yonder arguing with the construction crew? That's the cavalry, I do believe. Drove up from their mission in the Cities this morning. They call themselves the Soldiers of God. Yessir, Soldiers of God. There's going to be a war out there, Charlie, a 'fight for life,' and you got yourself a front row seat!"

Chapter 5

I sprinted out of Charlie's place so fast that the choir must have thought I was a man with an appointment. Which indeed I was. Dashing across the street, I stuck out my hand like a half-back trying to stiff-arm the oncoming traffic. Tires screeched three or four cars deep on each side, but—and this is one of the manifold mysteries of Minnesota—not one driver blew his horn. None, except one guy at the back, and I saw he had Illinois plates. The sea of traffic just parted and allowed me to pass. So I crossed over from the unanimity of the good old days back into the dissidence and division of the present. The tiff was heating up.

"I don't give a damn what it's going to be used for. I'm just a framer. My job is framing. Studs, joists, and trusses, that's all. No politics. And if you and your people don't get the hell out of here pronto, I'm going to have the cops on you so fast it—will—make—your—head—spin."

The hard hat was punching a stubby forefinger into the chest of a man twice his age and half his size, dressed in an ancient formal suit with wide lapels and knife-edge creases. It had once been blue but had long since turned metallic gray, probably from frequent ironing. His stiff white shirt was buttoned to the top. He wore no tie.

Standing around the two were a small crowd of gawkers and a handful of protesters. At the rear, I recognized the long-haired anorexic from Marian's funeral. Head bowed, she was rocking back and forth on her heels like a Moonie. Her lips were moving, but I couldn't make out any words.

This ragtag bunch were the Soldiers of God all right, all five of them, and the little guy was their Napoleon. You could tell that he'd been on the wrong end of more than a finger before. He didn't flinch. He didn't fight back. He didn't raise his voice.

He simply removed the wire rim glasses from his nose with his right hand and, with his left, withdrew a large handkerchief from his trouser pocket. He breathed on the lenses, wiped them, inspected them carefully in the light, and wiped them once more, as if everything depended on their being immaculate before he could proceed.

Then, replacing the glasses on his nose and looking serenely at the enemy, he folded his arms across his chest and said, "Then you might as well call the police right now, young man, for on this spot I will take my stand."

Vanquished by the handkerchief, the hard hat left the field and stomped off to make good on his threat, though no head-spinning was to be observed then or later in the bespectacled man. Quite the contrary, Brother Jeremiah Smit—as he styled himself—emanated the aura of invulnerability that comes from absolute certitude in the righteousness of one's own actions. He was plagued by no self-doubt, no skepticism about the great principle that he defended with single-minded devotion. His fearlessness was impressive, preposterous, frightening. He could be punched, kicked, imprisoned, but he was intimidated neither by amply muscled hard hats, nor pussel-gutted cops, nor all the assembled forces of Armageddon. Brother Jeremiah was a man capable of anything, and that was all the more apparent when he chose to do nothing.

Of course, I knew he was not doing nothing. He was fighting. His way. And he had just won the first skirmish of the war. The cops would arrive in a minute. He would get himself arrested—that is to say, martyred—and the only thing he wanted more fervently than martyrdom, I was sure, was to have it reported.

I ran after him with digital camera flapping at the elbow. "Hello! Hello, there! Evan Wade from the *Sentinel*. Would you care to make a statement? What do you hope to accomplish in Brainerd? Do you think that you're welcome here?"

Brother Smit abruptly turned away from the small band of faithful to meet the barrage of questions. Reporter lust: I had seen it a thousand times before. Fame or infamy, it didn't matter to them. Just spell my name right! It made you want to puke. The diminutive man eyed me for a moment and then did the unimaginable. He broke into a broad smile of recognition and extended the hand of comradery for me to shake.

"Wade! Wade! You have a name to inspire pride and confidence! The gutless cowards allowed Norma McCorvey to mask her shame behind a pseudonym, but Henry M. Wade had nothing to hide. He stood tall. He was a man of principle! You any relation to 'Hang 'em High' Henry?"

"None whatever," I replied in consternation, involuntarily reaching out to take that hand. Even if it wasn't the hand that killed Marian, I could care less about his cause, about Roe or Wade or McCorvey. He shook my hand warmly, giving me a half-embrace, half-pat on the back with the other. What made him think I was on the side of the angels, anyway? What's in a name? Even if my mother was a good Catholic, I wasn't there to enlist in his army, or carry a banner, or fling bloody chicken parts into the crowd. I was there for the story. That's all.

And that bothered me too. During all my years at the *STrib*, my interviewees never once took an interest in me personally or my lineage—never said, "He's the Wade boy," or "Give my respects to your mother." And that's the way it's supposed to be. One way or the other, in this business you've got to learn the difference between an interview and a conversation. An interview is never about the interviewer. He is detached, absent, elevated to another realm, from which vantage he can dispassionately survey the turning world. But here in Lake Country everything was different. I couldn't get out of the picture somehow. The byline was becoming the headline. This story, I feared, was not to be about Brother Jeremiah at all.

"Too bad," he added. "I didn't think Henry had any people up here. But you never know. Brainerd's not so far from Dallas. We have soldiers doing God's work all over the country. All over the world! Including right here in Brainerd."

"So I heard," I said. "Shirley from the preacher's circle tipped you off about the clinic, did she? Shirley…what's her last name?"

"You know, Mr. Wade," Brother Jeremiah paused to gaze pensively over my head toward something beyond. "I spent a little time of prayer and meditation at the Stillwater Correctional Facility, and my fellow sojourners there used very persuasive methods to teach me the rules of survival. Number one is: there's a ditch for every snitch."

"Which means exactly what?"

"Do you reveal your sources on request, Mr. Wade? Do you publicize them in your paper? We're fighting a war here, and it would be treasonous of me to give aid and comfort to the enemy. Don't you think?"

"I'm not the enemy."

"With a name like Wade, I should hope not. Then you're a friend to our cause?"

"No, not that either!"

"Well, this is puzzling. And disturbing. Come, which are you, Mr. Evan Wade? Are you blue or are you gray? Commit yourself! Are you cold or are you hot?"

"Neither one."

"Yes, so I feared. I know thy works, that thou art neither cold nor hot. I would that thou wert either cold or hot. But because thou art lukewarm, I will spue thee out of my mouth."

"I'm just a reporter."

"Ah, I see, no taking sides, just a reporter."

"Right."

"No commitments, just a reporter. You just stand back, observing the fray. No friend to the cause, but no enemy either. Is that it?"

"Exactly. I'm perfectly neutral."

"Just give your readers the facts, quite willing to let them believe what they like, come to their own decisions, make their own choices? " Brother Jeremiah's voice was becoming quieter and quieter, more intense and more soft with every word.

"That's right!" I exclaimed, triumphant.

"Then, Mr. Wade, I have some news for you," he whispered, "You are the devil incarnate! And you don't even know it! You have no idea who you are!"

"I know a bigot when I see one."

"Ah, yes, and I know a hypocrite!" he said, bringing his face so close to mine I could feel his hot breath. "You, Mr. Wade, are one of the hypocrites who condemn bigotry more than murder. Yours is the hypocrisy of enlightenment gone mad. Do-nothingism, that's your creed. You tell your readers: if you don't approve of slavery, don't buy any slaves. Do nothing! Don't like gas chambers? Then don't work in a camp! Just do nothing! If you don't want an abortion, don't get one, just be tolerant of those who do! At the New Holocaust Christian Center, we may be bigots, but we will never fall for that lie, that horrendous self-deception. If the old holocaust taught us anything, it was this one luminous truth: the only thing necessary for evil to triumph is for good men to be tolerant."

The dwarf's logic was so twisted and perverted it left me speechless. So he went on with his rant.

"I can be tolerant no more. I cannot stand by while one more abortuary is erected, for I have heard the silent dirge. I have heard Rachael weeping for her children, and would not be comforted because they are not. I have listened to the survivors of the new holocaust, as of the old, and I am haunted by their witness. The dead and the living implore us to stop the slaughter of the innocents. Their curse hangs in the air. Their accusation stinks in the nostrils of heaven. Their suffering cries out for vengeance. So I will not be tolerant. I will not do nothing."

"No," I shouted, "you will do anything, anything at all, won't you! That's your bigotry. You will stalk, and threaten, and even kill!"

"Yes, Mr. Wade," he hissed, piercing me with his eyes, "I will. The cause of life is worth dying for. And more, it is worth killing for. That is the nature of war. That is a soldier's duty."

"And were you at war with Marian Barclay?" I asked him with savage sarcasm.

"Oh, is that where you are, Mr. Wade? You and the cops and the reporters from the Cities?"

"Just answer the question!"

"Very well, I will answer, if you like. Yes, I was at war with Marian Barclay. She was the enemy, just like you."

"You bastard, you fool!" I exploded. "Didn't you know that she was on your side? You killed her, didn't you! And it was all for nothing, all a mistake! Didn't you know that she was an ObGyn?"

"Who do you think performs abortions, Mr. Wade? What do you suppose that she was doing that day at the Overdale abortuary? And it was not the first time. Why did they always sneak her in and out with a blanket over her head? Open your eyes, Mr. Wade! You know nothing whatever about her, do you? And you call me fool! Your ignorance would be touching, if it were not so pathetic."

With that, the cops drove up, and I was glad they did, because I swear I would have strangled that pygmy right there and then. Oh, Marian, to die like that! If they hadn't come, I would have done the world a favor and put an end to his miserable little life with my own hands. I swear I would.

But I didn't. The cops were closing in, and I grabbed my camera and began snapping away, picture after picture, moving over to get an angle, moving back further and further to get in the whole confrontation. And in retreating I almost backed into someone.

Turning to excuse myself, I found myself staring at the anorexic girl, her head still bowed and rocking, eyes closed, completely oblivious to my presence and to the imminent arrest of the incubus, her demonic general. Though she couldn't have been more than twenty, her skin was sallow, stretched tight over concave cheeks. Blonde, waist-length hair flowed over her skeletal shoulders like a white veil, so that with her head bowed, she looked like the skull of a madonna.

The girl rocked on, muttering to herself, saying the same thing over and over. I could hear it now.

"Pray for us now and at the hour of our birth."

"Pray for us now and at the hour of our birth."

"Pray for us now and at the hour of our birth."

"That's 'death,'" I said, correcting her.

"Yes," she replied, opening vacant eyes in cavernous sockets. "It is. For so many. Birth is death for so unthinkably many. But not for me. Not for such as me. Will you pray for us, Mr. Evan Wade? Pray for us now and at the hour of our birth."

Chapter 6

"Sherm, you're going to kiss my citified ass when you hear about the story I got for you today," I shouted gleefully, as I ran past Earlene in reception and threw open the door marked Editor in Chief. I couldn't wait to brag up my good fortune.

"I was wondering about that, Evan." Sherm looked up from one of the five piles of neatly stacked papers on his desk and replaced the Parker ballpoint in the wooden base proclaiming him recipient of the Pequot Lakes Distinguished Community Service Award, 1987. A snapshot of the "little lady," his wife, adorned one side of his desk, and his twin nephews with their parents appeared on the other. At ease with himself and with his life, Sherm rocked back in his chair, folding his hands behind his head. "Charlie called at lunchtime. He was on the cellular in his car, so the connection wasn't so good, but it sounded like he said you just up and left before he could tell you he sold his shop. What's up?"

"Sherm, forget about Charlie. Listen to the scoop I got from across the street! Pictures and interviews and all we need!"

"You mean the clinic they're putting in?"

"Why…yes. You knew about that?" I said, stunned.

"Sure, Nell told me about it the other night. She and Shirley Hoglund and their women's group called up this guy—Jeremiah Smit—from the New Holocaust Christian Center. Sounds impressive, but it's just a hole in the wall on 10th Avenue in St. Paul. He's going to front for them, so they can stay out of the picture. Could get a little hot down there. What's this got to do with Charlie, anyway?"

"You mean you knew the shit was going to hit the fan at this clinic, and you sent me to do a story on Charlie's barbershop?"

"Yup."

"What kind of a newspaper man are you, Sherm? Can't you smell a real story when it slaps you in the face? Have you been living in Podunk so long that you've lost your nose entirely?"

"Let's get one thing straight right now, Evan Wade." Sherm hurtled himself forward across the desk, sending his community service plaque skittling across the floor. "I don't live in Podunk, though it sounds like you think you do. I live in Pequot Lakes, and I'm proud of it. We've got a whole lot of shit around here, just like everyplace else in the world. It doesn't take a real sensitive nose to sniff it out. Now I don't know about down in the Cities, but when folks up here run across a pile of shit, they say, 'That's a pile of shit.' But they don't pick it up and rub it between their fingers and say, "Sure feels like shit," and they don't put a pinch between cheek and gum and say, 'Sure tastes like shit.' They just step around it, and move on."

"See no evil, hear no evil, report no evil. Is that it, Sherm? You know very well that the *Tribune* is going to have a reporter up here as soon as they hear about Smit and his merry band." I had no intention of letting Ben Drake steal my thunder up here, too.

"Evan, I render unto the *STrib* what is the *STrib*'s, and unto the *Sentinel* what is the *Sentinel*'s. When folks pick up our paper, they want to know who won the girls' soccer tournament—or they already know and they just want to see their strapping young daughter's picture in the paper, and read how she made the winning save in the big game. Or they want to hear about last week's fiery meeting of the Crosslake City Council where they're trying to block the Army Corps from repairing those old dams, dropping the water level three feet, and leaving their Chris Crafts stranded on dry ground. They want to know whether Jolly Young Saint Nicklaus is going to build yet another golf course that dumps tons of fertilizer into the watershed every year and that nobody who actually lives here can afford to play." Sherm's face was getting red, and he was starting to puff. "That's what people want to read about in the *Lake Country Sentinel*, Evan. They want to read about Charlie's barbershop, a venerable local institution that's about to vanish from the face of Crow Wing County, and that's what you'll be writing about if you plan to work for the *Sentinel*."

"Sherm, I can't believe it. You can't really want to leave this one to the *STrib*," I pleaded. "If you and the Missus are pro-lifers, I'd think you'd want to spill lots of ink on this protest and give it all the publicity you can."

"Evan, you're on thin ice. Very thin. Nell and I do believe passionately in the sanctity of human life. But my paper's not going to pimp for any cause, however worthy, especially if it's my personal cause. Didn't they teach you anything vaguely like journalistic ethics at the *STrib*?"

"Ok, ok. I'm sorry. But I bet the ladies didn't know that this Brother Jeremiah has a prison record when they invited them up north!" I confided this bit of insider information rather smugly, priding myself on being a top notch investigative reporter.

"Smit doesn't make any secret of it. He told *you* about it, didn't he, and he knew you were a reporter? "

"Well…yes. He did."

"And did he tell you that the dark crime for which he was incarcerated was the piddling little offense of criminal trespass? He acted with heroic disregard of the legal bubble zone the ACLU shysters erected around the abortion mills. For which act of moral fortitude he got six months, with time off for good behavior. But you! You heard he has a criminal record and jumped to the conclusion that he's capable of anything?"

"I didn't jump at all! He told me he is, Sherm! He told me that he is willing to kill for the cause. And he did! This guy as much as admitted to

me that he murdered Marian Barclay. He was stalking her. It was no criminal trespass but cold-blooded murder! We've got a chance here to...."

"Hold it! Hold it! Who is Marian Barclay?" Sherm interrupted. Briefly,
I explained her story, trying to keep myself out of it, but with every sentence his face grew more skeptical.

"And so this is the woman whose funeral you went to this week?"

"That's right."

"You knew her for just a couple months? Some twenty years ago? When
her parents bought a place on Woman Lake, which they then turned right
around and sold, almost immediately? The three of them weren't much
more than tourists around here, and now you're on a vendetta? What's
wrong with this picture? You want to do an I-Team report for the *Sentinel*,
so you can bring her killer to justice, who happens to have been invited
right here into our homes and bosoms by Shirley and Nell and the ladies
of the church?"

"Yes! Yes, Sherm," I said excitedly, only half listening to what he was
saying, "and I've got the interview notes and lots of pictures. What a story!
It'll be great!" I slid the memory stick from the digital camera into the PC,
and began bringing up one image of the arrest after another. "Look at
these, Sherm! That's Smit there in the blue. Looks a little like a Union soldier, doesn't he? There the cops are trying to push him around, but he
doesn't budge. There was this weird girl, too! Didn't get any pictures of
her, though. A couple of follow-ups and this'll be Pulitzer stuff!"

Sherman Helmholz was visibly unimpressed. "We can't use these pictures, Evan, even if I wanted to. See that gray semicircle on the right edge
here—and here, too?" He pointed to a smudge in picture after picture.

"Yeah, must be some malfunction."

"No malfunction, Evan. That's your finger. No sir, we're not going to
publish pictures of your finger, however fine a finger it is, and we're not
going to print stories that serve your personal mission. If I'm not going to
pimp for my cause, I'm sure as hell not going to pimp for yours!"

Then after a moment's hesitation, he added, "A cause which still does- n't make much sense. What am I missing here? What's the 'Rest of the Story'?" he asked in his best Paul Harvey voice, pulling his chin in the pose of intense meditation. I had no intention of letting him pump me, so I started attentively packing up the camera, piece by piece.

Sherm came around his desk and peered at me close up, with a little boyish smirk on his face.

"Were you getting it on with this young lady, Evan? Were you? That's it, isn't it! You were doing the Barclay girl when you were a young stud, and now two decades later, the wench is dead, and you've come down with a severe attack of the post mortem guilts. Isn't that right?"

Snapping the camera case shut with an air of finality, I did an aboutface toward the door to end the interview. Sherm's laughing voice followed me down the hall.

"Geez, Evan! You'd think you'd killed the girl! Just deal with it. But, please, go deal with it somewhere else. Not in my paper!"

At the reception desk, Earlene's head shot up and her jaw dropped open as I strode past, but before she managed to get anything out, I safely regained the street.

I drove home from the office cursing the bumpkin editor I worked for, bitterly disappointed about losing the story, the one honest to goodness, real story that I had sniffed out in months. The rusted out '69 Chevy in front of me didn't help matters either. Some old hayseed putting along at 40 miles per hour, with nowhere for me to pass. Sherm was a fool not to snatch up a story like that, and now Drake would have it. I tailgated the old fart. I laid on the horn. Nothing. Ever notice that these farmers drive their cars the same speed they drive their manure spreaders? Sherm thought he was pretty damn clever with all his amateur psychology, but he was way off base. He didn't have me pegged at all, but it was none of his business, and I wasn't about to go into the confessional with him or any- body else. I swerved out into the left lane, not seeing the oncoming car, and almost killed the whole lot of us before cutting back in behind Elmer again.

And just at that moment, apparently unaware that he had nearly met his Maker, Elmer made a quick right turn. Not onto the shoulder, not onto a side road. Without any signal, he turned right out into the middle of a freshly cut field of hay. Afraid the old coot was having a heart attack or something, I pulled over to the side, and the sweet aroma of fresh cut hay filled the entire car. It overrode the air conditioner, and it overrode the miserable events of my miserable day.

Like a time machine, the sweetness of the sweet grasses transported me back to the distant summers I spent with my teenage buddy Curt, making a few bucks by helping with the baling on this farm and that. The scene before me melted into those scenes, out in the field with the scorching summer sun glaring down on Curt and me, doing circle after circle, round and round the fields, and the hay bales piling up, horseflies wriggling out of them, mad as hornets for getting baled up inside, vengefully biting our shirtless backs, while we flailed away at them, and kept on baling and flailing until all the wagons were piled high and the sun dropped low in the summer sky.

A crack of self-recrimination and remorse blindsided me like a backhand across the mouth. To call this place "Podunk" was a sin against myself and what I knew to be true. None of Sherm's taunts justified committing it. Whatever this field was, whether sweet grass or the manure that made it grow rich and supple, it was part of me, part of the goodness in me, part of the bad. I swore to myself never again to forget who I was or deny where I came from in the name of citified sophistication.

I thought of Strawberry Delight, the Girl from Breezy, the woman in overalls even when she was in a business suit, the farmer's daughter. I didn't need to tell her anything about the meaning of hayfields. She knew the smell of hay and of molasses and a chestnut mare run hard, ready to be washed down. They were indelibly printed in her lungs and on her generous heart.

What was I waiting for?

Hearing a light tapping, I raised my head from my hands and saw the farmer peering in inquiringly at the car window.

"You all right there, son?" he asked as I rolled the window down.

"Fine, thanks. I'm much better now."

"Looked like you was having a heart attack or something."

"No. No. I'm ok. I just forgot something important, but I remembered it now. Thanks for checking."

"Good. Just wanted to be sure. Good. Well, I'll be on my way then. You drive safe now, hear, and watch those double solid lines!"

He knew about hayfields all right. He knew what was great about Greater Minnesota. A stream of SUVs flashed past us, racing northward to recreate the very suburbs from which they were fleeing. I eased out into traffic and headed home, my speedometer registering a steady 40 miles per hour all the way.

Chapter 7

Cruising down the highway, I was at peace with myself and the world. Broad green fields lining the open road stretched before me, and a two-mile string of cars lagged behind—tailgating, flashing their lights, and weaving wildly from side to side. But never blowing their horns. Turning my rearview mirror to the roof, I re-acquainted myself with the land of my birth, with the red hollyhocks that grew lush and tall on the west side of Erickson's garage, with the Jack Pine Inn, which cultivated the reputation among the tourists of having once been a loggers' bordello. Though it never was. We knew it actually started out as the creamery for the old Wilson farmhouse that burned down the day after Mrs. Wilson switched on the light bulb in the cool, moist darkness of her fruit cellar to discover her husband of fourteen years in an awkward but innovative position.

Yes, God's in his heaven and all's right with the world, I thought, and I continued to luxuriate in this state of sublime affirmation until a despicably gorgeous BMW roadster shot past with a guy in suspenders giving me the finger out the open convertible top. I didn't need to wonder who, or even where he was headed, but I had no idea why. Why was Ben on his way to my place? He must have gotten directions to the cabin from somebody up here, though they must have thought twice before helping out a braced and bowtied dandy like him.

"Hi, honey," I said to Libby, stepping up on the deck and giving her a little kiss on the forehead. The two of them were sitting in our captain's chairs drinking iced tea, drinking in the scene of the darkening lake, drinking up the last rays of afternoon sun that shone aslant through the needles of old-growth Norway pines and illuminated Libby's unruly locks like a golden halo. "Welcome to the Boonies, Ben. Get lost on the way to Minnetonka?"

"Not at all, Evan," he said, chuckling amicably and, without standing up, extending a hand for me to shake. I looked at it for a moment before accepting the invitation. No need to be churlish.

"I was visiting Brainerd, gateway to the Lake Country, for the day and thought I would drop by to see you in your native element. As a reward for the good thought, I was greeted at the door by this vision of rural loveliness who offered me liquid refreshment, sweetened by her conversation, while we awaited your eventual return."

Ben raised the tea-filled tumbler in toast to Libby. He couldn't keep his eyes off her. "I was just telling Ms. Farina that I would have arrived earlier," he continued, "if it weren't for the miserable traffic. You expect that kind of thing downtown. But bumper to bumper out here in the country! I had supposed an accident was tying it up, it was so bad, but it was just some old fart in a gray…."

Ben stopped in mid sentence when he spied my gray Ford in the drive. I just let him sit there and cook in his embarrassment for a moment before saying, "That's right, Ben. It was a wonderful day and I decided to stop and smell the hollyhocks."

"Sounds delightful, Evan, but hollyhocks, lovely as they are, have no aroma, and next time you decide to stop, you might wish to do so off the road."

"More tea, Mr. Drake? How about you, Evan?" Ever the peacemaker, Libby had an antenna for conflict and the tact to head it off before it got to boiling. I'm sure she'd had to give her diplomatic skills a daily workout down at Family Services, nothing being more in need of peace than most families.

"Sounds good," I said. "Make mine Long Island style. Want one, Ben?"

"Better not. I've got a long drive back, or I'd like nothing better than to watch the sun descend into the lake with you and Libby and a tall glass of Long Island iced tea. I'll have another regular though," he said, holding out his artificially frosted tumbler.

"Sure. Be right back," Libby said, as she left for the kitchen.

"Magnificent woman," Ben said, after a moment's silence. "Where do you find them? All innocence and freshness. Makes you want to suck in your stomach, throw out your chest, and smell the hollyhocks." He leaned back, shut his eyes, and inhaled deeply. Hannibal Lecter, I thought. "Yes, they do have an aroma, don't they? Very delicate bouquet. Very fine. I'd love to plant one of them in my garden of earthly delights, but I imagine they don't bear transplanting to urban climes. Oh, well!" Ben sighed as he watched Libby returning with the drinks.

"Thank you, my dear. Evan, I must have just missed you at the construction site. Smit left me a voice mail about the imminent 'Battle of Brainerd'—he call you too?—but Crow Wing County's finest had already carted him away and you had departed by the time I arrived. I always did need to get up pretty early in the morning to beat you to a story."

"The story's all yours," I replied, my ears still stinging from Sherm's boxing lesson. "I was actually on another trail when I happened to see the ruckus over there. So you're welcome to it."

"Another trail, eh? Well, now, the way I hear it, you and Smit were getting it on pretty heavy. Hard to believe! You actually accused him of killing the Barclay woman? What is this, a new interview technique? No indirection, no sly subterfuge, just bludgeon them into admission!"

"Evan, what in the world!" Libby exclaimed, totally confused. "Who is Smit, and what's he got to do with Dr. Barclay?"

"It's a long story, Libby, and I'll tell you later. But whatever the crudeness of my interview methods, they worked just fine. Worked to perfection. And since I'm not going to be writing anything about Smit or the clinic, I'll give it to you, Ben. Just a little present in return for keeping the cemetery business out of the paper. For which I thank you, by the way."

"Very welcome, I'm sure. What'd you get from Smit?" Ben was salivating in anticipation of the tender morsel I was about to serve up to him. I loved to watch him drool on his bow tie.

"All right, then. Brother Jeremiah Smit virtually admitted to me that he shot the Barclay woman."

"Well, my, my. Virtually admitted it, did he?"

"Yes, he certainly did, and I hope you and Queenie and all the good people down at the Bureau will make it so hot for Smit that he'll think he's in hell. Where he belongs, and where I devoutly hope twelve good folks and true will soon send him."

"Admitted it, you say, right out there in the parking lot?"

"Well, virtually admitted it."

"Not actually, though," Ben said skeptically. "He did not actually admit that he shot her."

"No, not actually, damn it, but in so many words. I pried it out of him all right."

"I see. In so many words, but not actually. Well, truth is, I would have been amazed indeed if Brother Smit had confessed that he shot her. Because if he did, then his aim must be even worse than mine. Not a single bullet hole was found in the body. The fact is, Evan, Marian Barclay was stabbed to death."

"Stabbed?"

"Yes, I'm afraid so. Many little details don't find their way into the paper. At Queenie's request. Perhaps if you're going to involve yourself in this story, though, you need to be a little better informed. Starting with the MO: seven puncture wounds in the stomach, inflicted with the much overused sharp instrument, and a pool of blood."

"How horrible!" Libby cried out aghast. Eyeing her distress, Ben became more graphic. "Not one of the seven was a mortal wound. Bled to death, in all likelihood, and not quickly. Lots of evidence of thrashing around. Blood sprayed everywhere. Scattered Reebok footprints, finally leading out the front door. Short strides. No hurry. Two partials in blood on the door pull. Smeared, unfortunately, but they're better than nothing."

"Stabbed or shot, what's the difference? Smit did it, and he should burn for it!"

"Well, perhaps, but then there's the little problem of the alibi, Evan. You see, Brother Smit has four of his 'soldiers' ready to take the stand and swear he was in their midst, planning out the Overdale Strategy, as he calls it, on the afternoon and evening of July 17."

"That bunch of loonies! They'll swear they've seen the dark side of the moon, if he tells them to."

"That may well be, but for now there's not nearly enough for an arrest. The stalking didn't amount to a criminal offense. He's got an alibi, however flimsy. And as for the two partials, as you very well know, half of Minnesota will match them. Even you, Evan! By the way, you didn't happen to be in the Cities on the 17th, did you?"

"Screw you, Ben."

"No, I didn't think so. Of course, not. Just a thought. Very silly of me, but always the newspaperman, you know. So sorry. Well, on that sour note, I'd better be heading down the highway. Thank you so much for the tea, Libby. Such a pleasant way to end the afternoon!"

"Come see us again, Mr. Drake." That smile of hers would bring him back if nothing else did.

"Yes, indeed I will. Tea for two. It was a delight. Goodbye then. Oh, and could you just point me in the direction of the old Barclay house? I thought I'd take a look at it while I'm in the neighborhood. Just background, you know. It's down the road here somewhere, isn't it?"

"Barclay house?" Libby exclaimed. "Somebody must be pulling your leg, Mr. Drake. The Barclays never lived around here, did they Evan!"

"Well...very briefly," I admitted, quickly adding, "They had the place on the point for just a couple months, a long time ago. That's when I first met Marian. You just turn left out of the drive, Ben, and...."

As I gave him the directions, Libby glared at me, long and hard. I walked him out to his car, prolonging casual conversation, hoping to postpone the inevitable.

Ben had been doing his homework all right. He was certainly a far better reporter than I had given him credit for. But who ever heard of background so deep that it included the victim's summer home of two decades previous? What did that have to do with anything? If he knew Marian had lived up here that summer, though, how much more did he know? I was glad old Hilda Hillstrom had long since gone on to receive her eternal reward—a pair of golden binoculars, inserted where the sun never shines, no doubt. Ben would certainly have found her and drained her dry of ancient history. But I was sure he'd been nosing around somewhere. I tried sly indirection to find out where—"Had a chance to meet any of the other folks up here?"—but he stonewalled, and if he hadn't suspected before that there was anything to the coincidence of my knowing Marian, he did now.

I had already been waving goodbye to the BMW far too long to be credible. I had to go back to the house. Libby was waiting in ambush, arms sternly folded, wearing her best "mad as hell" face.

"Why didn't you tell me, Evan?"

"Tell you what?"

"About when you 'first met Marian'! About her house just down the road! What happened to 'Dr. Barclay'? What happened to her living in the Cities? What did you have going with her? Whatever happened to being honest with each other?"

"Oh, Libby, I lived a long time and knew lots of people before I met you, and that was so long ago! You were only ten or eleven years old, learning to trot your dad's horses around the ring, and I was just out of high school. Since then, you've dated lots of boys—and men! I did, too. Women, I mean!"

"But I told you about them! I told you about Jimmy Smithers, that quiet boy from Jenkins who answered my Personal ad, and after six months still wouldn't touch me. I told you about Sam Nelson who kept trying to give me hickeys where they would show, so he and his jerkoff buddies could have a good laugh down at the Commander Bar. I told you about them all, Evan, and it's not fair that I should be shut out of your life after telling you all about mine. I feel like I don't know your past, and so I don't know you! It makes me wonder what all you haven't told me."

"Ok, you got me. It's true confessions time," I said, opening up my arms to her. "I'm sorry, Libby. Come here and interrogate me while I'm feeling guilty and vulnerable. What do you want to know? Anything. My dark and sordid past must come to light. Fire away!"

Libby pointed a finger at me, thumb up. "Bang," she said, and then squeezed her arms around my chest in more of a bear hug than an embrace.

"And you deserve it, too, mister. You've got a lot of explaining to do. First, who is Anne Chisolm?"

Ben, I thought. Ben, you dirtball.

"She's a reporter at the *STrib*, and a damned fine one. Yale, class of '86. Cut her teeth with the *New York Daily News* before moving to the Midwest. Anne did the series on the academic scandals in the U's basketball program, covered the construction of Highway 55 through the Native American sacred ground, as well as the Light Rail transit dispute."

"Enough with the resume," Libby interrupted. "What about the two of you?

"We lived together for about two years. Got along pretty well, too. Both liked Kirby Puckett and Spaghettios without meatballs. Problem was that Anne wanted the Charmin to unroll from the bottom, and consequently I could never find the end when I needed it most. We tried counseling, but to no avail. Our differences proved irreconcilable. There was only one bathroom, and things got so bad that we finally had to get separate apartments to meet our separate and individual TP needs."

"Why do I get the idea that you're not telling me the whole and unadulterated truth?" Libby asked, giving me a little bite on the chin.

"Adulterated? I should say not. Anne wasn't married, and me neither. What kind of man do you take me for?" I protested, my voice full of high indignation. "She's married now, I hear. To some English professor in Uptown, poor schmuck! Hope they have more than one bathroom."

"All right, wise guy, tell me about Marian Barclay then. Be serious! I want the truth now."

She wanted the truth. The shadows lengthened across the deck as the pinks and blues of twilight faded out and night descended upon the lake. Turning away from Libby, I looked out over the deck railing, down the seventy two steps, out into the dark water where I had never ceased to see the sculptured features of Marian's face.

"Was she pretty? Tell me the truth!"

Dark eyes returned my gaze, dark as bottomless pools, full of longing and loneliness, full of danger.

"Yes, she was very beautiful." Wet hair the color of obsidian. A simple white robe falling casually open upon golden olive thighs.

"Were you lovers?"

I sat silent, mesmerized by the dark lake. Libby only wanted the truth, no jokes, no evasions. She wanted to know my story. She wanted to know me, and wouldn't let go until she did. Why not just tell her? Libby grasped my head between her two hands, turning my face slowly away from the lake back down to her. Then she kissed me, briefly, tenderly, as if to free my lips.

"Tell me, Evan," she whispered. "Were you lovers?"

Chapter 8

The night we first made love the loons filled the air with their lonely, melancholy sound, calling and answering, pleading and responding, back and forth across the moonless lake. Just a single pair of loons was all, though the lakeshores echoed and reechoed their plaintive song. It seemed especially urgent on that late August night, for the white birches, always first to green in the spring, were now first to gold. And nothing gold can last.

During that summer, the laws of physics were suspended; the gradual progress of time was skewed. The summer flashed by in an instant. It dragged on in slow motion. Days were insignificant, nonexistent. Almost never did I see Marian during the day. She never went to town that I knew of, and thankfully never tried to see me at the Dairy Queen where I—to my enduring shame—was then in the process of learning to spin milk-shakes and sell my soul. Nothing, not my mother's poverty, not upcoming tuition payments, nothing whatever can justify or excuse the fact that for a few pieces of silver, I voluntarily and without threat of physical violence donned the mandatory DQ hairnet and brown polyester pants. So I was grateful that the days of summer never brought us together and Marian would never witness my shame.

Summer nights we rarely spent apart. We didn't have to arrange our rendezvous. I became accustomed to finding Marian sitting quietly, patiently on the dock, in nothing but a swimsuit and the anklet chain she always wore, with the delicate silver heart appended. Such nights, too soon over, slowly taught us each other. Marian felt the steadily increasing pressure of the passing summer, no doubt, the shortening days that would soon drive us south to the Cities and to the separate lives of college and ultimately career. But she would not be rushed.

Summer nights hurried us into one another's arms, but she disdained their vulgar insistence, for she had her own sense of time. Marian seemed imbued with an internal clock of rare device that ordered the pace of our endearments, regulating the steps with which we passed the successive thresholds of intimacy. I followed her lead in the dance, a slow dance in women's time. And so we came together slowly, very slowly, as if desire were cheapened if it was not prolonged, as if passion were not only heightened but sanctified by deferring consummation to the last possible moment.

That moment was long in coming.

I marveled at the woman beside me, radiant in the moonlight. Sitting in sand still warm from the afternoon sun, Marian threw endless pebbles with a plop into endless waves, while I sat looking on, endlessly. Tossing back her head, so that the long rope of her auburn hair swung down loose behind, she observed the whirling constellations pivot upon the motionless pole star. I lay alongside, head propped upon one elbow, watching her, admiring her serene self-containment, wondering at her choosing to be there with me. Lying back, Marian threw her arms out long above her head, and as her back arched up as if to receive the sharp-pointed stars, I saw her breasts rise, full and beckoning, and I reached out my hand to touch them, so marvelous they were, so fine. Then eyes, the color of the midnight sky, turned to meet my own. "Not now," they said, "not yet."

So the nights of warm anticipation passed, one by one. Then there came a time when Marian's nightly visitations abruptly ceased. After an hour's disappointment and surprise, I called her house, but there was no answer. Buddy and Francine were rarely home, and later when one of them picked up the phone, they just said Marian was out. They had no idea where.

I had no idea either. Next evening when she did not appear I took out the fishing boat and searched the lake, steering round and round the shoreline, in among the protruding docks and lifts. I imagined her welcome hand waving me over to a merry group around a campfire. I imagined a half-submerged corpse mangled by the old muskie that went after a toddler last summer. I imagined much else, but I saw nothing.

Marian wouldn't have gone to town, but on the following night I took my mother's car and searched there anyway. I looked in Silver Creek Traders with its candelabras shaped of deer antlers, and bejewelled ladies with silver hair buying Lake Country sweatshirts. I checked Sibley Station and saw only a single elderly man zealously spooning down his last few drops of Hungarian Mushroom soup, and I stopped in at the Butcher Block where a fat biker in beltless jeans exposed his butt as he leaned far over the beer-soaked bar, while behind him a hysterically laughing girl tapped the ashes of her Marlboro down his convenient cleavage.

Then I didn't know where to look. So I went home in despair.

And there she was, chatting with my mother.

"Look who's here, Evan," Mom said, the two of them grinning like co-conspirators who had just played a delicious prank on me.

For my mother this was all a novel experience. She knew that I was spending lots of time with Marian, and said nothing. She knew that the two of us sat for hours on the dock and beach, and she never thought up transparent excuses for bringing impertinent curiosity down the stairs, even though she must have been as excited and eager as a child at Christmas. She had more reason than most to know that it would either happen or not.

But to talk to a girlfriend of mine who acted like an adult, without adolescent squeamishness, without embarrassed giggling or an unseemly rush to escape her presence, gave my mother a new and unmixed sense of pleasure. I could see it in the serene joy of her face as she looked from

Marian to me. Not just the pleasure of conversation, I later realized, hers was the motherly pleasure of seeing her own son's growing adulthood, reflected in his capacity for knowing and valuing a mature young woman like Marian. It was pleasure in the prospect of my soon marrying and beginning a new family in the old family home, settling down on the quiet lake amid the august white pines and red oaks that bowed and waved to successive generations in the brisk night wind.

I couldn't wait to get Marian out of there and interrogate her.

"Where the hell were you, Marian?" I hissed as soon as we were out the door and onto the dark stairs. "I looked everywhere for you. Your parents didn't know where you were, and didn't care. I didn't know where you were, but I had to look for you. How could you just go off like that? Go off for days, when we have so little time left?"

"Shhh! Listen, Evan. Listen to the song of the loons."

Marian was one step behind me on the stairs, and I turned back and pulled her to me and held her there, hoping to extort a confession. "I don't want to listen to loons. I want to know where you were!"

"That's where I was, Evan. On my island, thinking. Listening to the loons. Hear how the two of them call back and forth to each other? 'Where are you?' 'Here I am.' 'Where are you?' 'Here I am.' They dive and surface, call once more and are answered. But after each plunge into the darkness, loneliness comes back and they have to find each other. They can never get enough assurance, because the loneliness never stops. So they call again. 'Where are you?'"

"Just riddles. You're talking in riddles again. What do you mean 'your island'? There aren't any islands on this lake."

Marian pulled my head to her breast and looked out over me to the lake. "None that you can see," she replied.

Oh, geez, I thought. That's great. Invisible islands, imaginary islands, fantasy islands. The loon music had gotten to her head.

"Come on, Evan. I'll show you," she said impishly, as she led me by the hand down to the dock in the darkness below. And there, moored at the end of it, was a pontoon boat the size of the Queen Mary. Actually, it was probably only thirty feet or so, but it looked immense on our little lake. A royal blue canopy stretched over the whole length; flexible plastic windows shielded the sides and rear, like a camper. You could live comfortably for weeks on a thing like that, though on our lake there was nowhere to go but around and around.

"It's my father's," Marian said. "Untie the ropes and come on." As I stepped onboard, I could see in the dimness that a canvas wall partitioned off the aft section, forming a separate, private room for sleeping. Forward was a wet bar, situated dangerously close to the captain's chair. At Buddy's request, no doubt.

Marian turned the key, and twin 90-horse engines rumbled to life. She eased away from the dock and, throttling up, propelled us swiftly into the darkness. I sat alongside, watching the deep wake flow out behind us, the only visible feature in the obsidian mirror of the windless lake. On this night of the new moon, the familiar shoreline of the cabin quickly faded out into a general blackness. With the shoreline gone, sky and lake became one.

No one was on the lake, as far as the eye could see. You would have expected a diehard fisherman like Werner Omdahl, trolling for walleye, but not tonight. Just the two of us, on a wholly private journey. The very solitude brought us closer together and, sensing that, I came over and stood behind her, letting her dark mane whip over my arms and chest, as the boat raced on, engines roaring. Marian steered straight ahead, toward no landmark that I could see, toward an invisible destination, perhaps an invisible island. I wanted to go there with her. I wanted her to take me.

The engines ceased, returning the lake to silence and the music of the loons. Marian rose and faced me. Her arms closing round my back, she brought me to her, and my entire body came alive at her touch. Eyes, the color of the moonless sky, the color of the moonless lake, looked deeply into mine, without asking any question or needing to. As I was about to speak, she raised her lips to mine, to silence them. She wanted no words.

And then Marian kissed me in the way a truly fortunate man is kissed once in his life. She gave me the kiss by which a woman plights her troth, that leaves no doubt, requires no explanation or certification, the kiss that withholds nothing.

I didn't know what to say. Somehow "thank you" didn't seem right. So I was silent. I just held her to me and waited.

"This is it," she whispered resolutely, stepping away. Around us, I saw nothing. "Give me a minute," Marian said and went into the room at the rear of the boat. After a moment she emerged, clothed only in the darkness of the night. Unashamed, unafraid, she paused, framed by the doorway, and let me gaze in wonderment upon her body.

I looked and was moved.

Then, striding across the deck, Marian dove into the black water. Down she went, soundlessly, and I lost sight of her almost immediately. I didn't know where she would come up. So I went to the other side of the boat, expecting a trick. Not there. I went to the front, I came back to the side. Twenty seconds elapsed, thirty, forty, and then suddenly she exploded up from the darkness, gasping for the air she wished she didn't need, wanting to fly on forever in the black depths.

"Where are you, Evan?" she called out, treading water and wiping the drops out of her eyes.

"Right here."

"Come into the water."

"Oh, no thanks."

"Come in," she repeated.

"I'm not much of a swimmer," I said, leaning over the side.

"I know, Evan. I know."

"I never liked the water much."

"I know. You can't swim at all, can you?"

"No. Not at all."

"I want you to come in, Evan."

"I really can't. Out here in the middle!"

"I want you to come in. Come in to me, Evan. Take your clothes off and come in. Take them off."

Desire and fear pulled me two ways like two teams of horses. I wanted her so much. I wanted to feel her naked body next to mine. I wanted to touch every part, kiss every part, possess every part. I was ready to burst with desire that had to be released. But at what price? I knew I would drown in that water. I had tried to learn again and again. Lord knows I felt my inability to swim was a slur against my manhood, a kind of impotence. I lived on a lake, for crying out loud! Why couldn't I do it?

Was it something only a father could teach? He would take me under his arm and say, "Here, son, here's the secret. You just have to do this. Watch me!" and then I would have it too. Mom tried, but it wasn't the same. She sent me to remedial swimming class, and on the first day the teacher had to bring me home after hauling me up, half dead, from the bottom of the pool. "Can't teach a rock to swim," he said.

And so I clung to life. "I'm sorry, Marian. I can't. Come back on board. I'm sorry."

"No, I will not," she insisted. "We will be in this together or not at all. I'm about to do the most terrifying thing I've ever done in my whole life, Evan. And so are you." Her voice was hard, threatening almost. "I'm afraid, but I trust you. I do! Those past few nights I spent here, thinking, deciding that it was right. Deciding you were right. I trust you entirely. With my life! And I want you to trust me. Wholly, completely. Take off your clothes now and come in to me."

Once she said that, I knew if I didn't I'd never be able to live with myself anyway, so I decided I might as well die right there. Just end my doomed life with a grand, heroic gesture. I didn't have many clothes on, but how I got those few off, I'll never know. I was trembling like a man palsied. My teeth chattered as in the dead of winter. I shook, and my clothes resisted, got caught, ripped, shredded. But I got them off somehow, and as I stood there, my body tumescent, on the edge of the boat and of my miserable fate, Marian looked at me. Her gaze swept over my whole body. I could feel her eyes brush over my manhood like the touch of soft fingers, and fearing I was about to erupt, I jumped straight out into the blackness.

I remember only thrashing wildly, pawing the water for very life, vainly grasping at Marian, who was only a few feet away. I flailed my arms, and went under horribly, coming up coughing and spitting and gasping for breath. But before I could catch any air, I went under again, filling my lungs with water. My arms and legs were all working against each other, so I could not even float. I went down, deeper into the blackness. I could not see her, I could not reach her, and still I went down and could not get up. I was drowning.

Then a miracle happened. My feet reached bottom, and I stood up, my head and nose and mouth just breaking the surface of the water.

I stood there coughing and spluttering and must have coughed for ten minutes before I could talk. "Your island?" I finally asked. "Your invisible island?"

"Yes," she said, and she gathered me, still trembling from terror and desire, to her body, the body of the long distance swimmer, long and lean, graceful, lithe. Underwater her flesh felt silken, fluid, like the water itself. She said, "Come into me." My loins strained to find her, to become one with her, to become one with the water. And she said, "Yes."

Embracing, intertwined, we danced upon the floor of the underwater island, moving with the currents of passion in the darkness, wreathed by seaweed among wondering fishes. Together, we were satisfied.

Afterward, we lay on the bed of the pontoon boat, remembering. Our hands explored shadowed contours, as the hands of the blind trace out the form and shape of what they would see and remember. We said nothing, as we tried in silence to become acquainted with the people we had just become. And with the people we were to be thereafter. The future loomed darkly. I trusted Marian, but did I trust myself? I did not know where I had come from. How could I know where I was going?

"I love you, Evan," I heard her say in the darkness.

I could barely make out the features of her face as I touched her lips and heard her speak of love. Were we lovers, then? What would she demand of me, this woman who had chosen me and trusted me? What was due to her in return? What price love? I did not want to know.

A single loon sang out across the moonless lake. "Tell me that you love me, Evan," she pleaded. "I never want to be lonely again. Promise you'll never leave me. I have given myself to you, and you alone. Stay with me forever."

I turned away from her and, looking out into the darkness, I was afraid, for I knew then what men have always feared, always denied, always known. The price of one moment is forever.

Chapter 9

What happy times together we've been spending.
I wish that every kiss was never ending.
Oh, wouldn't it be nice!

Saturday was laundry day, and drowning out the noise of the washer and dryer in the back room, Libby was belting out the Beach Boys. She always preferred golden oldies for the household chores. She never sang in the shower—unless she was cleaning it, that is, and then like always she'd turn the radio up, fill her lungs, and let'er rip. Always the same station, FM 107.5, The Power Loon.

"Come on, Evan," she hollered when I peeked into the laundry room. "Croon with the Loon!"

We could be married (Sing it, Evan!)
And then we'd be happy. (I can't hear you!)
Oh, wouldn't it be nice!

"I'll be on my way, Libby," I said quickly, before she had a chance to inquire of me whether it wouldn't, as a matter of indisputable fact, be pretty darn nice. I didn't want her asking whether I had fulfilled my promise to "think about our future together." But Libby was not a designing woman, or a nag, and she had more immediate sins of mine on her mind.

"Yeah, sure! Take off right in the middle of the bras and boxers! Oh, no, you don't, buddy. No way! Get your buns of steel over here and fold your own Fruit of the Wombs."

She was right about that. (Not the womb business, of course. Miss Libby Lutheran liked to twit me for my failure to renounce the faith of my mothers and embrace the one true church Protestant and local.) But she was right that I shouldn't run off leaving her pairing my socks or washing my dishes, even if she did enjoy singing to them. (I think they enjoyed it, too, in a quiet sort of way.)

Libby wasn't my maid. She was my...my what? She was not my partner (too legalistic), she was not my squeeze (too vulgar), she was not my significant other (pure psychobabble), she was not my friend (friends don't screw friends), she was not my lover (the first heats of passion had ebbed). So, pondering what Libby was to me, exactly, I set down my jacket and picked up my undies.

"I'm glad you're going over to see your Mom," she said quietly, turning the radio down and tucking a few uncooperative strands of hair behind her ear.

"Yeah," I said, repulsed by the very thought of Sacred Heart.

"I hope she's ok today. Say hello for me."

"Sure."

"You might want to turn those undies right side out before you fold them."

"Oh. Right."

"Whatcha thinking about?"

"Lots of things. About my mother." That wasn't a complete lie. Somehow my mother and Libby were bound up together for me in a way I didn't quite understand.

"Yeah. It's so sad. I wish she could be here with us. Here at home."

It was sad all right. Not just the Alzheimers or the home we had to put her in when she could no longer care for herself. It was sad that I owed my mother so much and had given her so little. I could hardly force myself to do the right thing by her, even once a week. It was sad that I wanted nothing more fervently than to avoid that truly depressing place. And more, it was sad that she had been left without someone to live with till death did them part. It was sad that she must have been desperately lonely year after year, and now she was ending her life in the still deeper loneliness of the mind, surrounded by eighty other desperately lonely people. It was sad all right.

"You ok, Evan?"

"Yeah. Fine."

"Don't forget next Sunday."

"Sunday? Sure, your parents' house for dinner."

"Actually they want us to come early."

"For what? Brunch?"

"For church."

"Oh, no, Libby! Gimme a break. I don't want to go to church. A Lutheran church? No way! Make my excuses, but no thanks. Tell them I'm a heathen, an atheist, a devil worshipper! Tell them I'm a Catholic, for Chrissake!"

"Unfortunate choice of words, Evan. But I will tell them nothing. They know exactly what you are, and they want us to go to church with them. You know, I'm not exactly the church lady type, but I will go because I love them, and you will go because you love me, and you will smile and be happy."

The ultimatum. The trump card. "Because you love me." It was a dangerous game for Libby to be playing, she knew, because when you play your trump, you have to be prepared to lose big, right there and then. But I didn't want a fight, still less an earnest discussion about "our future together," and so I caved in.

"Oh, all right. I guess I can endure it this one time. I'll go, and I'll smile. But I refuse to be happy!"

In fact, I was profoundly unhappy as I drove down the road toward the Sacred Heart Home, the same road that went to Breezy Point and the Farina's horse farm. I didn't want to go where I was going today. I didn't want to go where I was going next Sunday. I didn't want to go where I seemed to be going my whole damn life, but I couldn't ever manage to get off this road.

Didn't they know that this church thing was transparent? I felt like I was watching reruns of a bad murder mystery I'd seen too many times already, and the victim was me. The same old story. The age old plot was being plotted against me. Meet the family, have a meal, go to church, get married, be fruitful and multiply. Did they think I couldn't see through it? Why can't they just let you keep it simple, uncomplicated? Without church, without marriage and multiplication?

No, there's always the spider web. Touch it anywhere and you're stuck. You've got all these strings all over you, ligatures, obligations, responsibilities, connections. You feel like Gulliver tied down by Lilliputians. Nothing that amounts to a chain, really. They just run a million tiny threads all over you, and soon you feel like you're being woven up into a cocoon, a sack, a womb, and if you ever manage to get out, there's always one string still attached. Why, I wondered aloud as I turned into the parking lot, why can't they just leave you alone?

I wasn't left wondering long. As soon as I walked in the front door, I realized how profoundly, abysmally stupid that question was. For the smell of Sacred Heart hit me with the force of an epiphany, the smell of prunes, of disinfectant—and of eighty desolate people who were all being left alone.

My eyes teared up in anger at myself and everybody else too, and I tried desperately to keep myself from breaking down entirely before I got to my mother's room. Vacant eyes lined the interminable hallway, pleading for recognition. I nodded, smiled politely, and carefully scutinized room numbers to shield myself from the pathos of their mute and deafening appeal.

"John?" A stooped and shrunken woman accosted me outside my mother's door, reaching out a feeble hand. "Is that you, John?"

"No, sorry. I'm Evan, Evan Wade," I said, knocking. "I'm here to see my mother."

"See your mother," she repeated ominously, as I opened the door.

Mom sat in a shabby, overstuffed chair that faced the TV, but her head was turned away so she could see out the room's single window. It looked onto the brick wall of the men's building across the parking lot. Beside her was the sole piece of furniture she had insisted on bringing with her, the cedar hope chest that Roy Macklin had given her instead of a ring. All those years it sat in the living room and I never once saw it open. What was inside I didn't know. Maybe nothing. At home the chest had served only to gather dust beneath the living room window and hold the lamp that cast its futile beams into the darkness outside. She was not permitted to bring the lamp.

"Hello, Mom. How are you?" I said, walking over and giving her a kiss. "You doing ok?" The pointless, empty merriment of *I Love Lucy* filled the stagnant air.

"I wanted to stop over to say hello. See how you're doing. You doing ok? You're looking just fine."

The hollow laughter would not be silenced. A vast invisible audience greeted my questions with forced hilarity.

"Mom, it's me. Evan." I walked over and stood between her and the window. "Look, it's Evan. Your son." Her gaze was unimpeded by my body. I had been rendered transparent. She looked right through me with a daydreamer's eyes, open and unblinking but vacant. With the eye of the mind she was seeing another place, another time, another man. I knew who it was.

A very thick phonebook lay open on her lap. Her right hand, forefinger extended, rested on the left page, as if she had just left off searching for a number. Forty years of looking out the window, forty years of searching. I had had enough. It all welled up within me and I just exploded.

"Forget him!" I shouted, snatching the book from her lap. "You're not going to find him in there. He's not coming back. Forget him for once, will you? He's gone for good, long gone, and left us up in the air. Both of us."

No response whatever.

"It wasn't just you he ran out on. I feel like my whole damn life I've been dangling, dangling in the breeze because of him. I can't quite touch the ground. I can't get my feet under me, can't get going with my life. What made him do it, Mom? Tell me. Why wouldn't he marry you? I've got to know. Was it me? Did he know about me? Does he know I'm alive? Did you ever tell him?"

Silence, except for televised laughter.

"Look at me. Was that it? Did you tell him about me, and then he took off? Was it my fault? Didn't he want to be a father? My father? Why didn't he want me? I would have loved him. I know I would have. So many nights I lay awake imagining fishing trips and duck blinds, and loving him. Wondering where he was, who he was. I feel like I've got this big emptiness in me somewhere. Half of me is missing, just an empty outline, and I can't fill it in. Who was he? Tell me what he was like. Do you look at me and see him, see his eyes, hear his voice? I've got to know who that is I see when I look in the mirror. What was he like that he could just up and leave us like that? What was he like that you never gave him up? You must have wanted to, God knows. How could you have loved him so much that you gave him your whole life, married or not?"

"And you gave him my life, too! Do you know that? You gave him my life, too, because you kept that damned lamp shining in the window all those years. Why couldn't you just give him up and find somebody else? There must have been other guys. Why not find a father for me? Somebody to put his arm around my shoulder and bait my hook and hold my bike and teach me to swim the way only a father can?

"Is that too much to ask? Tell me, Mom. Why couldn't you? I have a right to know."

For a long time I remained standing there exposed to her unseeing eyes, weeping for this abandoned woman, weeping for her fatherless child. My mother's impassive face registered no explanation, registered no sympathy or guilt. She offered no apology for her life, or mine. But as I stood there, having emptied myself of a lifetime of smoldering questions, unanswered still, her vacant eyes unexpectedly came to focus, like someone awakening.

"Evan?" she said, and that one word, one look of recognition brought great joy to me.

"Yes! Yes, Mom. It's me."

"Evan, don't break her heart, will you? Such a lovely girl. Don't break her heart and mine."

It was too much. It was just too much to bear, because I knew it wasn't Libby. It was Marian she meant. Without ever asking, she knew what I had done; she knew what I thought was concealed from all but Marian and me. A wave of guilt passed through me, and I had to get out of there. Pursued by furies, I ran unheeding out of her room, down the gauntlet of pleading eyes and outstretched hands. I ran past empty chapel and full dispensary, all the way out to the main exit, and there my headlong flight was suddenly arrested by a picture.

Just a picture of the Holy Mother hanging in the foyer. Why I hadn't noticed it before I don't know—so many meaningless icons around these places, so much ancient drivel. But now this painting hit home hard and jerked me to a stop: the sacred heart of Mary, Lady of Sorrows, breast ripped open, her exposed heart transfixed by seven swords.

I knew what I had to do.

Chapter 10

Reluctantly, Sherm gave me a couple days of what he called "Personal Leave"—defined in his own idiosyncratic way. I told him I had to go back to the Cities to settle some pressing business. And he said, "I've got pressing business that needs attending here, too, Evan. We're short-handed already, and I can't do it all myself. If I can't depend on you, I'm going to have to take on somebody else."

And I said, "Sorry, Sherm. I've got to go."

"You're not still hung up on Jeremiah Smit and the Barclay woman, are you?"

"Yeah. Afraid so."

"For crying out loud, Evan! Then it's definitely a case of Personal Leave, because the sensible *person* I used to know has definitely taken complete and utter *leave* of his senses."

Libby didn't give me any leave at all, personal or otherwise. "Not again!" she cried. "You were just down there, Evan! How long are you going to be gone this time? You can't keep running out on me like this. Why do you have to go back? Forget about Marian Barclay. Why can't you just let it go? I want you here at home with me because I love you, Evan. I love you, and you won't go back down there if you...."

I put my hand on her mouth to stop her from playing her trump, because I knew it wouldn't work this time and the game would be over.

She would lose big. We both would. I was headed south, with or without her permission, but that didn't have to mean the end for us, so long as she didn't throw down another ultimatum. So I stopped her mouth and preserved a while longer the fragile tie between us. It was more than I had done with Anne Chisolm. I could have easily let Libby speak the words that would have sent our whole "future together" right up in smoke. And I didn't. I didn't let her end it. But she turned her back on me and stormed out of the room.

So I just assured her, "I'll be back in plenty of time for Sunday," and headed out.

Driving south, the gently rolling landscapes of Pierz and Genola and Buckman and Foley stretched out before me. The setting sun on that warm August evening magically transformed the featureless openness of mere farm country into a rich allegorical tapestry. Great golden rolls of hay cast lengthening shadows across cleanly shaven fields. Solitary farm houses rose from the earth, each nestled in its own windbreak. Against purple gray thunderheads gathering on the horizon, the low sun threw brilliant white silos into sharp relief. I could interpret these things and was comforted.

The beatific vision abruptly faded as I hit the suburbs, however. Darkness fell, the humidity rose, and the stillness of the night brought swarms of flying, biting insects into the oily air. I seized the opportunity to avenge tormented humankind and speeded up. Thick as rain, mosquitoes and moths, beetles and bugs lost their slimy lives on my invulnerable windshield. Like an avenging Rambo, I cut a swath of carnage down the whole length of Route 10 into the Cities. At length I sought rest from my labors at the Gopher Motel. There, at the foot of a thinly blanketed bed, a giant roach contemplated me with knowing malice, seeming to defer his revenge until I turned off the light.

My first stop, upon surviving the night, was at the Hennepin County Police Headquarters, where Queenie—all six foot three, two hundred sixteen pounds of him—did his best to instill in me all the trepidation of which I was capable. I didn't see any need to explain the exact nature of my relation to Marian or my interest in the case, but I knew enough to check in with him, at least.

"Keep away from Jeremiah Smit, Evan!" he thundered at me behind his closed office door. "I'm warning you. And while you're at it, keep out of the whole damn thing. I don't need you screwing up this investigation like you did the last one. I swear I'll have you up on obstruction charges if you don't stay out. The longer you live up north, the better friends we are. Let's keep it that way, huh? Nice and friendly. Now, why don't you just turn right around and head back to that little burg you came from and—who knows?—after a few years you and me might even get to be bosom buddies."

"You know how much I value your friendship and good opinion, Queenie," I began. Everybody called him that, even though Charles Cuene ("It's KEEN, damn it!") had been vainly trying to correct our pronunciation his entire life.

"Believe me, I'd like to stay out," I whined, "but I'm in it now because I got dragged in. Like I said, Smit told me that he stabbed Dr. Barclay. That's true, isn't it? She was stabbed?"

"Maybe."

"Now how would he know that unless he did it? And how would I know unless he told me? It wasn't in the papers, was it?"

"No," he grudgingly admitted. "We kept that quiet, along with a few other things."

"See?"

"But you know damn well, Evan, that what this loony did or did not tell you is just hearsay, as far as me or the court is concerned. We don't even have a real motive for Smit."

"He's a mad-dog pro-lifer, Queenie, slavering at the mouth!"

"So what? Just because this Dr. Slepian in Buffalo, and all the others going back to Gunn in '93, were killed by anti-abortion sickos doesn't prove diddly about Smit. And, besides, there's dozens of abortion doctors in the Twin Cities. He didn't kill all of them. Why this one? And even assuming he did tell you, I'm not sure I'd believe anybody who might find it to his professional advantage to be considered a murderer. He's got an alibi anyway. It's a dead end. So go back to Brainerd, Evan, and let us poor devils go about our business in peace."

"I can't go anywhere, Queenie. Because he told me. Me! You understand? I've got an in with him now. Let me try and help you."

"The kind of help you gave me last time just about got me fired, buddy!"

"But I'm off the *STrib* now! I've got nothing to gain here, and I swear I won't give Drake the time of day. Nothing. Zip. Come on, Queenie, let me try. Whatever I get I'll hand directly over to you, and if I come up empty I'll just swing the old gray Ford northward, and you'll be rid of me forevermore."

"Forevermore, you say? As in permanently? Gone for good? Out of my hair?"

"That's right."

"Tempting, but I don't believe it for a second. Nosing around down here, you'd be wasting your time anyhow, Evan. It's a complete dead end, I tell you."

"Maybe it is," I added, "but you don't need to worry then, because I can't do much damage on a dead end street, can I?"

"Suppose not," he conceded.

"You won't be sorry."

And thus it came about that Detective Charles Cuene, declaring "he was sorry already," told me what I already knew but had to hear him say. Queenie had a mean streak, and so I didn't want him finding out that I was dabbling around in the case behind his back.

"They swear Smit was right there with them. And I have to swallow it, until I can prove otherwise, which you can be damn sure I've tried my damnedest to do week after week. We're not going to let this one go. Not ever. Anytime you think about slacking off, you just have to see her lying there in a pool of blood. Seven wounds. And in the stomach! My God! However long you're in the business, you don't get over that kind of thing. Not ever."

Queenie was no fool and no slacker putting in time until retirement. We'd had our run-ins over the years, but I never had a question about his professionalism. I had not a moment's doubt that he had indeed done his damnedest on the case, and that fact nagged at me a little as I left his office and took I-94 to 10th Avenue in downtown St. Paul. Why should I be able to do anything when Queenie couldn't?

And that led me to wonder whether Queenie couldn't break Smit's alibi because there was nothing to break. But that was silly. Smit had told me he was willing to kill for the cause, told me that Marian was the enemy. What more did I need? And that meant either Smit's minons were lying to protect him, or that they were telling the truth, and the ME's determination of the time of death was wrong. Not likely, but I'd have to see what I could get out of Trish in the ME's office.

And there was another more serious question nagging at me. Why had I assumed without question that Marian was shot? Guns are effective, readily accessible, typical kinds of murder weapons, I guess. But there was another reason. I had assumed it was a shooting because, just like Queenie suggested, I assumed that the MO of the Buffalo assassination and others like it would fit here too. Or even if Marian had been killed with a bomb, like the clinic guard in Birmingham, that would have made some sense. Because these are killings at a distance. Like Slepian, for instance, who was shot not with a handgun but with a rifle through his living room window. Remote, impersonal is what these ideological killings usually are.

But stabbing is a very particular, very personal way to kill someone. You have to be right there, face to face. Did Smit know Marian personally, then? And even if he did, what in their relationship could possibly create all that anger? Because with a knife, one thrust is not going to get the job done. You have to be out of control. You have to be consumed with rage to stab again and again and again, while the victim is fighting you, thrashing, fighting for life.

A wave of nausea passed over me.

I had a hard time imagining Smit's calm, self-disciplined features contorted with murderous rage. But I had come much too far to leave without carrying it through.

The converted storefront that served as headquarters for the New Holocaust Christian Center looked as dour and forbidding as the function it existed to serve. The building had accumulated the soot of a thousand furnaces and the exhaust of a million cars. Whatever gay or solemn color it was once painted had long since turned to the color of old houseflies. I dreaded entering. I dreaded another confrontation with the dwarf.

A xerox sheet bearing the name of the Center was scotchtaped inside the window. Disappointed that I had found the right place, I took a deep breath and turned the handle. The door was locked. No open hours were posted. I put my nose to the window and peered in but saw no one inside. With a great sense of relief, I turned on my heels and almost bowled over Brother Jeremiah himself.

"Well, Mr. Wade! I am surprised," he said, as he took out a key and worked it in the lock. "After our last conversation in Brainerd I would have thought you'd be one of the last people to visit our Center. To what do I owe the…Well now, what would be the precise word on this occasion? To what do I owe the pleasure? Perhaps it's rather more of a displeasure. Wouldn't you agree, Mr. Wade? To what do I owe—shall I say—the honor, then? No, definitely not an honor either! Let me just ask, to what do I owe your presence on the doorstep of the New Holocaust Christian Center?"

This was not a promising beginning. "Let's just start over, can we, Smit? Try a fresh page? You've got a job to do, and so do I," I said, following him through the door into a large empty room with a circle of chairs. On the walls were posters calculated to upset the moral stomach. Mine was unphased.

"A fresh start would be very welcome, Mr. Wade. And very necessary, too. You see, after you falsely and maliciously informed your colleague Mr. Drake that I confessed to the murder of Marian Barclay, I am not much inclined to discuss our Center with you now or at any other time."

That's it, I thought. Ben had sabotaged me again. This interview is over. I've got nothing to lose. Why not switch the tack from "just need some background" to "in your face"?

"I told Drake exactly what you told me. Verbatim. You were fighting a war, and Marian Barclay was the enemy. She's dead. What conclusion was I supposed to draw?"

"You heard what you wanted to hear, Mr. Wade. Now, I must ask you to leave."

"I'm not going to leave here without some answers!"

"Goodbye, Mr. Wade." Brother Jeremiah was calm and unmoved as he turned to his desk.

"Tell me!" I shouted. "What did she do to you to make you hate her so fiercely? It's just you and me here! Tell me."

"We are not alone, Mr. Wade."

I thought at first that he was referring to the Divine Presence, and I involuntarily gazed upward to the tin ceiling. But then he nodded over toward the corner, where sat the anorexic girl, head bowed, her long hair spilling over her face.

"Does she live here?" I asked.

"I let Sister Amelie stay here when she has nowhere else to go."

"She's one of your soldiers?"

"Yes, and one of the victims of the war. One of the miracles." He walked over and put his palm on the still bowed head of the young woman, as if giving her a blessing, or receiving one. "Sister Amelie is a survivor."

"Survivor of what?" I asked in puzzlement.

"A survivor of the new holocaust, Mr. Wade, of the million and a half who are slain every year in this country alone. A survivor of mass murder."

"Abortion? Cut the bull. There are no survivors. That kind of crap may fuel your propaganda machine, Smit, but I know what the termination procedures are. I know that there's no way."

"You know nothing, Mr. Wade. Behold the living proof of your ignorance. Behold the one survivor born every day among us, the one in four thousand for whom our Lord in his wisdom chooses to stay the hand of the murderer."

"I never knew" was all I could manage to say.

"Yes, Mr. Wade. We call her Amelie because she is worthy to be loved. She is the miracle among us. Blessed with life, indeed, but cursed with a life most burdensome and tragic. Imagine it, can you? A child brought into life at the very moment she is consigned to death by her own mother! She needs our love. And our prayers."

Sister Amelie raised her head and, from out those cavernous sockets, simply gazed at me. She said nothing. She didn't need to say anything, because I could hear her deafening cry resound in the silence of the empty room.

"Pray for us, Mr. Wade. Pray for us now and at the hour of our birth."

Chapter 11

"Was Marian having problems at work you know of, Francine?"

"I don't know, Evan. I've been over all of this with the police, and I'm afraid I couldn't help them very much. Things are so hazy, indistinct. Now, with Buddy gone, I've been real low."

"I know, and I really appreciate your being willing to talk to me like this. Anything you can remember might help."

Even though it was late in the evening, I had stopped in at the Barclay's Kenwood house partly to dig up what I could, but partly to offer Francine my somewhat belated condolences. It had been a little more than a week since Buddy had given up Jim Beam and all his other worldly pleasures. He wasn't much as a human being, but he was all she had—except for the half million dollar house and investments worth three times that. She loved him, I guess, but nothing's simple; and other people's marriages are, with good reason, opaque to all but the eye of God. Francine twisted the gaudy diamond ring on her left hand, mindlessly slipping it up over the slender knuckle and then back down.

"No, nothing at work. No problems I know of. But we weren't real close in these last years. We were never very close. She always upset Buddy so."

Francine talked distractedly, dreamily, less to me than to the great picture window that formed one end of the palatial living room. The sun had set, and the twilight was fast dimming.

"Trevor and Marian did stop in once for a drink last fall, I remember. We were all on our way to the Walker for the opening of some exhibit or other. But she didn't say anything about the hospital. She didn't say much of anything at all. Even to Trevor."

Francine gently placed the fingertips of her right hand to her temple and let them slip slowly down her cheek until they rested on her neck. The skin of her hand had become thin and transparent, exposing veins and arteries, bones and sinews, like an anatomy lesson. But Francine Barclay was still an elegant woman. She sat forward on the sofa, and held her body erect. She still had her pride, despite everything Buddy had done to rob her of it.

"We always wanted Marian to become a doctor, you know. We were so proud when she got her white jacket." Francine receded into her memories and the dimness of the darkening room. "I didn't have a lot of education myself. A few night classes in typing and stenography. That was all I had the chance for, before I had to find work and went to Barclay Buick. But Marian was so smart. She always did real well in school, so we knew she could be a doctor and then we would have a doctor in the family. The Smithsons next door, you know, their children never amounted to anything. We wanted so much to be proud of Marian. I wanted Buddy to be able to say 'my daughter, Dr. Barclay' and smile from ear to ear! That was why we were so afraid when she dropped out of Carleton that first year."

"Marian left school in her first year? I knew it was a little rocky at first."

"Yes, but it turned out to be nothing. The end of her first semester was when it was. She said she needed some time to sort things out, and I could understand that, even if I didn't go to college myself. So she spent a month or two with a friend in New York somewhere. It was nothing though. She was back at Carleton the following fall, and it was smooth sailing from then on. Top of her class every term. Buddy and I were so proud of what she made of herself. But always from a distance, you know. We were never real close."

Francine's voice trailed off into the silence. Only the ticking of the grandfather clock filled the pauses. I could barely make out her features across the unlit room and so could not read her face. I sat there wondering if I should press her anymore, and decided against it. This was probably a dead end, too. Francine didn't seem to have any ideas, or even any curiosity, about Marian's killer. I thought about leaving but didn't want to be impolite. Then she picked up the thread again.

"We were so pleased when she married Trevor. Such a perfect match, with his position at the hospital. Director of something or other. Maybe if they had children, you know, that might have brought them over here once in a while, even if Buddy didn't get along very well with Trevor. Grandchildren could have cleared the air. There's so much room here for children to play. So many empty rooms. We never had any toys, but we could have bought some. Stuffed elephants, and swing sets, and coloring books, and little gas stations. All the things that make children laugh. We would have loved to have their kids around the house, hug them, and spoil them. Sometimes that can happen, can't it? All the walls between parents and children come down when it's just grandparents and grandchildren?

"Yes, I'm sure it happens sometimes," I said, though I suspected the opposite was more often true—that grandchildren were made into bricks in the wall between parents and children, pawns in games they couldn't understand, but Francine wasn't really asking for my analysis and continued without it.

"I never asked Marian why she and Trevor didn't have children. And her an obstetrician! I can't imagine they didn't want children. It might have changed things between the two of them, too."

"Things?" I felt ashamed as soon as I asked. If there was anything wrong between Marian and her husband, I had to know, even though, personally, it was none of my business.

"Well, sometimes you just have a sense about couples in trouble," Francine said, "but I don't know really. It wasn't my place to ask about their marriage. Marian would have just turned her cold eyes on me, like she always did. Not that she didn't have a right. We weren't ever close, us two. She was not my daughter and never let me forget it, never let me forget what a smart and loving woman her 'real' mother was, never let me forget that Buddy was not mine completely and never would be."

Francine twisted the ring up her slender finger and then back down, finally taking it off entirely and staring at the immense, gaudy diamond, now just a stone, catching no light. She went on, a disembodied voice in the semi-darkness.

"I wanted to give Buddy a son so we could start over, just the two of us and our son, a new family starting out together. That's what I dreamed of. But it was not to be. Not for us, and Buddy would not hear of adopting, even though Trevor told me once he might be able to find a way. But Buddy wouldn't hear of it. So we never did make a new start, and he stayed tied to a past that I would never be part of. But Marian was part of it. She was the tie. Buddy loved her so, and loved her mother through her. Never stopped really, even after we were married. He resented Marian for not being her mother, hated being reminded at every moment that Sara was gone. And I resented Marian too—for reminding me that Sara was still very much here, every night lying on that old four-poster bed upstairs, between Buddy and me. It's as if I couldn't have Buddy at all unless I was willing to share him. That was the price I had to pay, because now Sara and Marian are gone, but he's gone too. They're all gone."

The invisible clock tolled the hour and ticked on.

"And when they lay me down beside Buddy, the whole Barclay family will be gone. Not a single one left, and no one to carry on. The whole line will come to an end. It's so sad for the family just to die out like this and leave the world without a trace. It's as if you lived and died for nothing, to no purpose. You just vanish one day, like you were just an illusion and you never really lived at all. Everything you thought was your life—all the openings at the Walker, and the golf tournaments at Rush Creek, the fundraisers for Wellstone, and the dinners at Goodfellows—at the end of the day, everything you thought was real is just a mirage, unless you have children. Unless it goes on after you, your life's just an illusion, gone with a snap of the fingers."

That was all Francine had to say. It was enough. More than I had bargained for, more than I wanted. I was embarrassed by her grief or, more exactly, resentful because it was so intrusive and presumptuous. Her outpouring seemed to demand something of me that I didn't want to give, whatever it was. All I wanted was "Just the facts, ma'am"—anything that could help me find who killed Marian. I owed it to her to find out if I could, but not to pry into whether she wanted children, or her marriage was rocky, or her husband had his spats with Buddy. Who didn't?

Francine just sat there with the grandfather clock ticking in the darkness. Maybe she was still staring out the window. Maybe she was staring at me. What was I supposed to do or say? I'm not quite sure what it was about me that seemed to invite confessionals like this, but I was getting more than my share of them, who knows why.

The sick take "How are you?" for a real question about their ailments; the grieving mistake the empty formulas of condolence for real sympathy, and they just seize the opportunity. Their hearts are so full it doesn't take much to spill them. Once you utter even the hollowest expressions of sympathy, you're obligated to listen. You lose your right to shut the floodgates of grief once you've opened them, let come what may. So I sat there while Francine grieved.

Thankfully the doorbell rang. Francine switched on a lamp, and the room snapped back into existence. When she opened the door, I heard her say, "Come in. No, no, not at all. It's not too late at all." That was my exit line and I stood up.

An aging, portly man in a dark suit of the old cut backed into the room, saying, somewhat pompously, "I could see no lights on, and I feared I had missed you, Francine. But I'm so pleased to find you home.

You look somewhat drawn. Perhaps I have something here that would…" He was beginning to open a doctor's valise but stopped abruptly as he turned and saw me standing there. "Oh, I am sorry. I didn't know you had company. Please excuse me for interrupting."

"Not at all. I was just about to leave," I said, heading for the door. "Thank you, Francine. Thank you for talking with me during this hard time."

"Of course, Evan. This is Simeon…Dr. Simeon Landreau, our physician, our friend, for so many years. Simeon, do you remember Evan Wade?"

Apparently he did, because as soon as Francine pronounced my name, Landreau stiffened up like a board. He clasped his hands uncordially behind his back and by way of acknowledgement tipped his head in a way that was barely civil. Whatever I had done to get his hackles up, I had done a fine job of it.

"Yes, Francine," he said curtly, "I remember Mr. Evan Wade very well." The static in the air was palpable. "From Marian's funeral," he added.

"Oh, Simeon," Francine sighed. "Don't hold that against Evan. It wasn't his fault. You know how Buddy was sometimes."

"Indeed, I do," Landreau replied with inexplicable intensity. "I knew Burton for many years, Francine, even longer than you, and I was proud to call him my friend. I know he was always quick tempered, lightning quick, but never without cause. I know he was not one to make false accusations, Mr. Wade. You should be aware that I was well acquainted with his daughter, too, since the time when she was an impish child, the apple of her father's eye. I saw Marian through the loss of her beloved mother, as well as the troubled and tumultuous years of her adolescence."

Landreau put an arm around Francine, who stood at his side with her head down, unwilling or unable to stop his unaccountable rampage. "I was proud to watch her overcome all obstacles, finish her education, and ultimately enter my own profession, a mature young woman, wise beyond her years. I loved Marian Barclay dearly, Mr. Wade. I grieved her death as if she were my own daughter. You would do well to keep that in mind at all times."

What an ass! I thought to myself, though I replied as cooly as I could, having just been tacitly threatened for committing some unknown offense. "Dr. Landreau, I seem to have offended you, I'm not sure how, but I would hope to be on friendly terms with all who cared for Marian. For I did too, and that is why I am doing whatever I can to help Detective Cuene in his investigation."

"You?" he snorted, rebuffing my overtures. "You? A washed-up snoop, dismissed, discredited, disgraced as a reporter! A mere nothing! It's preposterous—the idea that you have anything at all to offer Detective Cuene! What, do you suppose that a two-month liaison with Marian gives you some privilege here? Some special insight? Some personal right to harass this grieving woman? You have none whatever, I assure you."

Francine began to weep softly as Landreau harangued on and on. "You are persona non grata here, sir. Your vacuous sympathies are unwanted. Your presence is an insult to Marian's memory and the memory of her father. The best thing you can do, Mr. Wade, is to crawl back into that leech-infested mud hole where you were spawned, and never return here. Never!"

Chapter 12

What the hell was that all about? I wondered, as I shut the massive double door of the Barclay house behind me and headed out to my car. Landreau was obviously feeling protective of Marian, and Buddy and Francine too, for that matter. But what gave him the idea that they needed protection from me? I couldn't imagine that he thought I had something to do with Marian's death, but then I couldn't imagine what he was thinking at all. I don't even remember speaking to him at the funeral, though the fracas with Buddy couldn't have made a favorable impression. And Buddy was not the type to soften his accusations later, supposing Landreau asked about them. But accusations of what, exactly?

Before I knew it, the old gray Ford was headed out of Kenwood toward downtown Minneapolis. It seemed to know the way, and so I let it take the familiar streets that converged on my old haunts, the landmarks of my city life as a reporter. I remember so vividly the early fall morning I drove down 35W into the Cities for the first time, full of Wheaties and ready to make my mark on the world. The silver IDS tower jutted up into the blue sky like Excalibur, challenging me to show my mettle. And I had acquitted myself well enough. Up until the end, at least. Well, maybe my first months at the U weren't anything to brag about either.

Now, though, everything had changed from that first day and the days of my triumphs thereafter. The Foshay Tower and Metrodome and all the rest of the urban landscape seemed part of a distant past, a previous incarnation, even someone else's life. Though I'd been gone less than a year, in that short time I had been reassimilated to the country, like a junker left sitting out in a field, and now a thicket has grown up around it, in it, through it, as if it had never known the city streets at all.

Minneapolis is a pretty tame, unthreatening city, as cities go, but even so I'd never felt at home downtown. The suburbs were bad enough, but for me downtown was always an alien place, no matter how long I worked there. I felt like an exile, a stranger in a strange land. Somehow I couldn't even get used to walking on sidewalks, funny as that may sound. Maybe my feet were just made for hayfields, but for some reason I kept turning my ankle downtown. I even broke it once on a piece of jagged concrete shoved up by the irrepressible life below. That's what's real, the tree root or whatever was down there, the stuff that they're always covering up with the concrete. Or trying to.

"The city comes alive at night," they say—and yet for me there was always something bogus about night life, artificial light, artificial gaity, artificial vitality. For all the bustle of the urban beehive, in the city I found only life-likeness, a plausible replica. And now the deserted streets of night, lined by the grid of criss-crossing streetlights, made me feel like I was the only living being in a cyberspace city, more virtual than real. Even a leech-infested mudhole was more real than this.

Besides there weren't any leeches in Woman Lake, where I was "spawned." No mud either.

"How did Landreau know where I came from?" I asked myself as the old Ford eased into a parking space beside my old hangout, Brit's Pub. How did he know about Marian and me? I never saw him at the Barclay mansion on the point. But that didn't mean anything, since Buddy and Francine—and maybe Landreau, too—were always at the Club. And I was inside the house only a couple times anyway. Even if he was an old family friend, though, what's Marian and me got to do with him that he should get so pompously indignant?

Marian and I were together for awhile. Then we parted ways. End of story. But not for Landreau apparently. How did he know that I'd been fired from the *STrib*? Had he been keeping an eye on me all these years, or hiring somebody else to do it? Ridiculous! Probably just a coincidence, but it did give me an eerie feeling. I had come down to the Cities to do a little looking around and see what I could see, but at every turn I saw other pairs of eyes peering back at me! And why?

Brit's Pub was crowded and noisy, as it was on every weekday night. I sat down on my usual bar stool. It was unoccupied like always, and I wouldn't have been surprised if no one had sat on it for the entire nine months I'd been gone, because this particular stool faced the beer taps. Not that I especially liked looking at beer taps, but the rest of the stools faced the mirror, and if you're sitting at the bar alone, there's one person you don't want to face all night long. I preferred the company of beer taps.

"Evan! How the hell are you, old fellow! Long time, no see!" The half-British, half-American pidgin of the bartender was unmistakable.

"Hey, Cyril. How you doing?"

When we first met, many years ago, he told me his name was Cyril, Cyril Braithwaite. Since he was no more British than me, despite affecting the King's English, and since no self-respecting American was ever named Cyril, let alone Braithwaite, I always assumed that Cyril was his "bar name," like a pen name or stage name for other professions.

But late one night as the two of us were closing up the place, he confided in me. After he had tended bar at Brit's for a number of years, pretending to be Cyril, he decided that Cyril was who he really was, and so he had his name legally changed. Being a Cyril, he decided, was just as necessary as wearing an apron for the honorable profession he had chosen. Cyril he wanted to be, then, and Cyril he was. The pretend man was the real one.

That's the city for you.

"Can I get you a Guinness, Evan?" Such was the opening line of a private drama that had been running for the last umpteen years between us.

"No thanks, Cyril. A Grain Belt sounds real good, though. I've got a mighty thirst for Grain Belt tonight." Now I knew, and Cyril knew, and Cyril knew that I knew that Brit's Pub had never carried Grain Belt or any other down home Midwestern beer, and never would. But our little drama was like a dance, a ritual of comradery. Always the same steps, the same code of recognition between two people who had no other connection.

"Oh, so sorry, old fellow, we're fresh out of Grain Belt. Just sold the last one to a bag lady. Yup, a bottle of Thunderbird and a Grain Belt, our very last one."

"No Grain Belt?" I replied, in feigned amazement and consternation. "What kind of a place is this! Oh, all right, make it a Guinness, if you don't have anything better."

"Jolly good, then. A Guinness it is." Already pouring the glass before I could get my last line out, he served it with just the slightest trace of a bow, like he was Jeeves—or, more exactly, like he was Cyril—and I tipped my glass to him, saying, "Good to see you. Good seeing you again, Cyril."

He winked and left me to my Guinness and my reflections. It hadn't been one of my better days. It wasn't just Landreau who depressed me but Francine, too. She was even more inexplicable than he. She wasn't just grieving over the death of Buddy, which must have actually been a blessing in certain ways. She was mourning her children and grandchildren unborn; she was mourning her barrenness as if it were her own death—as if her life were somehow dependent on the life of future generations.

And to me that made no sense whatever. The sex drive I understood well enough—well, somewhat anyway—but Francine seemed afflicted by something different, a drive to procreation, one that isn't satisfied by sex.

Is there such a thing? Maybe. I could see that the frustration of some such drive was eating away at her from within. Urge to procreate. Hard to imagine. I don't mean to say women aren't driven to have sex. But if that's separate, like for men, and if there's something else besides the sex drive in some women, many women, most women, something just as powerful, a drive to bear children that will be satisfied with or without a husband, then try to imagine what it's like for them to abort.

Nope, can't.

"Cyril, can I ask you something?" I stopped him as he passed by, wiping down the gleaming mahogany bar from one end to the other. "You got any children?"

He paused for a moment, meditated deeply, and then broke into a broad smile. "Not that I know of, old boy!"

"No," I laughed along with him, "me neither."

This too was scripted, I thought, though Cyril and I had never spoken the lines before. It's an old joke between men, a play so broadly and deeply familiar that every guy knows the lines. The script calls for a macho Johnny Appleseed, spreading his seed across the land, but in this play he has no idea whether there are any seedlings. Maybe there are, maybe there aren't. He just doesn't know. Only the seeding is his job, not the care and feeding. If there is a drive to procreate, separate from the sex drive, Johnny doesn't have it.

Roy Macklin didn't have it. My mind flashed to an image of him sitting at an unknown bar in an unknown city. "Nope, me neither," he was saying to the bartender with a big grin. "Not that I know of." He laughed. And they laughed together, and all the men at the whole bar laughed, loud and long.

I wanted to cry. I wanted to hurt him bad. I wanted to track that dirt bag down, make him eat that stupid joke, and rip his guts out for all that he had done. And not done.

"You ok, Evan?"

"Oh, yeah. Sure, Cyril. Just crying in my beer."

"Looks like it might be getting a little diluted there, gov'. How 'bout a fresh one?"

"Sure. Why not?"

"And how about you, Sheila? The usual?" Cyril was talking to the woman standing quietly behind me, waiting to get a drink in the crowded bar. I didn't want to turn around. I didn't want it to be that Sheila. I wished I was sitting on a stool in front of the mirror so I could be sure who it was without turning around.

"Right," she said in the familiar bark of the dog woman. Served me right for coming to Brit's Pub, and now there was no escaping. I had to just sit there with her eyes piercing me, like a knife in the back.

"Hello, Evan." My barstool turned involuntarily toward the one woman in the world that I hated, hated deeply with a gem-like flame.

"Sheila."

"Just getting a drink."

"Yeah, that's what people generally do at Brit's."

She couldn't get away until Cyril brought her drink. I couldn't get away as long as she was standing there, inches away, with her long nose and sharp chiseled features only inches from mine. We might as well have been in the same jail cell, except that with the noisy, jostling crowd pushing in, our quarters were even closer. My knees touched her thighs, and she tried to wriggle away, but there was nowhere to go. I stared at her silently. If her snout had been any longer, her eyes would have seemed like they were on opposite sides of her face.

"So," she said. And then something like, "Your backing pretty." The noise was deafening.

"What?" I shouted, leaning toward her.

"You're back in the Cities," she said, bringing her mouth to my ear.

"Right," I said in her ear, and then nothing.

"Oh, fuck it," she said, in the foul-mouthed way she found necessary when dealing with men. I assumed she meant she had had enough chit chat, and I was about to turn back to my drink, but then, unexpectedly, she went on. "Fuck it all, anyway, Evan. You're not a stupid man. You're not a stupid reporter."

"Thank you, Sheila," I bellowed. "I take that admission as a high compliment, coming from you."

"Cut the cattiness, Evan. I know you're not stupid. I've always known it. But what a jackass stunt that was, you know?"

"No, I do not know," I insisted.

"Yes, you do. You know damn well it was, because you're not that stupid. You know you've got to confirm something like that, something that can ruin a man. And you did ruin him!"

The din at the bar was still deafening, the crowd was still crushing in all around us, we were still shouting. But all of a sudden Brit's Pub and all the people in it just disappeared, and there was complete silence. It felt like it was just the two of us alone, like two fighters in the ring trading punches, and nowhere to escape.

"Oh, he wasn't ruined!"

"Did he get elected?"

"No, but he would have lost anyway."

"Is he going to get renominated?…Well, is he? You know damn well he's done in politics. Dead. Dead as a doornail, and you killed him. I want to know why. How could you have done it? I stood there and asked you, before we confronted him, where's the proof? And you lied to me. You just out and out lied to my face. Why?"

"I had to expose him. The voters deserved it."

"But he told you the kid wasn't his!"

"I knew it was his, whatever he said. What's he going to do, admit it when he's in the middle of a campaign? He wasn't about to give me a fucking blood sample! And I was sure anyway."

"But he was gay, Evan! The man was gay!"

"So what? I don't give a damn if he did come out of the closet to protect his ass when the story broke! That doesn't prove a damn thing. The kid is his, I tell you! And he just denied it! What a pitiful excuse for a human being! It was killing me to think of this asshole running for City Council when he's not fit to scrub city toilets. It was eating me up, and I'm glad I did it, whatever it cost."

"Whatever it cost *you*, you mean! If you wanted to martyr yourself, that's your privilege. But what about the rest of us? What about the paper? Did you ever think of that while you were dreaming up this pathetic little tale of child abandonment? You're not a stupid man, Evan, but you sure are an egotistical, self-centered son of a bitch. 'It was killing you,' you say. 'It was eating you up.' That's what this whole disastrous story was all about, wasn't it? You!"

Cyril came over with the drinks for Sheila and me. His cheery "Right-ee-o" broke up our intense little tete-a-tete before I could come to my own defense. It was just as well, because I don't know what I would have said.

So as Sheila wedged her canine nose back through the crowd, I turned back to the beer taps, hoping to be left alone for just a few minutes while I finished my beer. I had at most one more day in the Cities before I had to go back. I had better make the most of it. I owed it to Marian. I had to keep focused on her, and stop getting sidetracked with stuff like tonight that had nothing to do with her.

Reflected in the gleaming chrome of the taps, another face caught my attention. Oh, geez, who's behind me now? I wondered, grimacing. It grimaced back at me, this distorted cartoon face, drawn and elongated here, squeezed and fattened there. I put my head in my hands, hoping to make whoever it was think I was drunk or sick or crazy and just go away, but when I looked up again, the image, both clownish and monstrous, was still there. I peered closer and when it leered back more closely still, I could no longer deny that this face, at once pathetic and sinister, was my own.

Chapter 13

"Cesarean? Get real! Marian Barclay didn't have any children!"

I was stunned. But Trish had performed the autopsy, after all, and she had eight years of experience under her belt. The fluorescent lights glinted off her wire-rimmed glasses as she threw her head back in consternation.

"Keep it down, will you, Evan?" she hissed. From our hushed, conspiratorial tones, you would have thought we were in the back streets of Prague, walking hurriedly down dark, rain-soaked alleys. But it was just a Baker's Square restaurant in Minneapolis, with the dinner crowd lined up at the door and a pimply-faced waitress hanging around, waiting for us to vacate the table.

"You asked!" Trish exclaimed. "That's my best guess. What do you want? It was a four to five inch vertical scar from navel to pubis. Old. Most likely from a C-section."

"How old?"

"No idea. Pretty old."

"Ten years?"

"Yeah."

"Twenty?"

Let it not be twenty, I thought, with a rush of guilt and fear. Not twenty. Marian never told me anything, never hinted. But I had lost track of her completely.

"Could be twenty, I suppose," Trish said pensively. "It was an old kind of suturing pattern, now that I think about it. Pretty much obsolete these days. I didn't check any further."

"Why not, for gosh sakes? That's your job!" I was starting to have a horrible sinking feeling in my stomach.

"Don't you dare tell me what my job is! You don't have the first idea about it. We've got puzzles enough in the ME's office, Evan, and I don't have time to be inventing any more of them. Determine the cause of death. That's it. My whole job. What's the point of checking anything more when you've got seven puncture wounds staring you in the face and three more stiffs in the locker that you have to carve by dinnertime? I don't know whether the victim had an appendix, or tonsils, or any toes besides the one the ID tag was tied to. I do know she had seven puncture wounds in the lower abdomen, all to the right of the vertical scar. Various trajectories of penetration, suggesting various postures of the victim and/or perpetrator. Almost no blood pooling in the back or buttocks, indicating that she had lost most of it before circulation stopped. I concluded that, after a protracted struggle, the victim bled to death. That's all that finally mattered to me or Queenie. Now what's your problem?"

"No doubts about the time of death?"

"None."

"What do you mean 'puncture wound'?"

"Stabbed. She was stabbed. That's all." Trish lowered her eyes. I could see she wasn't telling me everything.

"Like with an ice pick?"

"Evan, you know I could get fired for telling you this stuff. You're asking me to break the law. Autopsy results are available only to the police—and the next of kin."

"Well, I could have been."

"What do you mean?"

"Forget it. I'm going to keep all this firmly under raps, for old time's sake. And, besides, you owe me. I was there for you and your daughter. Today's the day I have to call in the chits. Payment in full."

"Yes, you were there, and I'm grateful." Her eyes were glistening. "I owe you." Trish took off her glasses and ran the back of her hand across her reddened eyes.

"Big," I insisted.

"All right, I owe you big," she admitted. "And if I didn't, I wouldn't be sitting here, betraying myself and professional confidences. You need to know that my neck is on the block here, and I'm counting on you to protect me, Evan. Will you promise to protect me?"

"Of course. So, couldn't have been an ice pick?" I was getting pushy.

"Evan, the wounds were slits, not holes. But they were only ten millimeters wide, more puncture than slash. Besides, when's the last time you saw an ice pick, except in a Peter Lorrie movie?"

Our waitress danced over, a pad in her hand and a cutesy smile in her voice. "Now, did you folks save room for dessert? How about a nice piece of pie?"

"NO!!!" boomed our two voices in unison, blasting the poor girl away from the booth. But the desire for an empty table and another tip overcame her fear. She slunk back with the check, and placed it gingerly on the table at arm's length.

"Well, ok then. You folks have a real nice day now!"

Somehow I doubted that my day would be real nice at all.

"Ok," I said, returning to Trish and the business at hand. "No ice pick then. But a slender knife, though?"

"Very slender. What do you need to know for?"

"What kind of knife would leave a wound less than half an inch wide and only three inches deep?"

"A scalpel. The victim was stabbed seven times with a scalpel. Very little doubt about it."

"A scalpel! Are you sure?" I was amazed at her calm certitude.

"It's my job, Evan. I'm very good at it and will get even better—unless I'm fired first."

"We've been through all that. Now tell me the whole thing and be done with it."

"All right, all right. All the entry wounds were virtually identical. Each was made with a single-edged blade, approximately one or two millimeters in thickness. The blade's cutting edge was razor sharp. It left none of the microscopic tearing that is characteristic of common knives. In each wound, minute amounts of industrial disinfectant were detectable—the kind that manufacturers use on medical instruments before wrapping and shipping them."

"Don't hospitals sterilize those things before they use them?"

"Of course."

"That's it, then."

"That's it," she said. "Not really any doubt about it. A scalpel, unused and fresh from the packet."

"A scalpel," I whispered, standing up and throwing some bills on the table. "Seven times in the stomach. Holy Mary, Mother of God."

"Yeah."

"Trish," I said over my shoulder, walking toward the exit, "we're even."

I hadn't wanted to talk to Trevor Mitchell. We were hardly even acquainted, and the scene with Landreau had prepared me for the worst. But now I had to talk to him, like it or not. The scalpel had settled that, given Mitchell's job at the hospital. So I headed out to their Lakewood home. Not that I expected to find him there in the middle of the afternoon. I'd have to come back later when he'd likely be back from the hospital. But I wanted to look around the murder scene. You never know.

Lacking both lake and wood, the sprawling Lakewood rambler, its curved front walk lined with drooping petunias, still had yellow police tape across the front door. I wondered how Mitchell got in at night. I pressed the doorbell just in case, but nothing. Then I noticed the name under the button, "Dr. Marian Barclay." That's all. Looked like he didn't get in at night or any other time. Strange, though. Ben Drake's story had said that Mitchell found the body on returning home from work. Probably moved out after the murder. Nobody would like to relive that discovery every night in the living room. But if he left after the murder, wouldn't the doorbell still have his name posted, as well as hers?

The phone book at the SuperAmerica still listed Lakewood as his current address. The hospital directory was newer, though, and it had him in a townhouse in Fridley, where I decided to ambush him that evening. Fridley is a blue-collar suburb, a pretty far cry from Lakewood, and the Sixties vintage townhouse he lived in was a big comedown from the spacious rambler in Lakewood. Only the Mercedes in the driveway betrayed anything of former luxury.

My first knock produced Trevor Mitchell in the half-open doorway. He was suave looking, almost slick, still dressed in a natty pinstripe vest and suit pants, though his tie was loose and jerked off to the side.

"Yes?"

"Mr. Mitchell, I'm Evan Wade. Perhaps you remember me from the cemetery?"

"Yes, of course. How are you, Wade?" Shaking hands, I could smell the booze. I had no idea how I was going to get this guy to open up to me, but his breath gave me reason to hope. Mitchell opened the door and let me in. It must have been the maid's month off. Papers were littered all over the dining room table—if you could call it a room when it was just a corner of the main floor that was neither kitchen nor living room.

"Pardon the mess. I have to bring work home when I don't stay late.

"No problem. You should see my place! Junk everywhere." My mind flashed to Libby and the spotless kitchen. I yearned to get back to the cabin. I yearned to get back to Libby.

"What can I do for you, Wade?" Mitchell asked, motioning toward the couch.

"I've been working with Detective Cuene, doing what I can to help with the investigation. Not much help, I'm afraid, but I do what I can."

"Oh yeah? Cuene didn't say anything about you when he was questioning me downtown. Can you believe it? I suppose they have to cover all the bases. But me? I'm like the victim here, and they're giving me the third degree! Anyway, they get help from reporters?"

"No, not actually, but I'm not with the *STrib* anymore...and since I knew Marian way back, you know."

"Sure. Buddy mentioned you once." Mitchell eyed me with a husband's jealous eyes. He knew or at least suspected. It was coming back to him now, and his body language started to shout mistrust and suspicion. So I started back-pedaling.

"Dr. Landreau made it quite clear that my help was unwanted, Mr. Mitchell, and if you feel the same...."

"Landreau's an ass." He spat out the name. "Worse than Buddy, even. I shouldn't speak ill of the dead, especially my former father in law. But what a first class jerk he was! You knew him, didn't you? I saw him dressing you down at the funeral."

"Buddy? Yeah, a real piece of work all right. The first night I met him he said something so crude in front of Marian and Francine that he even made me blush. And I've never been the blushing type."

"That's Buddy, for you. Say, I was just about to fix myself a drink, Wade. Can I offer you a little hair of the dog?"

"A man should never be allowed to drink alone. That's my motto. Got any bourbon?" Comradery is good, I thought, but likker's quicker.

"A man after my own heart," Mitchell said. He went off to the kitchen, only five steps away, and started to rattle glasses and ice cubes. He didn't even have to shout to continue the conversation. "I don't know what it was about Buddy, but he never warmed up to me, even after Marian and me had been married for quite a few years. Hope you wanted ice. Here's mud in your eye, Wade!"

"Cheers, and call me Evan."

"Right, Evan. I'm Trevor," he said as he raised his glass once more and took a long drink. "And Landreau! I would have been thankful if he'd just been cool to me, like Buddy, but no! He was in my face from day one. We'd hardly gotten back from our honeymoon on St. Thomas when Landreau pulled her aside and started grilling her!"

"About what?" I asked with sympathetic indignation, only half pretended.

"About our honeymoon, the asshole! Maybe he had the hots for her himself! Wouldn't be surprised. I dunno what he said exactly, but that was just the beginning. It was like the deeper Buddy slipped into the bottle over the years, the more Landreau became Marian's Father Protector. He was always prying into our lives. Some pretty personal stuff, too. How'd you like your wife discussing conjugal details with a jerk like that! I wasn't cut out to be a parent, so it didn't bother me that she couldn't have children. I knew that before I married her."

"She couldn't?" I exclaimed.

"No." Mitchell said, glancing at me. "But what business it was of Landreau's I couldn't fathom. I felt like my sex life was under a microscope all the time, or telescope, or something. You ready for a refill?"

"Thanks."

I couldn't let the subject go. I had to keep Mitchell's tap running, and happily the bourbon was already doing more than I ever could. He brought the bottle out from the kitchen, and poured us both another, neat.

"I can imagine it must have been hard on Marian," I offered.

"What? Landreau?"

"No, I mean not having kids. I mean, when she was an Ob-Gyn and all."

"Sure, it was hard. Didn't bother me, but she never got over it, really. But she'd had a hysterectomy a long time back, before I knew her. And that was that. They were doing a lot of them back then. Got a woman problem? Rip out the plumbing! Presto chango, no problem."

A deep surge of relief and gratitude passed through me, drowning out what Mitchell was saying. His slurred voice kept droning on, but my mind was elsewhere.

Hysterectomy, that's what it was. Not a Cesarean. Just an abdominal hysterectomy. Or rather not *just*, since I knew—maybe even more than Mitchell did—that Marian wanted desperately to be a mother. She wanted to be, for her own child, what Sara Barclay had been, far too briefly, for her. She wanted to be the Sara who was married to Burton Barclay, not the Francine married to Buddy Boor.

Mitchell was still mumbling to himself and his bourbon when I tuned in again. "...contemptuous of anybody who didn't belong to the club. The M.D. Club, those arrogant sons of bitches! Always lording it over you, always reminding you that you're lacking certain initials after your name. But there's nothing wrong with being Director of Medical Records! The Director!"

"Certainly not!" I assured him.

"Landreau never came right out and said it, but every sneer told me I was just a leech, leeching off Marian."

"Yup," I said, "that's a favorite word of his."

"I wasn't, though. Just because her income was three times mine! That happens a lot with professional couples these days. Somebody's got to have the higher income. It didn't bother me at first. But it grates on you after a while, you know, getting introduced as 'the doctor's husband.' Marian didn't care about all that stuff, not at all. She was great, but Landreau and Buddy were always rubbing it in, letting me know that I just didn't measure up, that all the status and all the money were all on Marian's side. It's like having your dick cut off, inch by inch."

A knock interrupted our conversation. Mitchell didn't get up at first. He just looked in the direction of the door, as if confused and apprehensive of whatever was beyond it. A second, louder knock summoned him to unsteady feet, and when he opened the door he discovered that his fears were not entirely unfounded.

"Trevor Mitchell," Queenie announced, "I have a warrant authorizing your arrest for the murder of Marian Barclay."

Chapter 14

"I believe you said something about forevermore?"

"That's what I said, Queenie. And that's what I'm going to do. A promise is a promise, a deal's a deal, and a man's only as good as his word. I've checked out of my elegant quarters at the Gopher Motel and I'm headed for parts north."

It was already Saturday afternoon, and if I wasn't back home in time for Sunday with Libby's parents, I would be cooked meat. The very thought that I was about to partake of Welch's and Saltines with a coven of Lutherans made me shudder, but a man's gotta do what a man's gotta do.

"So you're not going to be back sitting here in my office two weeks from now, are you?" Queenie rocked his massive frame back in the oversize desk chair, and gave me a broad smile.

"Well, no, I don't expect to be back. No reason. You've got the right guy under lock and key, don't you?

"Yes, we believe we do. And so I don't want you coming back with some cockamamie story about the man in the moon confessing to you that he's the one, he did it."

"Ok, ok. Go ahead and rub it in. You've got a right. I was so sure it was Smit, and it wasn't."

"Doesn't look like it."

"You told me so. You were right. I was wrong, but at any rate now you're sure Mitchell's the man?"

"You still don't get it, do you? You think this whole thing is about being sure, and that's what makes you an amateur in a professional's world. Down here we're not in the business of being certain, however fortunate that would be for the cause of truth, justice, and the American way. Of course, we'd like to be able to put all our doubts to rest, but the longer you're in this business, the more you realize there really isn't much certainty to be had out there, Evan. And you'd be well advised not to make it up where it doesn't exist."

Queenie stood up, and then said with an air of finality. "When you're absolutely certain, chances are you're absolutely wrong."

"Well," I said laughing amicably but keeping my seat, "I'm not certain about Mitchell. That's for sure!"

"Good, because there's no reason to be. The evidence points in his direction. We've got enough for the DA's purposes, and when we do, that's our cue to move on to other cases. But certainty? Not hardly." Queenie started coming around his desk, with a rolling, sauntering motion meant to encourage me to be on my way.

"But I can't even see the dog on point yet," I said, refusing to budge. "Where's the beef? I mean, I know Mitchell's job gave him access to scalpels, even if he was in the records section. But what about motive? I know that he and Marian Barclay were separated. Had been for some months."

"Yes, you know quite a bit already, and the rest will come out at the trial. You'll be able to read all about it in the papers. So, I want to thank you for stopping in to say goodbye," he added, holding his office door open for me. "Drop me a postcard from Brainerd."

"Queenie," I pleaded. "Gimme a few crumbs here! I can't see how this all adds up to anything! At least I was trying to help you out."

"Now, Evan, neither of us believes that, and you've worn your welcome down pretty thin. The only thing you accomplished while you were here was to get Landreau pissed off enough to call in a complaint. What were you doing at the Widow Barclay's house anyway?"

"Just paying my respects."

"What do you mean respects? Why would you pay respects? You knew the Barclays? Wait a minute! Don't tell me. You knew Marian Barclay! Oh, no, Evan! You didn't see fit to mention that little fact the other day, did you? Of course not. No, it was all about Smit. 'He confessed,' 'he told me,' 'he's got me involved,' you said, but of course the question is why were you talking to Smit about the murder in the first place? You lied to me, Evan."

"No, I never…. "

"You knew that if you told me you had any connection to the Barclays, the jig was up. And you just kept mum about it. I can't believe how incredibly stupid I've been to let you anywhere near this case when you were personally involved. If the captain ever gets wind of this, it'll go in my file for sure! Oh, Evan! What kind of a man are you? To come to me asking—begging—a favor and then screw me over like this!" Queenie's voice had an almost pathetic incomprehension, as if he'd been blindsided.

"What did I do to you to deserve this?" he asked softly, holding the door open. "Who are you, Evan? I don't know who you are. Get out of here. Get out now."

I expected him to slam the door behind me, but he didn't. He closed it so slowly, so quietly that I could hear the latch touch the jam before it finally slid home. Somehow that gesture said more to me than any outburst of anger ever could.

But what, I wondered as I walked down the hall, was his problem, after all? I was using any and all means I could muster to get the information I needed. Two decades in the newspaper business had taught me that you can't be over-particular about stepping on toes. Who did Queenie think I was anyway, some Boy Scout? I would have handed over anything I got. I would have handed it to him on a silver platter. Eventually. Not that I did in fact get anything from this whole excursion. That's what struck me most as I exited the building into the parking lot. From all of this I really didn't get a damn thing.

"Hey, Evan, how's that breath of fresh air and sunshine you're shacked up with?" Ben Drake was just standing there, leaning back against the car he worshipped, looking like he was waiting for me to show. "When are you going to make Miss Libby an honest woman?"

"Screw you, Ben."

"What? Again? Yes, indeed, the same old Evan. Heard you were back in town. Heard you and the dog woman had a little pissing contest at Brit's the other night? Gotta be careful! The walls have ears."

"I've got nothing to say to you." I quickened my pace, trying to skirt around him.

"Nothing to say! Why, you've been nosing around down here for how long now? Three days? And you've got nothing? Now, I can't believe that! Not old Evan 'do whatever it takes' Wade. I thought maybe you wouldn't mind sharing the nothing that you got. Go halvsies? I'll show you mine if you show me yours? Just like the old days. Oh, that's right, I remember now. You never were very good at sharing."

"Not with people who screw me over, that's for sure. Why the hell did you tell Smit that I accused him of murdering Marian Barclay?"

"Oh, he mentioned that, did he? Bet he shut up tight as a clam after that. Just keeping my private sources private. That's all. You come down here, trying to horn back in on my territory, and you think I'm just going to sit around and let you steal my byline with a story of your own on the Barclay thing? No, no, I learned my tactics from a master, Evan. A master of the self-serving lie and half-lie. A master of the Royal Screw."

"I told you there's no byline for me in this. It's not business. It's personal." I turned and walked to my car.

"Ah, yes. Personal. So I understand," he said, strutting along a few steps behind. "One for the little girl who lived down the lane. Very personal, as your neighbors tell it. I wondered why you were at her funeral. I am positively amazed and deeply grateful how much those outstate bumpkins can remember and how much of the rest they can piece together. You just have to learn how to suck it out of them. The vampire, Evan, is a master of psychological manipulation. You must learn to discover the victim's deepest desire in order to offer the deepest temptation. You have to master the lie and skillful half-lie, the artful silence, the subtle prevarication, the leading innuendo."

"What the hell are you talking about?"

"I'm talking about two teenyboppers out on the dock, or anchored in the middle of the lake on this gigantic yacht, night after fucking night. Oh, I am sorry! That was too crudely put, but didn't I get it substantially right, Evan? Wasn't it night after fucking night?"

"You son of a bitch," I shouted, spinning round, ready to take a swing at the bastard. "Stay out of my life. And stay out of my sight, or I'll make you sorry you were ever born."

"Oh, I don't think so, Evan. You see, I have out-mastered the master. I know what you want, want so bad you can taste it, like a little puppydog can taste the bone held out to tease him. I can make you kneel down and beg. I already know things about Mitchell that you'll never be able to find out without me."

"Like what?"

"You'd like to know, wouldn't you, Evan? You want to know real bad."

"You don't know anything, Drake. You're just an asshole trying to pass wind."

"Oh, that's where you're seriously mistaken, Evan. I have sources that you'll never be able to touch, that you couldn't open if I gave you the key."

"Name one."

"Simeon Landreau."

"You have my attention."

"I thought I might."

"What did he tell you?"

"Ah, proposing a little sharing and caring session, are we?"

"Maybe."

"And what do you have to sell that would compensate me for any little nugget of knowledge I might be willing to impart?"

"The autopsy report."

"Well, well. Let's just step inside your office, so we are not accidentally interrupted during this transaction."

I unlocked the car door and as he was about to get in, he brushed off a pile of shriveled Subway lettuce from the seat with a look of disdain and deep offense. "The autopsy report! And I thought you said you had nothing. Have you been a naughty boy with Miss Tricia?"

"Let's cut to the chase, Drake. How did you manage to get anything out of Landreau?"

"Trade secrets, Evan. Trade secrets. Let's just say there are at least two people in the world that Landreau hates with a deadly passion. One of them is Trevor Mitchell. You are mildly acquainted with the other. At any rate, Landreau wants to see Mitchell hung, and we both know that a little public information spread in the right place at the right time can go a long way in preventing defense lawyers from confusing juries about the true nature of the facts. Offering my assistance in the interests of justice, I squeezed Landreau like a tube of toothpaste. What came out was not just who killed the Barclay woman but why."

Drake paused.

"I give up," I said, irritated. "Why'd he do it?"

"Ta, ta, Evan. I believe it's your turn. What did Trish have to say?"

"Scalpel. Seven times with a scalpel."

"My, my. Isn't that interesting. So Tricia's evidence connects the murder weapon to Mitchell, does it?"

"That is not for attribution, Ben. Strictly between you and me. Trish's neck is out pretty far on this one. She's pretty vulnerable, and I'm asking you to keep it quiet."

"Oh, Evan, I am disappointed. You know you can trust my integrity as completely as if it were your own!"

"Back to Landreau," I insisted.

"Yes, of course. It's an old story and a rather trite one. Seems that Mitchell wanted more money. I'm not sure why. Maybe he needed another Mercedes. You'd think that her salary combined with his would have made a tidy little nest egg." Telling his story, Drake wiped his fingertips over the dash of the old Ford and examined the dust that accumulated on them as if he were a connoisseur of dirt.

"Get on with it."

"Easy, easy. This delicious bit of information is like fine wine. Savor it. At any rate, Mitchell devised a little money-making scheme that wasn't quite illegal, just a little unethical. But then why should ethics get in the way of grabbing what you want? Right, Evan?"

"What scheme?"

"I'm getting to that. Like all Ob-Gyns, Barclay was besieged with sob story letters from barren couples. 'Dear Dr. Barclay, We are a highly educated couple, healthy and wealthy. We would love to give a child a loving, mortgage-free home. We've tried such and such procedure but it hasn't worked. We've tried such and such agency, but it takes so long and we are so desperate. Blah, blah, blah. We would be deeply grateful if you could arrange a private meeting, etc., etc.' These people will try anything. Now the good doctor never acted on such requests, but her not-so-good husband viewed them as a golden opportunity. He not only had access to her file of tear-stained letters but also to the maternity ward records, indicating which young ladies were generously willing to surrender their surplus offspring for a certain consideration. To make a long story short, Mitchell found ways to bring good people together, circumvent all public and private agencies, and arrange for private adoptions. You may be sure the healthy and wealthy couple were generously grateful."

"Tawdry, but what's it got to do with murder?"

"Oh, that! Well, apparently Dr. Barclay threw a hissy when she found out about hubby and refused to share bed or breakfast with him any longer. Confessing the whole sorry tale to Landreau, the lovely young doctor was advised that in order to preserve and protect her spotless reputation among the medical community, she needed to expose Mitchell to the Hospital Board. More compassionate than Landreau, Dr. Barclay gave her husband the choice of A) resigning from his directorship or B) facing termination in disgrace. But he, to our universal regret, chose C) neither of the above. Landreau told Queenie, then me. Not being sworn to secrecy, I'm telling you, and you're welcome, if you like, to tell the lovely Miss Libby Farina how marvelously successful you were in solving the mystery of the murdered Marian. But perhaps she's not particularly interested?"

It was almost midnight by the time I got back to the cabin. The house was dark. No lamp shone out the living room window. I quietly took off my clothes and slipped gratefully into bed next to Libby. Her body was warm and inviting. There was no denying I had missed her. A lot. She was lying on her side, facing the far wall.

"Libby," I whispered, curling up to her. "Are you still awake?"

There was no reply, but no deep breathing either.

Chapter 15

Libby was sitting in the bedroom chair looking at me when I woke up the next morning. Apparently she'd been there for some time, just looking, thinking. It's disconcerting waking up to discover that someone's been watching you while you've been sleeping. Maybe that's what it will feel like at the Last Judgment. You feel vulnerable, guilty of sins both remembered and forgotten. I had intended to start the day with an apology to get things off on the right foot, but I hadn't quite got my speech prepared, and Libby wasn't about to give me time to draft it. My eyes were still adapting to the bright morning light streaming in over her shoulder, when she said:

"I can't compete with a corpse, Evan."

"Oh, no, Libby," I stammered, not fully in command. The sun shone in my eyes, and though I put up my hand to shield them from the light, all I could see was a halo of radiant hair. Her face was dark, inscrutable. Her voice was flat and expressionless.

"I can't compete with a memory. I know that."

"You don't need to, Libby. I…"

"I still remember my first kiss like it was yesterday. My first prom. My first night with Brian Ferguson. So many years have come and gone since Brian and I held each other that night. You don't forget things like that. Whatever happens, it doesn't change a thing. Brian married some girl from Pine River, divorced her, and left her standing in the doorway with a baby on her hip. Makes no difference. I just remember his slow, tender hands, and I loved him with all my heart. Maybe still do, just a little."

"Libby, I'm all done...."

"Be quiet, Evan, and listen. I'm telling you the way it is. And will be. Because if you and I come to nothing, I don't want it to be because you didn't know or didn't understand. I can compete with any woman alive, Evan, but not with Marian Barclay, not with a memory. And I won't even try. Because the real question is whether you can have done with her and move on."

"Of course!"

"Can you, Evan? Because I've got to. Every time I wake up in your bed and watch the sun rise over the lake, I know I can't afford to wait much longer. You've never lied, never told me that you loved me. Is it because of her? I won't live in her shadow, Evan. I can't live out my life in the shadow of Marian Barclay. I've got to move on before it's too late."

"You're not in anybody's shadow, Libby," I protested. "Nobody at all."

"What is it, then?" she asked, coming over to sit on the side of the bed. "What are you waiting for?" Now I could see her face, could see the tears streaming down her cheeks, wetting her nightgown. She did nothing to stop their flow.

"Is it me?" she asked. "Is it that I'm not good for you?" As she bent over me, her tears fell on my face and chest, pleading for her, twisting in my heart.

"No, Libby. It's not you. It's me. You are good for me. Better than I deserve. I want you to stay with me very much. I missed you these last few days. Please stay with me, Libby."

"You just can't say it, can you?" Libby pleaded. "'Stay with me,' yes, but not 'Marry me.' 'I missed you,' but not 'I love you.' Why not, Evan? I don't understand. Why can't you love me? I just don't understand at all. I love you, Evan, and I will stay with you, but not forever. Not like this. Do you hear me?"

"Yes," I said.

"Do you understand?"

"Yes," I admitted. I understood her very well.

Standing up and grabbing a Kleenex to give her nose a honk, she added, "All right, then, get in the shower. We've got to hurry."

Breakfast was on the table when I got out to the kitchen, and Libby was in the bedroom getting dressed. I could hear her humming "get me to the church on time." So I knew she wasn't going to sulk, but she was not going to forget either.

I didn't know what to say to her by way of explanation, except that whatever I was waiting for was the same thing I'd been waiting for my whole adult life. Or, more exactly, I really wasn't waiting at all, not looking forward to anything in particular, or anticipating a better, fuller tomorrow. I didn't want anyone's future depending on me, because I had no reason to believe I could bear the responsibility. Dependability has got to be written in the genes, I truly believe, and my DNA was programmed for the road.

Libby didn't need me. She had been independent and self-sufficient ever since she finished up her social work courses at Central Lakes College and took a job in Family Services with the county. If I suddenly disappeared from the picture, she wouldn't have to leave a light in the window. She'd still have her job, and she'd get along just fine. That's why I could go on living with her. If for some unknown reason I betrayed her trust and hit the road one day, she'd be fine without me, just fine.

I could tell her none of this, though. She said she loved me, but the man she loved was a completely different person than the man she was living with, someone a good deal more reliable, trustworthy, and lovable. Pure wishful thinking on her part. In order to be that man, I would have to make a complete about-face, change 180°, become an entirely different person. But you still can't make a silk purse of a sow's ear. Gene therapy for that kind of thing is still a ways off, I suspect.

But I didn't want Libby to leave, and so I smiled at her while we were driving the few miles to her parents' church, and she smiled back. Pure white, the little country church was nestled in a grove of old-growth Norway pines that seemed almost black by comparison. It was a Currier and Ives church, snug and comfortable, but not awe inspiring. It did not speak to the Catholic imagination, which requires great size to remind the faithful of their insignificance, great age to remind them of their brevity, and great mystery to remind them of their ignorance.

In the parking lot I ran around to open the car door for Libby in a gesture of old-school courtesy, and held her hand as we walked up the drive. I wanted her to know I was trying and I cared. Truth is, too, I was just a bit anxious about entering her parents' church and didn't want her to get too far away. So I clung to her hand as to a lifeline. I kept expecting the solemn Lutheran elders greeting people at the door to detect a Papist in their midst, bar my way, and challenge me to recite the Wittenberg theses, all 95 of them.

What is it about these situations that makes you feel so uncomfortable and alien? For me, the little church in the vale might as well have been the blue mosque in Istanbul. Maybe it's not just that you don't feel at home but that you're not supposed to. You can't fully understand the purpose of religions and religious ceremonies, I think, unless you've seen them from the outside, as well as the in. Inside, the conventional verges on the natural. Everything seems as it ought to be. But from the outside you realize that every ceremony that fosters the sense of belonging among believers serves also to enforce a sense of exclusion among outsiders.

At any rate, even with Libby for protection on my arm, I was feeling so out of place that I was positively grateful to spy her father and mother waiting for us across the foyer. We hadn't spent a lot of time together, but I knew they were familiar, unpretentious, hearty people, strictly religious themselves but not judgmental of others, a rare and welcome combination.

Libby's father had a farmer's pride about him. It showed in his tall, upright bearing but even more in his hands and fingers. Broad, thick hands, with spatulate fingers. Rock-hard they had become from daily chores repeated day after day, year after year, chores that would be left undone if he didn't do them. You had to respect those hands. They were up to the task. And Libby's mother had her own kind of strength. Hers were the hands of an accomplished horsewoman. Though she never had the long lines of the equestrian that her husband gave Libby, she had the communicative hands that horses understood and obeyed without bit and bridle. She had the touch.

"Hi, Libby," her father said warmly, giving her a big hug. "Morning, Evan. Good to see you kids here."

"Kids," I thought as I was shaking hands. Twenty years of adulthood lost in one second. But I smiled and tried not to take offense, since he wasn't trying to give any. Seeing that, Libby smiled and gave my arm a squeeze. We would survive.

Libby nodded to old acquaintances as we entered the vestibule, her father leading us together down the center aisle, while an electric organ played the prefatory. There was no avoiding the ominous implication. It had to be that way. I knew it would be, but what I didn't expect was this: Libby looked up at me, her face beaming, and at that moment it struck me that she was a truly beautiful woman. I hadn't realized how beautiful before.

We were seated, the congregation sang a hymn or two, and the plate was passed. But wholly undistracted by the trappings of Lutheran ritual transpiring before my eyes, I continued to ponder her smile. Libby was not just Strawberry Delight, who looked so fetching in her white sundress embroidered with sunflowers. The woman radiated a depth of feeling from within that made her smile more beautiful, more profound than anything ever found on a magazine cover, or gallery painting, or statue. It spoke the depth of quiet joy she could feel, did feel as she walked forward down the long aisle. It would be sufficient for a man's aspiration, I decided, just to give her that joy; it would be enough for a man just to make her smile that smile, again and again, for a lifetime. As the preacher began reading the scripture, I wondered, Am I that man?

"Jesus answered and said unto him, Verily, verily, I say unto thee, Except a man be born again, he cannot see the Kingdom of God. Nicodemus saith unto him, How can a man be born when he is old? Can he enter the second time into his mother's womb, and be born? Jesus answered, Verily, verily, I say unto thee, Except a man be born of water and of the Spirit, he cannot enter into the kingdom of God."

Silence is the most powerful rhetorical device. After concluding the reading, the preacher raised his head and looked out in silence upon the congregation, simply gazed on us for so long that people began to squirm uneasily, wondering if the man had been struck dumb, forgotten his sermon, or decided we were unworthy to receive the Word. The anticipation was palpable. And so he had every ear when he began to speak:

"Born again. It cannot be. Born once, yes, but once only, not again.

"Nicodemus knew it could not be. He was a learned man, a scholar, a Pharisee, a ruler of the Jews. But it does not take a learned man to know that no one, neither you nor I, the rich or the poor, the mighty of the earth or the weak and powerless, no one at all can be born again.

"'Can a man be born when he is old?' Nicodemus asks. The question answers itself. An old man can only play to the inevitable end the play he has begun. He cannot be born again. He gets no second chance, no opportunity to wipe clean the slate or write his story anew.

"It is a sad fact, infinitely sad. Because we so desperately need a chance to rewrite our lives, each of us. But it cannot be. A man cannot return a second time to his mother's womb to be born again. Having once begun, he cannot start over, cannot even try to get it right a second time. For there is no second time. No, it cannot be."

Once more, the preacher let silence fall upon the tiny congregation, and the silence was the silence of those who had been born once, never to be born again, the silence of the damned. Then the preacher spoke.

"'It cannot be,' Nicodemus says. But Jesus, friends, Jesus says, 'It must be.' You must be born again, born of water and born of the spirit. For only the twice born can enter the Kingdom of Heaven. There must be hope, then, but at what cost? What, we ask, is the price that must be paid for the second birth?

"So many are without hope, so many condemned to be forever what they are. They are born once and once only, because they are unwilling to pay the price. We grieve for them, and we understand, because we know that the price is high. And so I must ask you today, my friends, are you willing to pay the price of hope, the price of a new beginning? Do you truly want to be born again? Do you want to be transformed utterly, so that you are entirely different from who you are? For if you do, then the person who you are must die. It must be. If the new man is to be born, the old man must go under the water, never to rise again.

"And that is the horror, never to be underestimated, my friends, the horror of going under, returning to the mother's womb, writhing in the throes of birth and death, fighting at once for dear life and against it. Those unwilling to face this double agony cannot enter the Kingdom of Heaven. They are without hope, condemned to die once and die forever, just as they are born.

"Let us pray for them now, friends. Let us pray that the weak may be granted the blessed courage to die, and be born again."

As the congregation filed out to the ringing of the steeple bell, I wondered whether they were more than usually quiet and somber, or whether the preacher was always this dark on bright Sunday mornings, as dark as the Norways surrounding the little white church.

"Heavy sermon," I said to Libby, trying to get a little distance and shrug off the pall that seemed to have descended on everyone.

"Yes," she said thoughtfully.

"Well, I'm sure looking forward to your mom's cooking. What's for dinner, do you know?"

"Sure, it was heavy, but there was something right about it, too. Something important that's not easy to talk about. That's what church is for, too, to help you think through things that aren't easy to get a handle on."

"Oh?"

"I was thinking about us, Evan. I'm sorry, and I won't be a nag, but I couldn't help it."

"That's ok. Me, too."

"I was thinking that I love you. You know I do. But when you were gone last week, I realized—I don't know how to say this so you'll understand—I realized that I love not so much who you are but who you could be."

Libby put her arms around my neck as I was driving down the road, and gave me a kiss on the cheek. "I'm in love with the man you could be, Evan. I know you can," she whispered in my ear. "I just don't know whether you will."

Chapter 16

Chatting with her mother about the chestnut mare and her gangly colt, the new internship program at Family Services, the lace tablecloth that needed to be spread, Libby was happy. You could hear it in her lilt of her voice as she brought dish after steaming dish to the table: she was happy to be at home, happy to be with her family.

I was trying to be.

Somebody had to entertain the old fella in the living room, and that assignment fell to me. I suppose he felt pretty much the same about the young fella. Mr. Farina had obviously been coached not to quiz me about marital plans, not to offer oblique advice or engage in abstract meditations about whether it is better to marry than burn. Out of kindness, such subjects were verboten; and with Libby's parents, kindness counted more than dogma. But all Mrs. Farina's well-meant efforts had an effect just the opposite of that intended. For, unlike the chain of free associations forming in the kitchen, in the living room the more her father and I danced around the one prohibited topic, the clearer it became that, regardless of what we were saying, we were talking about one thing only.

"Yep," he was saying, "Tess and I have been together thirty five years come September."

"You don't say. Thirty-five years! That's a remarkable feat, and it takes special people to accomplish it."

124

"Well, not really. I can see you brought your own butter with you today, though." The old man chuckled good humoredly and stretched out in a favorite brown easy chair; at its side was an end table with three fat photo albums on it. "In our day the world was a simpler place in lots of ways. Not a lot of ruminating and deciding. You'd just go to the stable, choose your mount, and ride off."

"I can certainly see why you would choose Mrs. Farina. She's obviously a fine…"

"Oh, no, Evan, I didn't choose her. Tess is the horsewoman in the family. She chose me, and we've been together ever since. This farm was her idea," he said wistfully, looking off toward the kitchen. "Back then I had a place in Onamia, raising fryers for Gold'n Plump. Doing pretty good, too. But this lady had an idea in her head, colts frisking inside long white-washed fences and a lone farmhouse on the hill. Tess had such confidence in me and in the future that I got pulled right along with her, I suppose. I didn't know much about raising horses at the time, but she told me I could do it, and she was right."

"Sure looks like it," I said. Out the picture window I could see four horses grazing in the lush green pasture. Beyond the dark woods that filled the valley below, Pelican Lake lay serene and pale on the distant horizon.

"All that was a long time ago now," Mr. Farina went on, "and I never looked back, never regretted giving her the reins."

"I know a lot of men who would guard that secret with their lives," I said, turning back to him, smiling.

"Suppose so, Evan. But I'll bet it's because a lot of men have that secret to guard."

"Dinner's on!" came the shout from the dining room. As Libby and her mother brought out the last two tureen dishes, they paused for a moment to look at the sumptuous table, ostensibly trying to remember whether they had forgotten anything—salt and pepper? green olives? gravy ladle?—but actually it was just to admire the wonder they had wrought. And it was wonderful, we men had to admit as we sat down to say grace.

We passed around the steaming plates of green beans and mashed pota-toes, the home-made rolls and creamery butter, marveling aloud at the sights and smells of Sunday dinner, and the more we ate and the more we marveled, the wider Libby and Tess would smile, and glance at each other and smile again.

'The way to a man's heart,' I mused, somewhat cynically.

Had Roy Macklin ever sat at such a family table, while my mother low-ered her head to conceal a shy smile and my mother's mother said, "Would you care for a few more green beans, Mr. Macklin? There's just a few more we need to clean up."

Maybe Roy Macklin didn't like green beans.

At the cabin, our great dinner table still stood on its lion's paw feet in the dining room, the family heirloom now grown superfluous. Mom almost never put the leaves in it when I was growing up. No need to, except when Uncle Karl came over. It was just me and mom, and yet since we didn't sit on opposite ends, it always seemed like an invisible third place had been set across from us. We never talked about it, anymore than we talked about what was inside the hope chest. So I tried to convince myself that just as the chest was really nothing more than a convenient stand for the lamp, so also it was good and right for just the two of us to be seated at Sunday dinner. Mother and son, a secular pieta with Joseph unremarkably absent.

The nuclear family, I used to joke at the office, is nothing more than a time bomb waiting to explode. But no matter how much I joked, I always knew deep down that the aching emptiness of a missing parent, like the ghostly aching of an amputated limb, was not to be laughed away. However fully I realized that my own bombed-out, post-nuclear home was both the ancient norm and the standard of modern times, I couldn't help wishing that someone were sitting before that invisible third plate at our great lion's paw table, spreading the white napkin in his lap, and say-ing, "Would you like to give thanks today, Evan? It's your turn for grace, son."

"A wonderful meal, Mrs. Farina," I said, as empty pie plates and coffee cups began to disappear into the kitchen. "You've been so gracious I'd love to help with dishes, if you wouldn't mind."

"That's so nice of you to offer, Evan, but Charles and I have grown into a little custom over the years since we've been empty-nesters. It's not hardly worth mentioning, but Sunday afternoons we do the dishes together, while we're having our last cup of coffee. And we talk about the week past and the week to come. Isn't that right, dear?" She turned to her husband of thirty five years, and at that moment I saw her reward him with her glittering eyes, with that smile of deep, wordless joy I had seen on Libby's face at church that morning. Libby had learned more than cooking from her mother.

"Yes," Mrs. Farina continued, "It's part of our quiet time together on this day of rest, and so if you and Libby would like to look through the albums or take a turn out in the yard, that would be just fine."

"Sure, Mom!" said Libby with a little smirk. "Family albums would be fun. Maybe I could get out the shoebox with the slides from our vacation in Itasca, too. That has the one where I'm straddling the Mississippi! Wouldn't that be fun, Evan?"

"Well, I..."

"Ok, Miss Smarty," her mother chimed in before I had to dance the dodge and shuffle. "Ok, then. But you know when people have a fire in their house? They think about saving three things, the children, the pets, and the photo albums. Because it's their life in there, you know, the story of their lives. And I thought Evan might like to know a little something about the Farina family history, especially if he's thinking about...if you two are.... Well, you know, it just might be nice."

"I think we'll go for a walk, Mom, especially because Evan and me are thinking seriously about...doing a lot of walking together."

And so Libby and I walked together, hand in hand, out the back door of the spacious two-story farmhouse and down the long drive that led to the stables and pastures.

What is it about green, green grass that refreshes the soul? Tall grasses waving in the afternoon breeze, close-cropped grasses revealing the contours of the earth like a green silk dress on a fine woman. No one understood grasses like Andrew Wyeth. Look at "Christina's World" and you'll see that he knew. Not just the house but the meadow is its portal, just as this pasture was portal to Libby's world.

"Now that wasn't so bad, was it?" she asked hopefully.

"Not at all. They really were trying hard."

"So were you, Evan," she said, giving me a little kiss. She smelled clean and astringent, like fresh-peeled apples. Taking her hand momentarily from mine, she freed her long strawberry blond hair from its clasp, and it billowed out westerly, along with her full sunflower dress. Libby, the girl from Breezy.

The woman.

"Mom was trying so hard not to be pushy. She can't help being a mother, though. It comes out at the edges. You'll have to forgive the albums."

"Nothing to forgive. They got me out of doing the dishes, anyway."

"Oh, you!" she said in mock annoyance, giving my arm a jerk in the direction of the long white fence that circled the pasture. "Come here a minute. I want you to meet a friend of mine."

Libby put a thumb and forefinger in the corners of her mouth and gave a sharp whistle that pierced the afternoon air. "Here, Peg. Come!" The chestnut Morgan across the field raised her head and paused for a moment before recognizing the voice and remembering sundry treats of days gone by. Then she sauntered over to us, stately, leisurely, as if unwilling to sacrifice her dignity by proceeding in unseemly haste.

"Hello, Peg. Hello, my love," Libby said, as the massive animal sidled up to the fence. You always forget how big horses are when you see them in books or on TV, or even in the sideshows with the Shetlands for the kids, but then when you get up close to a real horse like a Morgan riding horse, it's another matter entirely. Peg stretched her long neck well over the fence and nuzzled Libby's sides and sniffed her pockets.

"Oh, you think I've got a treat, do you?" Libby said, pulling out a baggie full of apple cores left from the pie. "You think I've got a treat, old girl? Well, let's see what we have here." She held out one piece of apple and then another, stroking the animal's neck, scratching her forehead.

"You remember me, do you, my love?" Great velvety lips delicately, almost sensuously lapped the morsels from Libby's outstretched palm. "I remember you. Yes, I do. We had good times, didn't we, Peg? Ok, one more. That's the last one now. The last one. No more!" Peg eyed Libby, and then Peg eyed me, patient, expectant.

"Do you want to make a friend, Evan?" Libby asked, looking up at me from the corner of her eyes. "You need to be careful now, because horses never forget."

"Like elephants?"

"Yes," she said. "Like people."

"Sure. I'm game."

"No game when it comes to horses, Evan. A friend once, a friend forever."

"Forever? What if I choose another mount one day, and ride off into the sunset?"

"Makes no difference at all. Peg will always remember you standing at this fence, remember the touch of your hand, the sound of your voice, and the smell of your Peppermint Patty."

"My what?"

"Here, take this," she intoned solemnly, reaching into her pocket once more, delicately unwrapping the votive offering and displaying it upon two upright palms. "You give this to Peg, and you will have a friend forever."

So I did it, somewhat gingerly, cognizant of flaring nostrils and great teeth that could have taken my hand off with a single chomp. But they closed without incident, and equine taste buds no doubt glowed incandescent as invisible glands released their happy juices. The pact between us was thus sealed, the ritual complete.

Except that Peg indicated that she was not entirely satisfied. One tiny peppermint morsel, she suggested, was hardly enough for a real horse, a mature Morgan mare, and so she muzzled wildly into my jacket, my shirt, my pants, shoving me roughly from one side to another, while Libby clapped her hands and squealed for sheer delight as I was tossed about.

"I knew it. Peppermint drives her wild," she hollered laughing, as I staggered backward. "Drives her crazy, but now you've got a friend for life."

"You've got a friend," Libby repeated, slipping her hands inside my jacket and up my back, snuggling up close. "Now how'd you like a lover?"

"Well, let me see," I said dispassionately, looking down into her eyes and letting her long hair whip about my face. "A lover. And for how long would that be, then?"

"Forever."

"Forever? Well, then, it depends."

"On what?"

"On whether you have any more Peppermint Patties!"

"Peppermint!" she exclaimed laughing, "No peppermint patties. All I've got for you, Mister, is pasture patties!"

"Oh, I see," I said, my voice full of sorrow and woe. "Just pasture patties. Too bad. 'Cause peppermint drives me wild!" I pulled her body to me and kissed her hair, her neck, her mouth, long and tenderly, as we stood embracing in the lane with the stiff breeze stirring the long grasses at the foot of the white fence, and Peg looking on.

"Ok, wild man," Libby said after a moment, "Feels to me like you're ready. Let's check out the stable." And as she led me back up the lane, her arm around my waist, Libby squeezed me tight and sang a little song in feminine rhyme.

When you take Libby, Libby, Libby,
To the stable, stable, stable,
You will love her, love her, love her,
If you're able, able, able.

I would love her, I silently vowed, if I could.

When we returned to the house later that afternoon, Libby's father was upstairs snoring and her mother was resting in the big easy chair with a photo album on her lap. If Tess Farina detected a stray wisp of straw in her daughter's wayward hair that day, she made no inquiries, no accusations. She just smiled to herself and said nothing.

A horsewoman understands these things.

Chapter 17

"Good morning, Earlene! Top of the morning to you!" Normally I wasn't quite so chatty or cheerful with the secretary. But it was in fact a glorious morning when I arrived back at the *Sentinel* offices—so bright, so cloudless the sky was just barely blue. Having gotten some closure on Marian's murder and survived the fury of a woman scorned, I felt like a great gray load had been lifted from my shoulders. Now with my city business behind me, my country business stretched out before like the yellow brick road.

"Good morning, Mr. Wade," Earlene said, giving me an arch and knowing look, as she arranged her scotch tape holder and three-hole punch. "Mr. Helmholz said you should stop by his office as soon as you got in."

"What's up?"

"You'll have to talk to Mr. Helmholz about that," she replied mysteriously.

"No problem. He's probably got another story assignment for me. I'll just put my things in my office."

"Actually, Mr. Wade, Mr. Helmholz said you should stop by as soon as you got in." The repetition irked me. As if I should just hop to. Sherm had given the order, and now Earlene assumed all the insolence of a butler relaying the master's wishes. But I wasn't going to let Earlene becloud this golden morning, so I strode down to Sherm's office and gave him a big, cheery hello.

"Hey, Sherm. I'm back. All done playing PI in the Cities and ready to get back to work. Wasn't Smit, after all. They've got Marian's husband in the clink. I suppose we should have looked at him for it right away. Nine times out of ten it's somebody in the family, you know. But all's well that ends well, and...."

I stopped short when I saw Sherm's eyes shift to the corner of the room behind me. There sat a fat boy with coke bottle glasses. Stout young man with corrected vision, I suppose I should say.

"Evan," Sherm said, gesturing toward him, "I'd like you to meet our new intern."

"How do you do, Mr. Wade," the corpulent young man said, lumbering up from the chair and offering a puffy, outstretched hand. "I am Nero."

"Nero?"

"Yes, that's correct." The hand was wet and fleshy and cold, as one would imagine the hand of a drowned man newly dredged up from the depths. The air-conditioning will do that sometimes.

"Nero comes to us from the Shadow Program at Family Services," Sherm explained. "I'm sure Libby has mentioned it to you."

"Ms. Farina has been an invaluable resource to me, Mr. Wade. Bureaucracies can sometimes be so obtuse and unfeeling, but she is a truly considerate as well as highly competent public servant."

"You'll do yourself no harm by praising Libby around here," I said, while noting silently that a little less stilted language would seem more sincere. "Glad to have you aboard, Mr. Nero."

"Just Nero is fine."

"Ok, then, Nero. Welcome to the *Sentinel.* What will you be doing during your stay with us?"

"That's where you come in, Evan," Sherm interjected. "I've assigned Nero to 'shadow' you."

"Me?" I stammered.

"Who better to teach a young fellow how to be a crack reporter? Nero will be following you around as he learns the ropes at the office, and of course you'll be taking him along for interviews, city council meetings, and such."

"Oh, I…I'm honored but.…Sherm, could I possibly talk to you for a moment?"

"Of course. Nero, why don't you go down to Evan's office and start getting settled in. Earlene has all the supplies you'll need. The desk on the left will be yours. Let me know if there's anything I can do for you, now or later. Anything at all. I want your internship with us to be a real learning experience. For all of us." Sherm shot a quick look at me as he offered his hand to Nero.

"Thank you again for your generosity, Mr. Helmholz. You are very kind to allow me this opportunity," the boy said, overplaying his gratitude just a bit. "Mr. Wade, I'm a genuine admirer of your work. I have so much to learn about you and the business of print journalism. I am eager to begin." Nero bowed slightly, adjusted his glasses, and shut the door on his way out.

"What the hell are you thinking of, Sherm?" I exclaimed once Nero got out of earshot.

"I'll tell you, Evan." Resolute but without heat, Sherm sat impassively behind his broad desk, straightening the community service plaque before him. "I'm thinking of helping a young man get on his way, a young man who hasn't had it easy in life. He needs a helping hand just like you did a few months back, and we're going to give it to him."

"But Nero! Nero? Who would name their kid Nero?"

"I assume nobody. He probably had it changed. Like Cher or the artist formerly known as Prince. What difference does it make? What's in a name?"

"The kid's a weirdo, Sherm. I can smell it. 'I am Nero.' What kind of shit is that? Like Lon Cheney, 'I am Dracula.' If he's Nero, I'm Caligula. Weirdness, I tell you."

"Won't be the only weirdo we've got around here. But weird or not, we're in the business of words, and the kid's got words, Evan. You can hear it when he talks."

"Yeah, it sounds like he's reading, not talking. Speaking lines from a script or something. Not his own words but somebody else's."

"Just needs a little polish. If somebody hasn't got words, then there's nothing for him in this business. But this kid's a wordsmith in the rough, just like you were once, my friend. You can polish him. You can teach him how to write for the *Sentinel*, write so it sounds like just folks. Or the way folks would like to sound if they could."

"Oh, Sherm, you know I work alone!"

"I know you used to work alone. When you worked at all."

"Ok, ok, point taken. I'm sorry I skipped out on you last week. It was something I had to do, and I know how it must look on your end, but I can't have responsibility for this kid on my hands. I'm no babysitting service."

"No, Evan, you are not." Sherm picked up the picture of his wife from the place it always occupied on his desk and looked at it for a moment. "If Nell and I had been blessed with a baby to be sat, you can be damn sure we wouldn't call on your services. I wouldn't put my baby in your hands. Because you're not really very dependable when it comes right down to it, are you now, Evan?"

"Well, at least I'm up front about it. No promises, no lies."

"You think that makes a difference? I need you to be here when I need you to be here, Evan, and promises or no promises makes no difference. You know, I didn't learn a whole lot in college, but one thing in my political philosophy class stuck with me like pine sap. You ever hear of something called the social contract?"

"Of course."

"Well, I'm glad, because then you ought to know that this so-called social contract is the only contract that's absolutely binding on you, whether you sign it or not, even whether you've heard of it or not. You can say, 'the laws don't apply to me. I never promised to obey any such laws,' but it makes no difference whatever. The law still applies to you."

"Your point being?"

"My point is this: just because you're up front about your undependability doesn't mean squat, because people have to depend on each other whether they like it or not. And you can say in your truest and bluest tones, 'Don't depend on me, folks, I'm truly undependable, unreliable, irresponsible,' but the fact is that folks don't have any choice but to rely on you. And if you prove unreliable, you can't just excuse yourself by saying, 'Sorry, but I told you so.' No, Sir, you're just as much a slime ball as if you had made a promise and broken it. Because you did promise, Evan. Implicitly. And that's the social contract for you: you're always contracting obligations to me and everybody else around you whether you want to, or mean to, or say so, or not!"

"Very enlightening, Mr. Plato."

"Just Plato will be fine, thanks. At any rate, what Nero needs is a role model, as they call it, a professional role model. It's your job to supply it."

"My job, is it?"

"Yes, it is."

"Must be that my job description is sort of like the social contract, with all sorts of stuff I agreed to do without ever knowing it."

"Only if you want to continue in the employ of the *Lakes Area Sentinel*."

"Gimme a break, Sherm! You want me to play the father figure to this kid, Jabba the Hut, the weird waif?"

"Put it any way you like, Evan, but when I said I wanted this to be a learning experience for all of us, I meant just that. You can give Nero a chance to learn the news business, and in return he'll give you a chance to start acting like an adult role model, and I'll get a chance to practice the virtue of overlooking shortcomings. Yours in particular."

"No further discussion possible?"

"None."

"Then thank you for granting me this learning opportunity, Mr. Helmholz. I am profoundly grateful and eager to begin."

"Glad to hear it, Evan. Why don't you begin by dropping the sarcasm and checking out what Our Lady of Sorrows has planned for Bean Hole Days this year."

"Right you are, Sherm. No need for sarcasm there."

As I walked back down the hall to my office, Earlene kept her head down, shuffling papers intensely at her desk, studiously oblivious to me in every way, except that she was whistling "Me and My Shadow." Not to be undone, I whistled back a salvo of "I Did It My Way," whereupon she escalated by threatening me with "You'll Never Walk Alone," and if the hall had been long enough we could have waged an entire musical mini-war, a whistling version of *Casablanca* with "Deutschland, Deutschland" pitted against "La Marseillaise." But I declared a unilateral cease-fire upon entering what used to be my private office.

Nero sat upright on the edge of his desk chair. Maybe he wanted to look eager. Maybe he had to sit that way because the chair wasn't quite big enough to accommodate his massive butt. Even if I was inclined to be polite, I couldn't honestly say he was "big boned." Nero was short, squat, and fat. And fat people always evoked in me a deep, visceral disgust. I suppose it was just that my own propensity toward overdeveloped love handles had always made it necessary to exercise a certain discipline at the table, and so I felt a Puritanical contempt for those incapable of similar self-restraint. But for whatever reason, Nero's doughy gut, overflowing his belt so far that it splayed out his knees, repulsed me to the bottom of my soul. For me, just containing my disgust was an act of uncommon virtue.

Reflected glare from the sunlight coming through the window rendered his coke bottle glasses completely opaque. I wondered that he could see out of them because I certainly couldn't see in. It was strangely disconcerting, not being able to see his eyes. The 'windows of the soul,' people used to call them. There's something to that, I suppose. Why do troopers look more ominous and threatening when they're wearing shades? Why does somebody who won't 'look you in the eye' seem like they've got something to hide?

What was my shadow thinking behind those opaque glasses, that less revealed than concealed him, just like the poncho of fat he wore over his squat frame? What was he actually feeling that remained inarticulate, unexpressed by the stream of inflated words not really his?

I couldn't tell and didn't care.

He turned his head slightly toward me and the thick glasses went clear, suddenly revealing and magnifying the dark, almost jet-black eyes behind them. They looked monstrously large and deep, those eyes, both vulnerable and dangerous at the same time. But though Nero was looking in my general direction, his eyes focused only vaguely, as if he weren't really looking at me at all but at something or somebody behind me. I was tempted to turn around to see what he was looking at, but I didn't, not wanting to seem rude. Still, I couldn't shake the feeling that the closer I looked at him, the more he was looking through me. Weirdness, I thought.

Apparently Nero traveled light. His desk was bare, except for half a Mars bar, a yellow legal tablet, and a row of new pencils fresh from the box which he was sharpening with his penknife. I wondered if he could type.

"And that makes seven. All set, Mr. Wade," he said, finishing a last pencil over the wastebasket.

"I see that you are. Those are quite the glasses you've got there."

"Yes, sir. I can see very little with them, but I can see nothing without them. ROP."

"ROP?"

"Yes, sir. Retinopathy of prematurity, stage 4."

"You were a premature baby, then?"

"Yes, a twenty-six week preemie. Twenty three is about the minimum. I am particularly fortunate, however, because many ROP victims are afflicted with amblyopia and strabismus."

"But you were spared their fate?" I inquired, wondering what in the world he was talking about.

"That's right. I got away with just myopia. My mother did all she could. She tried cryotherapy, but to no avail."

"Looks pretty severe."

"Oh, I don't know. Many people suffer short-sightedness to a greater or lesser degree. I would even wager that you are a little myopic yourself, sir."

"Me?"

"Do you ever discover that you can't see what is right in front of you?"

"Not really."

"Then you are either very fortunate," Nero said, his glasses going opaque once more, "or even more myopic than I. At any rate, I wish to assure you that my handicap will not prevent my fulfilling a reporter's duties and obligations, however demanding. Has Mr. Helmholz designated our first assignment, if I may be so bold as to inquire?"

"He has indeed, and it's a dandy."

"Something investigative, I hope?"

"You might say so, Nero. You'll need to bring your pad and all your pencils, because our assignment, should we choose to accept it, is to investigate Our Lady's Bean Hole."

Chapter 18

"'Like many country traditions of unknown origin, the earliest celebrations of Bean Hole Days antedate the memories of today's participants.'" Articulating each word carefully, Nero ran the paper past his stationary nose as if he were a human scanner. "What do you think so far, Mr. Wade? I know that's just the beginning, but is the language concise, elegant, and efficient?"

"I tell you what, Nero," I said, wincing, "it's hard to know from just one sentence. Why don't you read on a little more, and I'll give you my best judgment." I leaned back in my office chair and placed my hand over my face, trying to prevent myself manually from breaking out in an uncontrollable guffaw.

"All right," he proceeded, "here goes: 'Asked by this reporter to recount the genesis of the annual, late-summer event, Queen Bean Nina Arnulfson responded, "I dunno. There's always been a Bean Hole!"' —That's an exact quote, Mr. Wade. Very authentic, but do you think I should correct the grammar?"

Without replying, I allowed one noncommittal eye to peek through my extended fingers.

"Ok, ok. I'll go on. – 'One source, who asked to remain unidentified and whom we shall call Father X, hypothesized that the ceremony has a religious origin. 'After all,' Father X observed, 'the beans are lowered into the burning pit, covered with earth, and then they rise again after....'"

"Thanks. Thanks, Nero." I said, interrupting him before I lost it entirely. "That's fine. I think I've got a good idea of the piece now."

"So, what do you think? Is it any good?" Nero's glasses glinted and his fatty white cheeks trembled in anticipation. He wanted so much to win my approval. I wanted so much to stifle my groan.

"Well," I said, searching frantically for something, anything at all, to compliment. "Well, it's an excellent start."

"Oh, I'm very relieved, sir. I did try to combine the virtues of reportorial accuracy with a certain stylistic panache."

"Yes, I can see that, but perhaps we can start right there with some improvements. You know, 'panache' isn't a word we have much use for in the Lake Country, or in the *Lakes Area Sentinel* for that matter. The same goes for 'antedate' and 'hypothesize.' What with McLain's crack-brained ideas about the death, burial, and resurrection of little brown beans, that kind of language makes your story sound like an anthropology article about North Country vegetation rituals."

"I see what you mean. You recognized Father McLain, then? I **was** trying to protect my sources."

"Well, when Our Lady is the only Catholic church in town and there's only one priest in the church, you know! Besides, he's tried to fob that story off on any reporter who'd listen. Maevis Sterns, our county librarian, dug up a 1937 article with the real explanation how the whole thing got started. It seems that during harvest the grateful townsfolk of Pequot decided to reward the grain threshers with a bean dinner."

"I see what you mean." Nero slumped down in his undersized chair, melting over its edges like Cheddar cheese on a hot burger. "I'm afraid I got carried away."

"Hey, no problem. Live and learn! Where did you get all those ivy-league words anyway?"

"I read much of the night. I love to read. I can't get my fill of reading. I consume history, drama, and poetry voraciously, and fiction I simply inhale. My mother's influence, I suppose. She loved to read to me when I was a child. I remember late in the evening, after dinner dishes were done, Mom would sit down with me on the big overstuffed couch with her arm around my shoulder. I turned the pages at her signal, and she would read aloud chapter after chapter of *Lassie, Come Home* until the pages of the novel blurred out in the tears we shed for that lost collie and the boy who loved her. And then with a big hug and kiss, I would go to bed and cry some more about an inconsolably lonely little boy with a beautiful, loving mother."

Listening to Nero reminisce, his fat seemed less obtrusive, less disgusting somehow. For I remembered another boy, likewise inclined to pudginess at a certain age, likewise acquiring an insatiable taste for language at his mother's knee, from his mother's tongue.

I thought of her, staring out the window, with canned laughter mocking her inexorable descent into silence.

"You do understand, don't you, Mr. Wade?"

"I suppose so. Sure."

"I knew you would," he said, pausing for a moment and smiling slyly. "I'm your Shadow."

"Well, Shadow, you can start writing more like a newspaper man by lightening up your prose."

"Do you mean I should attempt humor?"

"Sure, that would be a start."

"I have some notes here somewhere," he said, patting down all his sundry pockets back and front, high and low, looking for all the world like an obese dwarf trying to dance the Macarena. "Here, these might serve the purpose," he said, as he produced the pile of scraps he had gleaned from the search.

"Good," I replied. "Why don't you take those back to your desk for a few minutes and work on lightening up a little."

Occasionally glancing in his direction, I could tell the task didn't come easy. Nero's face underwent contortions that I hadn't believed possible before, though I can now testify that with sufficient concentration the human tongue can extend almost to the earlobe. Broken pencil points skittered across the floor, the penknife slit the pencils back into shape, and a few minutes dragged out into more than an hour, as Nero attempted to lighten up.

"I'm sorry, Mr. Wade," Nero said upon returning, holding out a crumpled and much-erased sheet of paper as proof of his labors. "I'm afraid that levity does not come naturally to me. Everyone thinks corpulent people should be light hearted, gay, and amusing. I am not."

"You're not the type to fiddle while Rome burns?"

"No. And my namesake wasn't either."

"He wasn't?"

"No, that fiddling business is pure fiction, probably deriving from a translation error. But if I were more inclined to fiddling, I might have more success writing about Bean Hole Days. Is there some technique I should know? Some trick you could teach me? I do want to learn," he pleaded.

"It's not a matter of tricks but of learning a trade."

"I know you're very busy, but could you teach me, Mr. Wade? Could you show me?" Behind his coke bottle lenses, Nero's big, puppy-dog eyes entreated my assistance. He needed me so much that it was pathetic. I was not about to put my arm reassuringly around Nero's shoulder, but I could at least give him a sample of the kind of thing the *Sentinel* printed.

"Well, let's see what I can come up with as a model." I leaned back and shut my eyes, composing myself and my first paragraph.

"How about this?

What would you do if one day you found yourself with an extra 440 pounds of beans on your hands, along with bacon and brown sugar to suit?

Well, the citizens of Bobberland, as the town of Pequot Lakes calls itself, know exactly what to do on such occasions. They do it every summer.

You start by digging a big hole with a backhoe—a long trench, actually, five feet wide and four feet deep. You fill the bottom with lake rocks and pile it high with brush and logs to burn and heat the rocks. Then you find yourself five beanpots. They can't be any ordinary, kitchen-variety beanpots, of course, but five massive, black iron beanpots big enough for Paul Bunyan to heat his porridge.

You add the beans, bacon, brown sugar, and many secret ingredients also beginning with the letter B. Stir thoroughly with a canoe paddle. Then after lowering the beanpots into the hole, cover them with plywood, top with sand, and simmer for 16 hours. As they bake, the aromas of rock and wood and earth, the savors of the Lake Country, permeate every bean.

All that's left is to invite 2000 of your close, personal friends to join you at high noon, when a powerful wench hauls the steaming pots from the earth, and everyone gathers round to enjoy a bean feast extraordinaire!

"That's amazing, Mr. Wade!" Nero exclaimed. "And all of it extemporaneous! Light, yet detailed and informative. Perfect without revising a word!" Sherm had sauntered up and stood listening to us, arms crossed, in the doorway.

"Just takes a little practice," I said, bowing my head and trying not to brag. But I suppose there's nothing more boastful than false humility.

"There's just one thing I don't understand, though," Nero said hesitantly. "I wonder where they ever find a young woman strong enough to pull those immense pots out of the trench."

"What young woman? There's no woman!" I couldn't fathom what the idiot boy was talking about.

"Oh, I must have misunderstood," Nero said in puzzlement. "I thought you said that a *wench*....You perhaps mean the pots are raised with a *winch*, a mechanical device with cable and pulleys, whereas a wench is..."

"I know the difference between a winch and a wench, and I don't need any lectures on vocabulary from...."

"'Fraid he's got you there, Evan," Sherm said, roaring with laughter as he trotted back down the hall. "This is going to be a learning experience for all of us, all right."

"Oh, I am sorry, Mr. Wade! I certainly didn't mean to embarrass you. And in front of your boss, too."

Nero's apology failed to smooth my ruffled feathers. In fact, nothing he said sounded quite sincere, and his apology served more to heighten the offense than excuse it. Magnifying his midnight blue, almost black eyes, his glasses made him look like a bug-eyed Martian, examining me dispassionately, expressionlessly, disjoined from whatever he happened to be saying.

"Don't bother yourself about it," I replied.

"I'm so sorry. It's just that I happened to be reading Eliot last night. Do you like T. S. Eliot, Mr. Wade? I was reading the poem that begins: 'Thou hast committed— Fornication; but that was in another country, and besides, the wench is dead.' You see! I just had the dead wench in my head, that's all, and so when you said 'wench,'...."

"Forget it. No problem."

"Are you sure? I'd hate to fall from your good graces so soon."

"You haven't."

"Well, I'm glad, because I find it so informative and satisfying to be your Shadow. That's why I was reading Eliot in the first place. You know his poem 'The Hollow Men'?"

"It's been a long time." In fact, it must have been a previous life, for I never read any poem whatever if I could help it.

"Of course," he said, his voice full of understanding, maybe even a little condescension. "It's the poem that ends, 'not with a bang but a whimper.'"

"Oh, right. I've heard of that."

"It contains these haunting lines about the Shadow: 'Between the conception and the creation falls the Shadow. Between the desire and the spasm, between the potency and the existence, falls the Shadow.'"

"What's all this got to do with the Family Services Program or your job here?" I asked irritably.

"Why, nothing, nothing at all!" he replied with utter nonchalance, looking at me and, as he so did so often, through me at the same time. "It was just all whirling in my mind like a vast bean pot, you know. The desire and the spasm, the fornication and the dead wench, the conception and the creation. And between them all falls the Shadow."

Chapter 19

Something was up. It didn't take Sherlock Holmes to figure that out. Libby had been putzing around the cabin all morning. A little dusting, a little mopping, a little baking—nothing very unusual for a Saturday. But not a single note of the Beach Boys all morning long. The place was like a tomb that smelled of Pine Sol and chocolate cake.

I wasn't aware of having committed any offense that would repress either the lady's spirits or her vocal cords. But a man's unconsciousness of guilt, I had long since learned, is no proof of his innocence. Who can know the true depth of his sins? Perhaps I had forgotten an important occasion, like the anniversary of our first date, or today could have been her sister's birthday or something. I doubt it, though. I don't think Libby had a sister. But just to be sure I tiptoed around the cabin like it was a minefield.

I could imagine what would happen if I tried to confront and interrogate her: Ok, Libby, spill it. Why, whatever do you mean, Evan? You can't tell me that something's not up. What do you mean up? I mean something's going down. Down? Yeah, if something weren't up or down, I'd be hearing the Power Loon crooning all over the house this morning. Oh, you mean that. Yeah, that. So sing it or spill it.

Not likely to be a very profitable conversation. So, while the vacuum cleaner whirred and purred about my feet, I went on pretending that

147

everything was hunkydory and finished the BLT on rye Libby had made me for lunch. I knew something was wrong, though. I could feel it. And all pretense of domestic bliss was shattered when Libby shut off the cleaner, turned to me all full of innocence, and fired her first salvo. "Evan, could you run down to Monty's and pick up some walleye for dinner?"

Now, Monty's Fish House was some thirty five miles away, requiring a round trip of almost two hours. Just for a couple of walleye. So Libby's seemingly innocent request, as she very well knew, amounted to a transparent provocation, a flagrant shot over the bow meant to start a fight. But Libby was no match for me. I decided to outwit her by employing the old switcheroo. She thought she had me pegged. But instead of manfully resisting unreasonable female demands, as she fully expected, I simply agreed to them.

"Sure. Glad to," I said.

"You sure you don't mind?" she replied, with a smile that artfully concealed how deeply frustrated she was.

"No problem," I replied, with a little smirk.

"Because it's a pretty long way to Monty's if you don't want to," she said, pretending to backtrack and let me off the hook. That's when I knew I had her, all right. Libby was trying to pull a double reverse on me. Me, the grand master of reverse psychology! But I was a little too quick for her there. I wasn't about to go for the fake. No, I would catch her at her own little game. I would play the victim, and she would end up owing me big time.

"As a matter of fact," I said pensively, "the Gophers are playing Iowa this afternoon, and Floyd of Rosedale is up for grabs again."

"You mean that pig they play for?"

"Not just a pig, Libby. It's Floyd, or a statue cast in loving memory of Floyd, actually. The original passed away some time ago, and now he's a bronze statue."

"You mean they bronzed a dead pig? Like baby shoes?"

"No, no. Never mind. The point is that it's kind of a personal tradition with me, Libby."

"What kind of people would play for a bronze pig?"

"Forget it. You don't understand. You see, I've caught the Iowa game every year since I left the U."

"I bet it's just guys, isn't it? Do the women at the U play for a pig?" She just wouldn't let go.

"Of course not. Let's see. I'm just about to turn forty three. Monday, in fact. So this year would make it twenty three. Twenty three years without missing a game!"

"Pretty sexist for a University tradition, if you ask me," Libby said laughing. "A sexist pig tradition!"

"Oh, what the heck!" I said, pretending to give in. "I guess I can miss the game just this once, especially if we're out of walleye." I tried not to gloat while savoring the sweet smell of success and deciding what compensation I would exact for my self-sacrifice.

"Good," she said, looking away and adding vaguely, "I've got a couple errands to run this afternoon or I'd go myself." I wasn't going to ask what errands. I knew it was a ruse. There really weren't any errands. Only fictitious errands. No errands worth mentioning at any rate. At least, if there were any real errands, she didn't see fit say what they were. I may have been slightly curious about any and all errands that Libby chose to shroud in secrecy, but I certainly wasn't about to play her little game by inquiring as to the exact nature of errands so momentous they had to be concealed from me.

Thus, by dint of sly intelligence and powerful self-restraint, I won this particular battle in the ongoing war between the sexes. But as I walked out to the car, I had to confess a certain admiration for Libby's utter nonchalance. In fact, she seemed on the surface completely oblivious to my victory, betraying no sign of what must have been for her a deeply humiliating defeat.

On the way to Monty's, however, I decided, for reasons best understood by myself, to stop in at Northern Hydraulics, a man's store if ever there was one. Specializing in wood splitters, go-karts, and pneumatic devices of all descriptions, Northern does not exactly prohibit women from entering the premises but does discourage them in subtle ways. Take demonstration days, for instance. They are something like Saturday sample days at County Market, where malicious ladies with baggies on their hands display plates full of shrunken wienies pierced by toothpicks and sliced up in ways that can make grown men waddle down the aisles with knees pinched. So too Saturdays at Northern are demonstration days, except that their demonstrations are specially designed for male patrons and may not be suitable for viewing by young or unaccompanied women.

On this particular Saturday I was especially fortunate to be present, the young greeter informed me, because the staff were demonstrating wood splitters. And since I've always wanted a good, strong wood splitter myself and secretly envied men who had them, I was glad to watch these husky fellows demonstrate the various splitting positions: first, the standard horizontal position, where the gleaming, wedge-tipped rod drives inexorably forward until it cleaves even the tightest of logs, and second, the fascinating vertical position, surprisingly effective even with rod down, for use as desired and convenient. I was tempted, I confess, to purchase one of these magical machines right there and then, but I managed to satisfy myself with one of the chisels they were handing out as door prizes.

Reassured by this detour, I made my way as quickly as the old Ford would carry me to my appointed destination. Monty wasn't there, of course. On his office door he had a cute little wooden fishing pole sign with a note on the line that said "Gone Fishing." Monty was actually "Gone to Dry out at Hazelden," but there was something endearing about the idea of a fish store proprietor out catching some fresh wares. Perhaps Monty was forced by geographical necessity to import frozen shark and tuna, shrimp and oysters, dolphin and flounder, but these exotic fishes were not my quarry today. I had come for walleye, the national sport fish of Minnesota. Not that I had ever caught any. Quite a lake boy, I was. Couldn't swim, couldn't fish, but I did love to eat fresh walleye. And so when I managed to pry the gangly clerk with the little sailor hat away from the Iowa game he was watching behind the counter, I asked for:

"Minnesota walleye, please."

"Minnesota?"

"Walleye. Yes. Minnesota walleye. Is there a problem?"

"We don't have Minnesota walleye."

"All out today?"

"Actually, sir, our walleye are flown in from Manitoba."

"Manitoba walleye?"

"Or Saskatchewan. That's correct, sir."

"I can't believe it," I said indignantly. "No Minnesota walleye here in Bobberland?"

"Oh, there's plenty."

"But they're still in the lakes?"

"You're very quick, sir."

"Do you sell bobbers, then?"

"No, sir, you'll have to go down to Marv Koep's for a bobber, but you don't catch good eating fish that way anyhow."

"No?"

"Around here," the kid said with a broad grin, "the only fish you catch with bobbers are crappie."

"Funny," I said, disappointed to have come all that way for two dubiously fresh (Manitoban or perhaps Saskatchewanian but at any rate very unMinnesotan) walleye. As I drove homeward, past the famous bobber-shaped Pequot Lakes water tower, I pondered all these things in my heart and came to a much keener appreciation why some folks in town earnestly desired to repaint the town's landmark bobber as a golf ball.

I didn't look forward to explaining all this to Libby, and it turned out I didn't have to, because at the very moment when I opened the cabin door, an entire throng of familiar faces shouted, "Surprise! Surprise!" And Libby, her vocal cords fully recovered, led them all in a boisterous chorus of "Happy Birthday."

Chapter 20

"You trickster! You just wanted me out of the house, didn't you? So you sent me on a fishing expedition!" I said, with my catch still under my arm.

"You really had no idea?" Libby asked with a big grin on her face.

"Not a clue," I admitted. I thought it best not to mention how I had actually interpreted her little subterfuge.

"Well, let me put these in the fridge," Libby said, taking the fish, "and come look who all is here."

She had managed to assemble a small group. Strikingly small, I reflected. There wasn't much she could do to expand it, though, for truth was, I didn't know many people. Not well enough to have them into my home anyway. I didn't go to church, didn't belong to the volunteer firemen, didn't throw dinner parties, didn't attend the book club, didn't invite neighbors to cozy campfires on cool summer nights. Work and Libby, work and Libby, that was all. It occurred to me that this was a new way of determining age: not chronologically by the increasing number of years but inversely by the decreasing number of friends. By this measure I was already ancient and decrepit. For in fact I had only one friend left, other than acquaintances and relatives. Just one.

And what if she left me? What if the circle, never large in the first place, shrunk down to a single point of light, and finally just disappeared with a blip and rush of static, like a TV set going dark for the long night?

This party was not an entirely happy surprise. But I was grateful and determined to make the best of it.

Charles Farina and his wife led the band of well wishers. ("Forty three, eh, Evan? Young, still pretty young, not at all too old to....All right, Tess, all right. And Libby is—what is it now—thirty one? All right, Tess, I know! Say, Evan, why don't you stand over there with that young lady and her mother so I can I get a picture.")

Sherm and his wife were there, too. ("Hi, Evan, Happy Birthday! The little woman here was just asking about the difference between a winch and a wench. Do you have a minute to run over the fine points with her?") Bending over to give Nell a welcome hug (she actually **was** a little woman), I laughingly referred her to Webster for enlightenment on this important and frequently misunderstood distinction.

"Look who else is here, Evan," Libby said. Nero shyly shuffled forward, his thick glasses like an opaque mask in the afternoon light. ("Thank you so much, Miss Libby. I'm deeply grateful for your invitation to join this family celebration, this commemoration of life and birth. Congratulations, Mr. Wade. Please accept this gift betokening my recognition of your contributions to my education and very existence.") At arm's length, Nero held out a flat, square birthday present, obviously a CD, wrapped in the Sunday comics.

It was only when I had thanked Nero and he had stepped aside that I spied the guest of honor, seated in her favorite chair beside the hearth. Fetching her from Sacred Heart must have been one of those momentous errands Libby had concealed.

Without rising, she held out her arms to me. "Evan," she said. I knelt down to embrace the emaciated female form that was my mother, and she whispered, "Happy birthday, son!"

"Mom," I said, and that one word was all I could say for a while. A big lump rose in my chest and tears welled up in my eyes. Not just because she recognized me or because it was one of her good days. Seeing her once again in that doily-covered rocker, the chair she would always occupy in my memory and imagination, made it seem as if my long exile in the Cities had been erased, as if the dark night of Alzheimer's had never descended upon her, as if the child Evan had returned once again to sit at his mother's knee.

Looking on from behind the others, Nero seemed even more touched by the scene than I was. His fat heaved. Great sobs bubbled out him. I resented his repulsive blubbering, his unwelcome intrusion into what should have been a private, or at least uninterrupted, moment with my mother.

"I'm so glad you're here, Mom," I finally managed to get out. "What's a birthday party without the woman who gave birth?"

"Gave life," Nero interjected somewhat loudly from the rear. Everyone turned round to stare at him, and abashed by the startled faces, he immediately tried to take it back. "Oh, I'm sorry. I've got no business....Please forgive me."

"Not at all, Mr. Nero," my mother said, releasing me and diffusing the tension. "You're quite right. Life! That's the real birthday gift."

"Yes," Nell said, looking at the floor, "a gift that can only be repaid by giving it again in turn." She took her husband's arm, and he lightly patted her hand as it rested there.

"Why, I remember that afternoon so well," my mother mused. "I remember the exact day, forty three years ago, everything about it. Lying in the tiny labor room at St. Joseph's with acoustic tile on the ceiling—the walls, too, as a matter of fact. Airless, and hot as the dickens it was in the August heat. My mother sat at my side, dabbing my drenched forehead with a cool cloth, squeezing my hand in hers when I cried out. 'Saint Joseph!' she said bitterly. 'He's the only one. Ain't none of the rest of 'em saints. That's for sure. Not a one. You don't need that man, Evelyn. He's gone and good riddance to him, I say. You're going to be just fine, dear, just fine.' And she was right. I was just fine."

No one spoke. What was there to say?

The birdsong clock in the kitchen broke the silence as the thrush sang out three o'clock.

"This is it, Evan," my mother said, looking up at me with a smile. "The hour of your birth."

"And the hour for birthday cake and ice cream," Libby chimed in. "Everybody to the table now, and we'll serve up the goodies."

So everybody gathered around the great lion's paw table, which hadn't accommodated that many people since Grandma Wade's funeral. Libby brought out a half-gallon of vanilla ice cream and a chocolate cake with thick chocolate icing. My favorite. I should have guessed what was up from the very beginning.

"Look at all those candles," Sherm said, trying to count them. "Hardly room for one more."

"Good thing I'm not eighty three," I said.

("Sure is!" I heard Libby's father blurt out under his breath.)

"We'll just bake you a bigger cake," Libby said, as she sliced the chocolate, scooped the vanilla, and handed the plates around. "An eighty-three-candle-size cake, and you'll have to eat it all, and you'll enjoy it as much as Nero here."

"Me?" Nero asked, rising up from his plate, icing on his glasses, his mouth stuffed full of cake. Everybody looked at me, looked at Nero, and laughed and laughed. Everybody, that is, but me and my shadow.

It wasn't long before the guests were standing up, offering their parting thanks and congratulations. Libby and I saw them out the driveway and returned inside to clear away the last of the dishes. Then we were alone with Mom, sitting again in her favorite chair, rocking, musing, reminiscing. Neither Libby nor I had the heart to propose taking her back to Sacred Heart just then. So we let her sit there, looking into the cold fireplace as if warmed by fires gone by, while familiar surroundings summoned memories from near and far.

"What are you thinking about, Mom?" I finally asked after a number of minutes had passed, as much to determine whether she was alert and aware, as to satisfy my curiosity.

"Oh, just thinking, remembering," she said, still staring off into empty space or, rather, into the fullness of time. "It's been a long while since I thought about my mother sitting next to my hospital bed like I did today. I'm afraid I didn't repay her kindness very well."

"What do you mean?" I exclaimed. "You took care of her to the very end, sitting at her bedside just as she was at yours." I couldn't let her slight herself, for I too had memories of Grandma Wade's last days. I could still remember a great fetid stench rolling out of the back bedroom where the old woman lay after she lost control, memories of my mother cleaning up, without hesitation, without complaint. Greater love hath no man. My mother repaid everything she owed, and then some.

"Yes, dear. But I meant she wanted me just to forget about Mr. Macklin and move on, begin again. It was good advice, I'm sure, and I wished I could some days, wished with all my heart, but I never could do that, you know."

"Yes, I know," I said. In fact I knew it all too well—it was one of the burdens of my existence—but not because she had told me. She never discussed Roy Macklin at all.

"I just couldn't," she went on, returning her gaze to the cold fire. "I couldn't move on from him, anymore than I could move on from myself."

"You were hardly more than a girl back then," Libby offered.

"It's true, dear. A little slip of a thing." She smiled and reached out to Libby, who took her hand. "But being just a girl doesn't let you undo what you have done. Because what you have done is you. And you have to live with that. You have to live with yourself, for better or for worse. There's no second chance. You write your own story, and write it any way you like, but that's why you can't just write 'the end' in the middle of it and turn a new leaf, start a new page."

"Then there was you, too, Evan," she continued. "Even if I could have found someone new and started over somehow, you couldn't. Your father is who he is. You can't start over with someone new. You can't undo who you are, any more than I can. And it would have broke my heart to see you grow up in shame because of what I had done. So I was not about to make you ashamed by trying to move on myself, when you could not. I was not about to start a new page, even if I could."

"And I didn't want to. That's what irked Mother the most, I think. I didn't want to forget him. 'After that man just left you!' she used to say, time and time again. 'After he up and hit the road!' She was right, of course. But it's no worse that he left me when he did, than five years later, or ten, like when Grandpa Wade left her to waste the rest of her life in bitterness. I was not going to do that, let it consume me like she did. And leaving wasn't the only thing about him, or the most important. Does everything else get erased by that one thing? Whispers out on the dock, a shared laugh in his fast, fast Corvair convertible, rowing late at night up the inlet to Star Lake, just us two."

Now was the time for questions, if there ever was one. When exactly did he leave? Did he know you were pregnant? What did he say? Did he promise to come back? I wanted to know everything. I asked nothing, however. I could not interrogate her. So I just let her go on.

"I loved your father, Evan. He had so much about him that was fine and admirable. It wasn't all a cheap and dirty trick like Mother said, was it? Does everything good have to last forever, or else it's just a lie, and always was?"

I made no reply. I didn't say that for her, it did last forever, because I wanted to believe Roy Macklin had something resembling a heart, some glimmer of decency, just a glimmer. I wanted to believe it for her sake. And for mine. I truly wanted it to be so, because neither of us could sever the tie with him.

And did he really manage to leave us entirely, I wondered? Was he out there never giving us a thought, dandling some Johnnie or Mickey on his knee, waiting for a warm voice from the kitchen to call out, "Supper's on, you guys. Come and get it"? Or, as he lay back on the unmade bed of some squalid motel with the neon sign outside blinking "Vacancy! Vacancy!" did he ever think back to the cabin on Woman Lake, hoping that a lamp still shone in the window after all these years?

What if he suddenly sat bolt upright, pulled on his jeans, and pointed his eighteen-wheeler north, to the North Country and the family he had never entirely left behind? And when he held out his hand in the doorway, saying, "Hello, I'm Roy Macklin," would I take him to me, saying "Father, father"? Or with one fell blow, would I drop him where he stood?

Mom was tired. Her head was drooping, and Libby was trying to catch my eye.

"Ready to go back to the home, Mom?"

"I am home. This is my home," she snapped, without raising her head.

"Of course it is," I agreed, standing up. "I just meant...."

"What is it with people nowadays? They put away their babies, and their parents, too? That place isn't a home. It's a warehouse with wallpaper."

"Oh, Mom!"

"Let me stay here with you and Libby, Evan," she pleaded. "There's plenty of room. I promise not to be a bother. I won't get in your way."

"Oh, don't, Mom! Don't say that! You're never a bother, but we can't take care of you here. You know that. We've talked about that. What if you had a bad day while we were at work? Sacred Heart has nurses for you and everything."

"I'm afraid when I'm there, Evan. I'm terribly frightened. All the time."

"There's nothing to be afraid of there! Nothing at all." I stepped over to the closet to get her sweater. "They're all there to help you."

"No, Evan, there's no help for what I've got. And it's not the people I'm afraid of. It's just the waiting and waiting for the end. Long days of waiting. Sometimes just blank days, and I wake up from the blankness, lying on my bed or sitting in my chair, and I wonder, did I die then? Am I alive?

I get so confused and angry. I don't want to die in that place, son. Won't you let me stay with you and Libby? If you send me back there, it will kill me! I know it will. Your own mother!"

She knew how to twist the knife. But Libby and I tried our best to sooth and reassure as we helped her on with her sweater. There was no arguing, but no giving in to her pleas, either. Her living with us just wouldn't work. But that didn't make her tears burn any less hotly as we drove her, weeping softly in the rear seat, back to Sacred Heart.

In my anger, I couldn't keep myself from blaming her for crying and not understanding the dilemma we were in, blaming Libby for bringing her to the cabin and opening old wounds, blaming myself for not being son enough to attend to his own mother personally, without hesitation, without complaint, to the very end.

Libby and I kept our thoughts to ourselves on the way back to the cabin, but when I saw the CD wrapped in the comics lying unopened on the buffet, all the resentment that had been building in me just burst out.

"What did you have to invite him for, Libby? I can see Sherm and Nell, I guess, but Nero? He didn't belong here."

"Oh, Evan, I just thought it would be nice for him. He doesn't have family or friends around here. And besides he was standing right there when I stopped in to talk to Sherm about the party."

"You could have just waited a minute."

"Actually, I did, but he didn't seem in any hurry to leave us in private. And I wasn't going to snub him, especially when I knew how much he looked up to you."

"Me?"

"Sure, when he applied to the Shadow Program, he talked about wanting to be a reporter. He wanted to know whether we had any internships with newspapers, and I told him, Sure, the *Brainerd Dispatch* had a couple that might be possible. But he said, no, he was more interested in the *Sentinel*. More interested interested in working with Evan Wade, who wrote all those stories in the *Star Tribune*! Isn't that nice? You're famous! So I told him I'd check with Sherm, and you know the rest."

"Just what I need—a groupie! What does he know about me? A sick groupie! Did you hear the fool blubbering when I was talking to Mom? And what was that little outburst of his? It was disgusting."

"A little bit of sympathy might be in order, Evan. He didn't have it easy."

"Didn't have it easy," I said, mimicking her. "Everybody keeps telling me he didn't have it easy. I can't see that he had it any harder than me or lots of other kids."

"What do you mean?" said Libby, startled.

"Well, he told me about his beautiful, loving mother, who read *Lassie* to him at bedtime. Sounded like pure Norman Rockwell to me."

"I don't know, Evan. But I saw Nero's Family Services record going all the way back, and he's been in one foster home after another, a couple of them abusive, or close to it. Nero never knew his mother."

"Weirdness. I told Sherm the kid was weird."

"Give him a break, Evan. Maybe you misunderstood or something. Look, he brought you a present. I told them all that presents weren't necessary, but he went and got one anyway. Open it, why don't you."

I assumed it would be Jimi Hendrix, or maybe something arty like Count Basie, if he overestimated my age. But I would have never guessed a CD of the *Orson Welles: The Golden Age of Radio*, disk 2. Nero couldn't have thought I was that old. But then I understood. On the disk was not *War of the Worlds*, as you might expect, but two digitized episodes of *The Shadow* from 1936, with Welles playing Lamont Cranston. I knew how it would begin even before I put the disk in the machine. Welles' great basso and fiendishly threatening laugh rang out like a vaguely familiar voice from another life.

"Who knows what evil lurks in the hearts of men?

The Shadow knows!"

Chapter 21

For Sherm, the annual meeting of the Minnesota Association of Print Journalists was a cross between the Academy Awards and a Shriner's convention. He abstained from the pleasures of the flesh on these occasions, but he made up for it with the pleasures of Grain Belt. I enjoyed his company, and I had reasons of my own to want to get back to the Cities. But I knew better than to ask Libby for her permission or simply take off without it. She was already beyond ultimatums.

"I can't go, Sherm. Libby would kill me. Or worse!"

"Listen, Evan," Sherm insisted, coming out from behind his desk and sitting on the front edge, "the APJ comes but once a year. Like Christmas. Tell Libby it's business. She'll understand."

"She'll understand all right. And I'll be bobbitized when I get back."

"No problem. I know a guy that sells snap on tools. Say, you know why Bobbit couldn't get into the night club? The sign out front said Private Members Only!"

"Do you think these up yourself, Sherm, or do you collect them from the net?"

"Oh, Evan," he said, ignoring my sarcasm, "just tell Libby whatever you have to. Because if you can't figure out a way to get to the APJ, you don't need to worry about what will happen when you get back because you've been bobbitized already."

"Thanks, Sherm, you're a pal. What did you say to Nell?"

"I just told her it would be bad luck if the *Sentinel* weren't there to accept the award."

"We're not up for an award."

"Sure we are, and we've got a great chance, too. The category is 'Local interest, animal or vegetable; circulation less than 50,000.' For 'Bay of Pig.' Jake wrote it just before he left."

"The drowned porker that Wally Knutson snagged off the end of his dock? Where'd that thing come from anyway?"

"Who knows? Must have fallen in the river somewhere upstream. Jake did a real nice job with it. Photos enough for a full spread. Lucky for us, it was a very photogenic pig. The thing was puffed way out, with four stubby legs sticking out like a Macy's parade balloon. Must have been six hundred pounds of ham hocks. Nobody could find a wench strong enough to lift it out."

"Enough with the wench, Sherm."

"Right. About all they could do was tie the carcass to Wally's dock where it floated around for a week like a giant pink and purple bobber. Boy, was that thing aromatic when the DNR finally came and hauled it out! I wanted to call the story 'Bringing Home the Bacon' but 'Bay of Pig' won by a snout in the office pool."

"That's great, Sherm. A sure winner, unless we're edged out by a calf with two heads or giant pumpkin that looks like Jesse Ventura! But none of this helps me with Libby."

"All right, let's put our minds to the task before us." Sherm assumed his chin-on-knuckles imitation of Rodin, ruminated on the problem, and, with a strain like defecation, produced an epiphany. "Hmm. No. Well. Ok, ok. I've got it. NERO!…"

"Sherm, no." I wanted none of this.

"No, listen. This is it. Nero's the key to this whole thing. We'll take him along, and of course he's got to have somebody to shadow."

"Out of the question. Bad enough that Libby invited the weird waif to my birthday party. I don't want him tailing me all the time. I'm starting to feel like I'm on the run, pursued for crimes and misdemeanors unknown. You know what he gave me for a birthday present?"

"Evan, do you want a free ride to the Cities or not? You know Libby's soft on the kid. He's your ticket!"

Sherm would not take no for an answer. And thus it came to pass that, after complimenting Libby on her cheese ravioli and spinach soup that evening and offering to sing harmony to "Good Vibrations" while drying the dishes, I broached the forbidden subject.

"Libby, Sherm asked me to take Nero to the journalists' meeting this weekend. What would you think about…?"

"This weekend? Well, no, I don't see any problem with this weekend."

I had hunkered down, prepared to face a tornado of wrath, a tsunami of indignation, and meeting no resistance whatever, I almost pitched forward on my astonished face. Couldn't be another birthday party that she needed me out of the way for. That would have been a surprise, all right. So I thought for a minute that Sherm was right—Nero was the ticket— until Libby added:

"Where will we be staying?"

"Staying?"

"It's going to be wonderful, Evan. Sometimes you are so thoughtful. If we're out by the Mall of America, I could pick up that set of Williams-Sonoma I've been looking at. You know, the Pugliese pasta bowls. Great for ravioli soup! But I could take a cab even if we're downtown at the Radisson. It's no problem. Anywhere is fine, really, and we can go out to romantic dinners in the evening when you're done with convention business. And at night! At night!…" Libby wriggled up next to me in a full body embrace, the stimulating effect of which was not at all diminished by the apron I was wearing. "Did I ever mention how turned on I get by king size beds in king size hotels with king size men?"

This did not seem an auspicious moment to point out that Libby was not expressly invited to share in the king size pleasures of Minneapolis, nor did that moment come later when she called Nell to ask what she would be wearing, and Nell said, "Oh, a weekend in the Cities! What a wonderful idea!" But Sherm reminded me that this was not intended to be a family outing when he called to inquire whether I had a brain in my head and to suggest that if I didn't acquire one pretty quick, in the future I might have no occasion to attend the meetings of the Minnesota Association of Print Journalists.

Given the turn of events, Nero was no longer absolutely necessary to our scheme. But Sherm wanted to bring him along anyway. And since Sherm offered to take Jabba in his own car, I didn't protest too much. Nero was thrilled when I informed him of his good fortune.

"Oh, I would be honored to accompany you, Mr. Wade." Nero always jiggled when he got excited or nervous, and now he was jiggling like a bowl of jello.

"Actually you'll be with Sherm most of the time, Nero."

"What an opportunity to meet so many distinguished members of the profession! How fortunate I feel to be your shadow." While talking to me, Nero was searching through his desk drawers one after another. Finally he fished out a bag of chips and began chowing down. "What a learning opportunity this will be. Will you be pursuing your investigative work while you're in the Cities?" he asked, his mouth full.

"What investigative work?"

"Well, the Mitchell trial is set to begin soon, and I naturally assumed...."

"What do you know about me and the Mitchell trial?" I snapped. The Shadow knows a little too much, I thought to myself.

"Why, nothing, Mr. Wade," Nero protested. "I don't know anything. But you were telling Mr. Helmholz about Trevor Mitchell's arrest when we first met in his office. 'Most of the time, it's somebody in the family,' you said. I thought that was so astute. Don't you remember saying it was somebody in the family?"

"I suppose so," I replied, reassured that Nero hadn't been snooping. "But for me this weekend is pure R and R," I said. "Just a few beers and a few laughs with colleagues past and present. That's all. No work, investigative or otherwise."

"Of course," he said, coke bottles glinting in the sunlight. "Well-deserved R and R. I understand entirely, and I promise not to be a bother. I want to assure you that I won't get in your way at all."

"No. You won't," I said with an air of finality that sent him hustling back to his potato chips.

Why was it that everything Nero said seemed to have an edge to it? No Orson Welles laugh, of course, but an undertone of the sinister nevertheless. Just passive aggressiveness, I decided. Who could blame him, I thought, looking like he does? 'Cower or be kicked' seemed to be his recipe for getting through life, though it did imply he considered me definitely the kicking type.

I had never said or done anything that I knew of to deserve that opinion. I had gone out of my way to repress all urges, however powerful, to steal his Mars bars or leave him in a cloud of dust, waddling slowly behind, feet splayed, stiff arms pumping, pendulous stomach swaying, as his weight rocked from one stumpy leg to the other.

Maybe I should cut him a little more slack, I thought. But then there was the *Lassie* thing. That was something else, well beyond passive aggressive. Delusional? Neurotic? Made no difference to me, I decided.

The cavernous foyer at the Radisson was the right size for the conference: it offered just the right amount of room for finding the conventioneers you wanted to find and avoiding those you didn't. Across the crowded room, filled mostly with shuffling men in tousled hair and the customary uniform of corduroy jackets, jeans, and sneakers, I had spied Sheila Hund. The dog woman stood out, conspicuous for being the sole person in the room wearing a sportcoat and necktie. She looked a little like Boy George.

Of course, Ben had a bowtie. Without it and his matching red braces, he could have gone incognito. At the moment he caballed with a knot of chums and chumettes in the corner. I couldn't avoid them for the whole weekend, but keeping my distance for one evening would be pleasant.

I didn't worry about avoiding Anne Chisolm. Maybe that was why, when I lowered my first empty Grain Belt, there she was in front of me, glowing.

"Hello, Evan." She smiled her little understated, Jane Austen smile, and it came back to me what a great woman she was. Or could be. When she didn't have her claws out.

"Hello, Anne. You're looking great. Married life must be agreeing with you. How's...what's his name? Sorry. I didn't mean to be snide." I'd never met her husband.

"That's ok. What's his name is fine, and so is what's his name junior." She made a discreet gesture toward her stomach, and I noticed that she was just barely showing.

"That's great, Anne! I'm really glad for you. When are you due?"

"January. January 12, give or take."

"Wonderful. Can I give you a hug for old time's sake?"

"Of course," she said. I put my arms awkwardly around her, afraid to break something. "A hug for old time's sake, Evan, and new time's, too. Life goes on, doesn't it? Begins and then begins again. For Charles and me it was time to decide about beginning a family. Now or never. I'm no spring chicken."

"Certainly not," I agreed, remembering the way she pounced, talons flashing, on some pretty tough old birds. "A spring chicken hawk, maybe. But chicken? Hardly!"

Anne smiled. "Chicken hawk. I like that. With a covey of baby chicken hawks hatching! Yes! And how about you, Evan? What's beginning in your life?"

The conversation ended somehow, I don't know how, and she drifted away to other partners, other conversations. I just remember being strangely wounded by her question. Not the obvious "How are you doing?" Or, "What's new with you?" Or, "Are you with anyone now?" No problem there. But Anne's stilted, unidiomatic, piercing question left me standing alone in the middle of the vast Radisson foyer with an empty beer bottle in my hand, while numberless corduroy jackets circled aimlessly around.

I just stood there because it occurred to me that I had nothing in the ground. As Johnny Appleseed, I was a complete failure. Not a single living, growing seed in the ground. What's beginning in my life, Anne wanted to know. Nothing, I had to answer. Exactly nothing.

And so what? What's wrong with that? What's wrong with just continuing, with ongoing? What's the big deal about beginning? And is it really so easy to start a new life as Anne seemed to think? Just say "The End" and move on?

Mom didn't think so. Having been robbed of a future, she clung to the thief who stole it, because that was who she was: the woman who had been robbed by Roy Macklin. Only death would end her unfinished business with him. Short of that, she never could start over and begin anew. Was it always that way, I wondered? Short of death, no birth?

"Buy you a beer, Evan? Looks like you could use another."

"No thanks, Ben. I've got to go and meet Libby in a second."

"She here with you? Lovely as springtime, that woman. But spring doesn't last forever, does it? The seasons pass and fade. You will let me know when you're finished with her, won't you, Evan?"

"You **are** a slime ball."

"Me? Why, of course, but then I have no pretensions otherwise! I didn't mean to offend, however. Perhaps I misunderstood the nature of your intentions concerning Ms. Farina. Did you have in mind something more permanent and binding for the future, perhaps?"

I made no reply.

"No, I thought not," Ben said dryly, tugging on his bowtie. "Wasn't that your ex I saw you chatting with? You and Anne were together...how long was that? I can't remember exactly. Six months, was it? Seven? I do admire your taste in women, Evan, though Anne was always a little on the catty side for me. Slice you up like a veg-o-matic. I can understand why you wouldn't want to leave your zucchini in there very long. Unless you like puree."

I turned and began to walk toward the elevators. Ben didn't move from his spot. He just called out, "I suppose you don't want to know about Trevor Mitchell, then?"

"What about Mitchell?" I asked, as I turned and walked slowly back, hating myself for letting Ben play me like a yo-yo.

"I take it your friend Queenie hasn't kept you fully apprised of his progress?"

"We don't talk much these days." In fact, I would have been amazed if Queenie ever spoke to me again, after his mood when I last saw him.

"Well, Mitchell's off the hook. The couple he claimed to be with on the afternoon of the murder finally turned up. Seems that they were one of those wealthy but childless duos he was dealing with, and weren't very anxious to talk to the police. So!"

"So what?"

"So the case is in the toilet. Informed sources say Queenie returned to the Overdale clinic last week. Now, it seems unlikely that Mitchell has any connection with that place, and so I guess Queenie must be looking at Smit again. Whatever the reason, it can't be a good sign if they're having to go back to square one."

"And square one is Overdale?"

"Well, Medaille and her staff at the clinic were the last ones to see Dr. Barclay alive, as far as I know. And that, according to perennially proven police procedures, is generally the place to start. Don't you agree? I ask you, then, as a deeply interested, unusually well informed, and personally involved party to this investigation, what could Detective Cuene be after?"

"No idea, Ben. Let me know when you figure it out."

Chapter 22

I had no idea what Queenie could be after. But as I rode the Radisson elevator up to our room, the only thing I knew for a moral certainty was that Marian was not, could not possibly have been, performing abortions at Overdale. Could she? The woman I once knew was prime motherhood material. Could she have changed that much? Become a different person? Kicking my shoes off and flopping back on the king size bed, I reassured myself that it was not possible. For better or worse, people don't change that radically. Maybe don't change at all.

So what other reasons could Marian have had for being there? I had no idea, and I sure as hell couldn't ask Queenie. Mitchell might know, but not likely, since they were already separated by that time. No way around it: I had to go to Overdale. No one would miss me at the conference. I could slip out on the "Enhancing Digital Images" demonstration and the panel discussion on "Right to Know vs. Right to Privacy," and no one would be any the wiser.

A great commotion at the room door announced Libby's return from her first shopping expedition. Bags and boxes bounced against the door and tumbled to the floor while she tried to figure out whether the right or left side of the key card went in the slot, then whether top or bottom went in the slot, and then whether back or front went in the slot. Complex as this process may sound, scientists at MIT have determined that there are in fact only four possible insertion positions for key cards. Therefore hotel guests with sufficient time and patience need merely apply a simple and systematic process of elimination, probably already familiar to mathematicians and users of ATMs, in order to illuminate the little green light and open the magic portal. Since Libby's little red light was already glowing, however, I thought it best to defer explaining this process, and just open the door.

"Oh, Evan, thanks," Libby said, gathering up the scattered parcels. "Am I crazy, or were keys much easier than these card things?"

"Yes, they were, but you're still crazy. What's all this stuff?"

"You'll see," she said, giving me a little kiss on the cheek as she rushed past, arms full of packages. "All in good time. Just a little surprise."

"Only a little one?"

"Ok, a big surprise, then." I peered gingerly into the bags, Saks, Williams-Sonoma, Victoria's Secret, Wicks 'n Sticks.

"Hey, get out of there," she exclaimed, laughing and folding shut the bag tops. "No peeking! You hurry up and get changed. We're going out for a night on the town that you'll never forget. I guarantee you."

Libby took the Saks bag and disappeared into the bathroom. I figured I was in for a wait, so I lay back down on the bed.

"What would you think about eating at the Black Forest tonight?" I shouted through the closed bathroom door.

"Nope," the door replied.

"They've got some great Rindsrouladen. You know, that's…"

"Beef rollups. I know. Nope. No Rindsrouladen."

"But they've got this neat little arbor out back where you can eat outside. Very romantic."

"Nope, no romantic arbor." The door seemed very opinionated tonight. "Are you dressed yet? Don't forget to put on a coat and tie!"

"Libby, I didn't bring a tie," I said, grinning smugly from my supine position on the bed. "I only own one, and I left it home."

"Well, can you imagine that!" the door exclaimed in amazement. "In that case, you'll find your first surprise in the Nordstrom's box on the table." Afraid that I had been outfoxed, I got up and looked. There, among others, lay a tie box, of course.

"Oh, Libby, you shouldn't have. How could you have guessed I'd need one?"

"The Shadow knows, Evan. It is useless to try to escape. You are in my power."

With these words, the door opened and laying eyes on Libby, I had to admit that she was right. I was in her power. A little black nothing of a dress, low scoop front, lower back, accented every delicious curve. Libby did a quick turnaround and gave me a come-hither look over her shoulder that would raise the dead.

"My, my," was all I could get out.

"Oh, you wordsmith," she said, encircling her arms around my chest and leaning backwards until I had to catch her from falling. "Your eloquence just sweeps a poor woman off her feet. Kiss me lest I swoon!"

She let her head fall back, her strawberry locks almost reaching the floor, and I kissed her ear, her neck, her chest, and lingering there, I caught the scent of a new perfume that might well be recommended as an alternative to Viagra.

Then she stood up. "Wait just a minute, Mister. Didn't your Mama tell you that you can't have dessert til after dinner?"

"I don't always do what Mama told me," I said, giving her another kiss. "And, besides, you don't want to go to the Black Forest."

"Nope," she said, with a little playful smugness, "we're going someplace you've never been." Libby took the silk tie out and tied it round my neck in a perfect Windsor as she talked. "And since the Shadow knows you've been around the block once or twice, I asked the Concierge to recommend someplace special. The sky's the limit, I told him. The sky, Madam? Maybe even beyond the sky, Sir. I understand, he said. You are looking for a place that would give a fellow's rockets a booster? Exactly so, I replied.

Then Goodfellows is the only place for you, he said. And the cab will be waiting for us at 7:45."

I couldn't help but laugh. "You've got it all planned out, don't you, Miss Farina!"

"You don't know the half of what I've got planned for you tonight, Mr. Wade. You don't know the half of it." And the fun of it was I didn't know, but if this was just the prelude, I could hardly wait for the climax. So I happily went along with Libby's big plans, and shortly after the dining hour, we arrived at Goodfellows.

As soon as we opened the door, I was afraid I was in over my head. I gazed up at the impressive Gatsby décor. Vast etched mirrors multiplied the angular metal furnishings in black and gray. "Libby," I whispered, "this may be a little more than I can afford."

"Shhh. Not another word about money. Tonight is about us," she said, as the maître d' approached. Bowing, with hands clasped before him, he discreetly admired the wonder of Libby's chest. I couldn't blame him, really. The summer sun had covered it with multitudinous freckles, like a June pasture sprinkled with buttercups. Once as Libby was sleeping on the beach, I spent an hour counting her freckles one by one. Then she opened her eyes and, catching me surveying her, she smiled her Libby smile and said, "Well, what do you think, Evan?"

I thought of June.

Now, too, as she turned and followed the maître d' to our table, I imagined painting Libby in all her summer glory. She lay unclad in a breeze-swept meadow, her long, firm body dissolving into invisibility among the myriad buttercups of June.

Mark would be serving us this evening, the maître d' predicted, and Mark it was. He greeted us warmly enough, to be sure. But the barely detectable hint of condescension in Mark's voice thoroughly intimidated me. Libby seemed right at home, though. She held her chin pretty high for a girl from Breezy, as if everything common were beneath her notice this evening, including Mark, whose upper lip intimated that, unlike the glorious creature who inexplicably accompanied me, I might feel more comfortable at some other establishment, somewhere like Brit's Pub, perhaps, where impostors were more welcome.

That was why I was overjoyed to catch him out in his little masquerade of culinary expertise. Ignoring me, he addressed himself to Libby:

"May I recommend the Pequot Lakes Pheasant this evening, Madam? It is served with pecan-spiced butternut squash and dried cherries. The David Bruce Winery has a particularly fragrant Pinot Noir, one of my personal favorites from 1997, that would complement this entrée."

"Wait a second, Mark," I interrupted. "Did you say Pequot Lakes Pheasant?"

"Yes, Sir. Goodfellows prides itself on gathering the genuine tastes and aromas of Minnesota and raising them to the heights of dining pleasure."

"Well, you may have a little problem with the genuineness of your Pequot Lakes Pheasant."

"How is that, Sir?"

"Well," I said, leaning back on the back two legs of my chair, "I was raised in the North Country, and during my youth I was a hunter of sorts. Pretty good one, too. But anyone who has ever escaped the provinciality of the Cities knows there are no pheasants in Pequot Lakes. It's too cold for them anywhere north of Pierz. And so I suspect these pheasants of yours are like the Minnesota walleye that come from Manitoba—more likely to be from Peoria than Pequot."

"Ah, I see the problem, Sir," Mark replied with a tone of deep pity for the pervasiveness of ignorance in the world. "But you are referring to wild pheasants, of course. And wild fowl are characteristically tough and gamy, quite unfit for the tastes and standards of Goodfellows' patrons. Their usual patrons, I should say, who prefer their pheasant free of No. 6 birdshot. Ours are shipped to us freshly dressed from a game farm in Pequot, just down Route 16, three miles east of A-Pine Restaurant. Perhaps, as someone who has escaped the provinciality of the Cities, you've heard of Wild Acres?"

"Sure, Evan," Libby chimed in, "you know the place back in off the road, near the Breezy township line?"

"Exactly, Madam. Now, if I may continue...."

So Libby ordered the genuine Pequot Lakes Pheasant with pecan-spiced butternut squash and dried cherries, while I dined on crow and humble pie. Nobody, I can affirm, prepares them better than Goodfellows.

Nothing could spoil the evening, though. Libby was in high spirits, enhanced by the Pinot Noir. She laughed at me a little, and I laughed at myself. She joked about bringing bad boys to Goodfellows. I told her that I liked her cooking better than theirs, and she told me that I was a shameless liar, but a sweet one.

And just to please me, Libby said, she'd made her afternoon's pilgrimage in search not of the Holy Grail but pasta bowls.

"Now we can have ravioli soup every day," Libby joked. "I love the Williams-Sonoma dinnerware, Evan."

"What's wrong with our jelly glasses?"

"Have you ever seen their Charleston Saffron dinnerware?"

"Oh, I'm just mad about saffron."

"Good, because someday I want all Charleston Saffron dishes on my table. Our table, Evan. And we can invite Mom and Dad over for Sunday dinner."

"After church?"

"Yes," she said, reaching out her hand across the table to take mine. "After church."

"Well, lucky for me Pequot doesn't have a Williams-Sonoma store." I gave her hand a squeeze.

"Unlucky for you, Evan," Libby quickly replied, "Williams-Sonoma has a website, and on that site is a gift registry, and using that registry people can miraculously order gifts without ever once entering the store."

"Now, why would anyone be ordering gifts for you, Miss Farina?" I said, accenting the Miss.

"We'll see," she said, as she caught Mark's eye for the check. "We'll see."

It started to sprinkle as we left; occasional flashes of lightning lit up the Mini-apple like a strobe light. On the way back to the Radisson, we snuggled and giggled and fondled each other in the back of the cab like a pair of horny teenagers. No wonder cabbies have so much to talk about. Libby wouldn't let me pay for the cab any more than for the dinner, and so as I was systematically running through the six basic positions for inserting the key card in the lock, I said, "Oh, I know what you're after all right. Girls like you! You think you can take a guy out for a nice dinner and a bottle of wine, and pay for the taxi, and take him to some fancy hotel room, and now it's his turn to pay. Is that what you've got in mind, missy?"

"It's payback time all right," Libby said, "and the price is high. I want all you've got. Now, if you'll just step into the waiting room...." She gestured toward the bathroom door. "I'll call you when I'm ready."

Minutes dragged, and standing naked before the bathroom mirror, I sucked in my stomach and threw out my chest. Not so bad, I thought, so long as I hold my breath. I tried twenty seconds, then thirty. Thirty-five seconds was max. Would she notice my still youthful physique, or just my beet red face? I was getting impatient. But Libby was taking the lead in this dance, and it was my part only to follow. Finally I heard her say, "Ok, you can come in now."

Opening the door, I at first saw nothing. The room was dark, lit only by two candles on the bedstead. As my eyes adjusted, I saw the covers had been turned back, and on the bed lay Libby in a midnight blue silk chemise that was barely long enough to conceal Victoria's secret. At first she said nothing, merely watched me standing there, rising to the occasion.

"Dinner's over," Libby finally said. "Time for desert."

"And what's for desert this evening, Madam?"

"Strawberry delight, Sir."

With that, I was upon her. Or was it she who was on me? Rough, almost violent, she was, like the angel wrestling with Jacob. Sometimes I felt as if I were taking her by force, such was her resistance. At other times, she clamped down upon me so hard that I moaned as much out of pain as passion. Libby was not a weak or timid woman. She knew how to use the force of her body, lean and muscular from farm labor, and she knew how to ride. Together we rode hard up the hills, peaked, and coasted down the valleys, struggling against each other, raising each other up to where the lightning flashed in the night sky, then falling back into darkness. Again and again. Enough, I wanted to cry out, I'm too old for this. But Libby refused to let me go until the candles on the bedstead burned low and passion succumbed to exhaustion.

We lay there spent and silent for many minutes, until I said, "What a night! Unforgettable, just like you said."

"Yes," she said. Her head lay heavily on my arm.

"A night of surprises," I said.

"Yes." She fell silent for a moment, looking over at me, wondering, making a decision. Then she added, "And they're not over yet."

"No?"

"No, they are not." In her eyes seemed to be some doubt, some question she needed to have asked but feared to have answered.

"What have you still got up your sleeve, Libby? Oops, sorry, no sleeve! No blouse either!"

"Tell me, Evan," she said with no trace of humor, staring at the empty ceiling, "I want you to tell me now that the corpses all are buried."

"Corpses?" I exclaimed, completely taken aback. She just looked at the ceiling, silent, expressionless, waiting for me to remember my return from the Cities and our conversation weeks previous.

"Oh, you mean…." I couldn't tell her that in just a few hours I was headed to Overdale to dig one of them up again. "Yes, completely gone."

"Completely?"

"Dead and buried. No ghosts, no shades or shadows." I shut my eyes, hoping Libby wouldn't be able to see I was lying. Marian was only one of my ghosts, but lying about my unfinished business with her was like lying about being unfaithful, and I was ashamed.

"I'm glad, Evan," she said sternly. "Let the dead bury the dead. We have to live. And so it's time now, Evan."

"Time for what?" I asked, almost frightened what she would say.

"I've waited for you and waited, and now it's time for you to decide. Past time, and I can't wait any longer. We're good friends and great lovers, but that's not enough. You know it's not. We're going nowhere. All our tomorrows are like yesterdays. It's like we're drifting out on the lake. It's a breathless day, and we're drifting aimlessly in a dead calm, going nowhere. It's time to move on to a new life. It's time for you to ask me, Evan Wade. Will you? Right now. Because if you don't, I'll ask you."

Libby looked steadfastly into my eyes. I didn't press her, didn't quiz her as to what she wanted me to ask her so urgently, because I knew full well. Before she said it, I knew with the certainty of prescience what she was about to say, and I couldn't stop her, couldn't strike her dumb before she spoke the words that would drive us apart.

"Evan, will you marry me?"

Great tears welled up in Libby's eyes and flowed down her cheeks. She rolled over and put her head on my chest, scarring it with her hot tears. "I'm so afraid. I want to marry you so much. You know that, don't you, Evan? I want us to be a family and have children. I'll love them as I love you, and I'm so afraid you'll say no. But I can't wait any longer. It's time for yes or no. Please say yes, Evan. Tell me you will. We could be married, and we'd be so happy. Wouldn't it be nice, Evan? Wouldn't it?"

Chapter 23

When I last spoke to Marian it was November, a barren, lifeless month that could be dropped without loss from the Minnesota calendar. The gray-blue sky and waters of the Lake Country wore the look of pale dreams. Ungainly docks and lifts littered the gray shoreline like jurassic skeletons stranded on the beach. The birches had long since gone bare. Mom's brilliant yellow mums had gone gray. Hard frosts had embalmed the whole landscape, draining it of life and color. Only the red oaks, stubbornly clinging to the last few rust-colored leaves, insisted that summer heats had been more than a delusion.

September had taken Marian to Northfield and me to the Cities, where it was Carleton for her and the U for me. She went under duress, as if to prison. I, by contrast, felt totally emancipated. At the U, I was free of the cabin, with the pathetic Wade family history grimly figured in two chairs at the lion's paw table. I was free of my mother, too, with her petty household economies, her unspoken but suffocatingly desperate hopes for my future. And if the truth be told, I was grateful to be free of Marian.

Her boundless loneliness needed boundless reassurance, and after that first frightening dive into the water, we came together on the pontoon boat with a frequency that left little to be desired. As summer days grew shorter, wild nights grew wilder aboard the "Queen Mary"—which I rechristened the Queen Marian. But the pleasures of possession dimmed the keener pleasures of anticipation, and I began to understand the mean-ing of the old Lake Country proverb: the two happiest days of a man's life are when he buys a new boat and when he sells it.

Cold, late summer nights extorted the usual promises from us as we cuddled beneath blankets, floating aimlessly, unanchored. The frigid air sucked the last warmth from the steaming lake. Fog gathered around the boat, flowing over the deck, into the cabin, between the two of us lying on the bed. The moon grew hazy, indistinct. I promised that I would always this, and never that, and the other thing would surely last forever.

These scenes, however vivid at the time, were instantly displaced by the excitements of life at the U. I loved my dorm, Sanford Hall. True, Sanford offered no place to study, but I didn't need any, because after midterms I found I had no need for books or classrooms either. True, it was the cheap-est dorm, packing in two rich or, as in my case, three poor sardines to a room. I didn't mind the close quarters, though, because my roomies were usually gone when I was there. True, almost every night false alarms roused groggy residents from their beds during the early morning hours. But the sirens, the fire trucks, the cursing freshmen forced out into the cold night air didn't bother me; I and my fake ID had rarely floated back from Fowl Play by then. During the days, though, the dormitory lived up to its true and original function: with no roommates, no fire trucks, and no academic interruptions, it was the perfect place to sleep.

So I was sleeping the sleep of the dead when Marian's call came that late November afternoon.

"Marian!" I said, startled by her voice into sitting prematurely upright. "Good to hear from you this morning." My head throbbed like it was in danger of falling off, and I had to lay it back down on the pillow for safe-keeping.

"Is it two already? All right, good to hear from you this afternoon, then." The grayness of the unremittingly gray day made it impossible to tell nine in the morning from four in the afternoon.

"Well, a little extra shuteye never hurt."

"*Yes*, until two o'clock! Why not?"

"Oh, not much. A few beers with the guys. Then a few shots. Fowl Play. You know. The usual."

"Pretty often, yeah. In the evenings."

"Yeah, that's why." I fingered through a pile of Marian's unreturned phone messages that my pathetically scrupulous roommates had left for me.

"Sure I tried! But you were always in class or something."

"No, of course not. Don't be silly. I still do. I've just been out with the guys a lot. That's all."

"Sure I do, when I get the chance. I grab a few minutes here and there, and then I hit the books really hard. But I'm not really into the academic thing. I've got a couple real losers for profs anyway. You should hear this bozo in Ethics lecturing about social obligation and the Absolute Good. Absolute crap, if you ask me! Asshole gave me a D on the midterm essay."

"'Freedom and Responsibility.' Not going to win me a Nobel prize or anything, but a D? Gimme a break! I wasted half the night on that thing!"

"Yeah, probably so. I got a warning letter from my advisor last week. So probably next quarter at the latest. But who gives a shit? I'm a free spirit, footloose and fancy free."

"Nope. Won't miss it a bit."

"I don't know. Travel around, I guess. How about you?"

"No, I mean your classes."

"None of them? I thought you liked Bio?"

"I miss you, too. But you're not going to flunk out or something?"

"No, I didn't think so."

"There sure are. Lots of things more important than this diddley shit. Now, for the first time in your life you feel really free, the whole world is yours, and then they saddle you with all this…."

"No, I haven't forgotten at all."

"Sure, every word of it."

"Absolutely, I still want to. In a few years. We talked about a few years. When the time is right, we said."

"Christmas? Jesus, Marian!"

"I know I said I'd be thrown out at the end of the quarter, but...."

"What's the rush? Did you talk to your father? I can just imagine what him and Francine would have to say: 'Why, Marian, whatever can you be thinking of! Don't you remember what we said about med school?'"

"Ok, forget Francine, then. Forget med school. Do what you like! You're free, too, free as a bird, and you've got the scratch to fly away any time you want. Fly away little bird!"

"Ok, don't fly, then."

"Sure, I want one too."

"Of course I know how important a strong family is!"

"And you will! You'll be a great mom. No doubt about it. Just like your mother."

"Yeah, mine too."

"I'll sure try to be. But fatherhood is a big responsibility. None bigger, maybe. And so you have to be absolutely sure before you jump in. And you know how I feel about jumping in! You could drown out there!"

"I *am* serious! Never been seriouser. You don't want to get into this kind of thing and then decide you want to back out of it. No, it's once and for all. No turning back. No starting over. You write your own story, and then have to live it out to the end. That's why you have to be sure."

"I love you too, but we have to wait until the time is right, Marian. Until the time is right."

"I don't know. When we're a little older, I guess. We'll know when we get there. But not now, not Christmas."

"Don't, Marian. Please don't. What's the big deal about Christmas? Why not Spring, or Summer, or whatever? I don't get it!"

"I know, I know, but don't lay this on me! We've got our whole lives to be sure about this. There's no rush. We've both got things to do before we get tied down."

"I mean *married*. That's what we're talking about, isn't it? Tying the knot, getting tied down, the tie that binds and all that?"

"No! I haven't changed my mind at all."

"I can't, Marian. Not right now. I really can't. It's just not something I can do right now."

"Well, it's still no. Not yet."

"Of course! Of course, we will. You bet! Just not right now. Next year maybe. Yeah, maybe next year. What do you think about a year or two?"

"Yeah, it will be great then. Just you and me."

"Right, and baby makes three. But in a year or two, and then we'll know if it's time."

"You ok then?"

"That's my girl. Got it back together now?"

"Sure, I will. Next Tuesday. Week from today. Is this a good time to call?"

"Ok. Good. Talk to you then."

"You too. Bye."

That was a long, long time ago. The week slipped by, and I forgot to call Marian at the appointed time. Slept through it, and only remembered the next morning, when I grabbed the phone and dialed furiously, furious with myself for having forgotten, furious with Marian and all her insatiable needs, her senseless proposals. When she didn't answer the phone that day, or the next, or the next, I knew she would be making no more tearful pleas. My buddies down at Fowl Play congratulated me. "A man's got to be free," they said. I was free all right. But for all our beery laughter, I mourned her inwardly and grew to despise my miserable freedom.

I never talked to Marian again, though a few weeks later I did receive a letter from her. An envelope, actually. When I opened it, I thought it was empty, just a stupid joke. But, about to throw it in the trash, I peered inside. There I saw a finely wrought anklet chain, slender and strong as a silken thread, and on it a tiny silver heart.

I kept the thing for a while, in a drawer with extra buttons, socks with no mates, and undeveloped rolls of snapshots I intended to put in an album sometime. The trinket finally got lost somehow over the years, but that doesn't matter. And over the years Marian married Trevor Mitchell, and I found Anne and Libby, but that doesn't matter either. For however far apart the events of our separate histories had driven us, Marian Barclay and I remained tied together always, indisseverably joined by one summer, one night on her invisible island, one moment of union that could never be broken or denied. The price of that moment was forever.

I had told Marian that if we got married, we would have to live with it to the very end, till death do us part. Which is true. Divorce is a fiction, as far as I can tell. Even without children, married couples are never really free of each other in any but a legal sense. So I thought I could keep my precious freedom by staying single, never getting married in the first place. What I didn't understand is that it's not marriage but the decision itself that ties the knot, and you are bound by your decisions, either way. You're even more strongly bound by the negative ones, perhaps, because they seem to be no decisions at all. I was tied to Marian, though not by marriage, it is true. It was precisely my refusal to marry her that bound us, and I'd been reliving that refusal for the rest of my life.

And, more, it galled me that this was not the beginning, a free decision, a decision for freedom. It felt more like enslavement, a lock-step march to the same old destination. For I knew I'd been performing an all too familiar play that had been running before our brief liaison and would go on after it. The script was written by one R. Macklin, or his father, or his father's father, and had become a classic, a genre piece in a tired repertoire, which, however banal and predictable, would get repeated inexorably, inevitably, unhappily forever after.

First Marian, then Anne, and now once again I was alone, staring out the window of the Radisson, seeing nothing but the slow rain drizzling down the pane in grimy rivulets. Always the same paths, the same dirty streams. Behind me, reflected in the gray window, was the open, half-empty closet. On the king-sized bed lay the silk tie, still knotted in a perfect Windsor, the only memento Libby had left behind.

Chapter 24

"Why, good morning, Mr. Wade! Enjoyable and informative meeting, isn't it?"

Ambushed. I had tried to escape the Radisson without being accosted by Sherm or, worse, Ben Drake, who caught my eye from a second-floor balcony, as he surveyed the mezzanine. I couldn't explain my morning's errand to them. I could hardly explain it to myself. But here was Nero shuffling out to ambush me from behind one of the hotel's great marble urns filled with dried trees and flowers. A veritable thicket had been imported to flank the entrance, like Birnam Wood come to Dunsinane. So I never saw Nero until he was upon me.

"The meeting's fine," I said, dancing this way and that as I tried to get around his broad circumference. "But excuse me, would you, Nero. I've got to be somewhere this morning."

"Somewhere. Of course. Didn't mean to get in your way. We'll have plenty of time to talk later. I guess I'll be riding back in your car, now."

"Oh?"

"Mr. Helmholz says his wife gave Miss Libby a ride home, so we'll probably be riding with you. Unfortunate that she had to leave. But that'll give us a chance for a good talk. He didn't explain why Miss Libby had to return so unexpectedly. A family problem, was it?"

Nero paused. His coke-bottle glasses magnified his eyes until they looked many times their natural size, like twin lakes, deep and midnight blue. Deciding that I was not about to volunteer any information, he went on: "I trust it's nothing serious. I had hoped to find opportunity to thank her again for being so helpful to somebody like me. But yesterday I couldn't find her anywhere. Miss Libby is such a wonderful woman, so kind and caring! Like my mother in lots of ways." Nero looked off into the distance, on his face a wistful smile. "But listen to me go on! You know all about her, of course. Who knows better than you? Right, Mr. Wade?"

"About your mother?" I had a mind to tell him right then to cut the crap about this fictitious mother. But all I wanted was to get out of there as quick as possible and be on my way to Overdale.

"Oh, no! I meant Miss Libby, of course. Miss Libby!" His fat bounced and jiggled, as he laughed at his little joke, laughed a little too long. It was all I could do to keep from snapping at him.

"How could you know about my mother? No! You didn't know her at all, did you? No, not at all. But Miss Libby! Who knows more than you, Mr. Wade? By the way, did you enjoy your birthday present?"

"Yes, thank you, I did, but got to run now. See you later." I maneuvered round him and gained the street, with Nero waddling a few steps behind.

"Didn't mean to get in your way," he shouted. "Will you be attending the awards ceremony when you get back from...?" Waving, I pulled my windbreaker up over my head and ran out into the drizzle, leaving Nero standing in front of the hotel. He was still standing there, talking to the bell captain at the cab line, when I headed the old Ford out of the ramp.

The Overdale Women's Clinic occupied a squat, graceless building of Seventies' vintage in a once fashionable suburb of the city. Recessed from the street somewhat further than its neighbors, it appeared inconspicuous, though by no means secretive. A painted, black and white sign plainly announced its name, and a swarm of protesters denounced its function. Distanced exactly fifty feet from all who entered, they prayed, they pleaded, they prophesied divine wrath in charismatic phrases hallowed by

Jeremiah, son of Hilkiah, as well as his modern namesake: "Before I formed thee in the belly I knew thee; and before thou camest forth out of the womb I sanctified thee," read one of the more eloquent placards.

The clinic's secluded parking lot was located around back. The rain had pretty much stopped. So I took off my jacket and, throwing it in the front seat, strode up the long sidewalk that led to the front door, for security reasons the sole access to the clinic. I imagined Marian entering there, shrouded by the ineffectual blanket. She must have rushed through the gauntlet of "sidewalk counselors," amid cries of "Your baby wants to live!" At first, no doubt, they would have taken her for a somewhat older patient, until one of them—if not Smit, then another—followed her home to discover that the babies she delivered were not her own. But if in fact she was neither a patient nor a doctor there, why the secrecy and concealment? Was she just prudently shielding herself from mistaken inferences?

The little general was nowhere to be seen, but I recognized Sister Amelie, eyes closed, hanging back at the edge of the group. Her waist-length hair was bedraggled and matted by the slowly falling rain. Her lips moved soundlessly. I tried not to listen, but her words drowned out the shouts of her vocal compatriots. I tried not to look, but I couldn't help myself when her eyes opened and she looked directly at me. I nodded. Giving no sign of recognition, she closed her eyes again, and I felt horribly alone.

Inside the clinic, I felt even more so. This was no man's land. No man had any business being there. Women were arranged, mostly in pairs, around the circumference of the waiting room. One typically kept her eyes on her lap; the other glared at me with contempt and accusation that let it be known my presence, any man's presence, on this ground was an outrage.

The sullen, gray-haired Medusa at the reception desk could scarcely be civil to me, but I had brought my mirror, and could give as good as I got.

"Yes?" she spat out.

"Dr. Medaille, please."

"Do you have an appointment?"

"No."

"The Director is very busy. What do you need to see her for?"

"It's a private matter."

"I'm sorry, sir, but you'll have to...."

"Tell Dr. Medaille I'm here, please. Now."

The receptionist eyed me for a moment, smoldering, then punched a few numbers in the phone.

"Doctor? Wilma at the front desk. Sorry to bother you. There's a man out here."

"Name," she barked at me. I told her.

"Says his name is Wade. Won't say. Private, he says." She listened for a moment.

"All right, Doctor," she said and returned the phone to the hook. Without looking up, she snarled, "First door on the left."

In the doorway stood Dr. Sharon Medaille, a petite woman but stocky, square-jawed. One look at her face and I knew that I was no match for her. She had seen too much, endured too much. Her face was furrowed with bullish perseverance, and tension, and sheer will. What bowled over the receptionist would just bounce off this woman.

"Dr. Medaille, thank you for allowing me to intrude on your time," I said, extending my hand for her to shake. Instead of accepting it, she pointed to the chair in front of her desk and shut the door. The office was spartan, unadorned with decorations except for the diploma on one wall and on the other a Georgia O'Keefe print that depicted either a flower or a vagina. Littered with yellowing file folders, her desk had a plexiglass cover. Underneath it was a schedule of varying prices arranged according to trimester and kind of procedure. At the top it said, "Our Business is Caring." At the bottom, "Payment Required in Advance."

"What is the nature your private business with me, Mr. Wade?"

"Marian Barclay," I said, sitting down on the edge of the chair.

"Your associates were already here once today. Identification, please."

"I'm not with the police."

"In that case, you have no business here at all, and I must wish you good day."

"No, wait! Just give me a moment to talk to you. You see, Marian and I were...."

She waited a moment before saying, "You were what, exactly?" Sarcasm dripped from her words.

"We were...very close."

"You're telling me you were involved with Marian Barclay?"

"Yes."

"Get out, Mr. Wade," she shouted, standing up. "I don't know what your scam is, and I don't care, but I know you for a liar. Leave now or I will call security!"

"No, no!" I pleaded. "You're wrong! If Marian were standing here today, she'd tell you it's true."

"She had ten years to tell me, Mr. Wade. I knew Dr. Barclay as a colleague and close friend for ten years. More than ten, and she never mentioned your name. Not once! Now get out." The doctor was already returning to her paperwork, expecting my immediate exit.

"It was before then that I knew her," I spit out. "In 1976. The summer of '76. I'm telling you the absolute truth. It was the summer after high school, two decades ago. We grew apart, but I never forgot her. Never got over her. Have you ever felt like that about anyone, Doctor? The memory of Marian Barclay preys on me, haunts me. I've been going around in circles ever since, going nowhere, repeating the life I had with her, as if she had a hold on me still. It's worse now that she's dead, and won't let go even from the grave. Please help me. I've got to know what happened. I'll never be able to get on with my life until I find out."

Medaille just looked at me, without response. Her face was neither livid, as it had been a moment before, nor sympathetic. I took heart from the change.

"1976," was all she said.

"Yes. So many years ago, and I…."

"But you were never married."

"No."

"I'm sorry, Mr. Wade. Marian's death is under active investigation. I cannot violate its secrecy, even if the reputation and viability of this clinic were not directly involved."

"Don't you believe me?"

Dr. Medaille stared directly into my eyes, her face growing darker.

"Yes, as a matter of fact, I do believe you. You have said the one and only thing that would convince me that you and Marian had a relationship. And that is all the more reason why it would be highly improper for me to communicate anything to you. You, of all people."

"I've never told these things to anyone, Dr. Medaille. Never opened up these old wounds to friends, let alone strangers."

"I can appreciate that Mr. Wade, but my hands are tied."

"I have nowhere else to turn. You're the only one who can help me!"

"I'm very sorry."

"Just tell me one thing then! It will help. Tell me that Smit and his crew are wrong about her. I can't believe Marian was working here."

"I don't know why you shouldn't be able to believe it. Our full-time staff has never been large. Since its opening, the clinic has frequently required help from outside physicians. Like them, Marian understood the need for the clinic's services, Mr. Wade. She understood it full well. She never objected to our offering properly counseled women the option of first, or even second, trimester terminations. But she never performed them herself. I honored Marian's decision, though I had made a different choice."

"I knew it," I said quietly, my head down. "I knew it. It would have been unthinkable. She wanted nothing more than to be a mother, wanted to have a baby and give it the love she once had, but lost when her own mother died. I knew it."

"You knew that?" Medaille barked. "You knew that a child and a family was all Marian Barclay ever wanted! You knew that and you still...."

"Sure. But what was she doing here then, if not...?"

"You fool," she sneered. "You despicable excuse for a human being. You knew Marian, and you cared nothing for what she wanted? Did you love her not at all? Not even a little?"

"What do you mean? Of course I did. I...."

"You couldn't have," Medaille snapped. "But I know she loved you. I know today why she never spoke your name all those years, and I have no interest whatever in loosening her grip on your life, even if I could."

"But why? Why wouldn't she have mentioned me? I never stopped thinking of her. Every night at the lake, I saw her face. I dream of her constantly, even more after she died. Isn't that love?" I turned and started to leave in despair, but her response pulled me up short.

"Love? More like guilt, I'd say! Not dreams, but nightmares!" Medaille hissed. "That's what brought you here today, isn't it? Ghosts and demons and furies that you'd dearly like to exorcise. You know that's what it is! You wheel your sick conscience in here on a gurney, looking for a cure! You'd like me to say the magic words to save your soul, wouldn't you? You come to the confessional wanting the stranger to pronounce the *ego te absolvo*. Well, you'll get nothing from me, nothing to soothe your mind, Mr. Wade. Your conscience will get no salve here. Only salt!"

"Cut the fucking riddles, will you! Why are you torturing me?"

"The code of ethics prevents me from revealing anything whatever on this subject. That's what I told Detective Cuene this morning. That's what I assured Marian a month ago in this very office. No one will ever find out anything here. Our records are permanently sealed, I told her, protected by doctor-patient privilege, even beyond the death of the patient."

"Patient?"

"They can be opened only by her or the attending physician, even files dating as far back as February 3, 1977."

"What?" I exclaimed. "No! It can't be! I don't believe you! No!"

"Yes, Mr. Wade, yes!" she whispered fiercely. "You want the solution to your fucking riddle, and you think it's at the Overdale Clinic? You make me want to vomit, you and your fucking buddies! All of you! Marian's in her grave, and you come in here wanting me to loosen her grip on your life? I wish her grip were on your fucking throat!"

Chapter 25

"But why didn't she tell me? I don't understand!"

Unmoved, Dr. Medaille watched me writhe and whimper like kicked dog. Then she stood up abruptly, her head tilted to one side, listening. Outside the sound of approaching sirens filled the air. "Not again! The idiots!" she exclaimed in disgust. Raking my face with her contempt one final time, Medaille shuffled and reordered the yellowed folders on her desk and ran out the door, leaving me alone in the bare office, staring blankly at the folders and O'Keefe print. I scarcely heard the sirens. I just sat there stunned and muttering, "No."

Not just Marian dead, her child, too. My child! My own baby! That was why Marian never mentioned me. She never forgot, never forgave me. How could I blame her, though, knowing what I knew about her past, her wants and hopes? But what did she do it for? I didn't make her get an abortion! It wasn't my fault. No way. I didn't even know, for Christ's sake. Why didn't she ever tell me? Was I supposed to guess? She could have just said, "I'm pregnant. We have to get married." All she had to do was tell me.

But never. Not one word. No, she just said "Christmas." It had to be Christmas. If she'd only told me, I would have married her, Christmas or any other time. I know I would, and she must have known it too. But she never said the word that would have made me tie the knot. Nothing.

Why not, though, if she wanted to get married so bad?

Was it that she wouldn't use the baby to tie down the man? She had heard enough about my precious freedom, I suppose, to know that marriage would have felt like a straight jacket, a baby like a ball and chain. Yes, that's the way it would have felt for me. There's no denying it. I wasn't adult enough to take on a wife and family. Wasn't man enough.

Did that make it my fault, though? She aborted her baby to spare me? It died for my sake? No! Even if she wouldn't force me to marry her, that didn't mean she had to have an abortion. There were other options, lots of other possibilities! Adoption, maybe. Or why not raise it alone? "It"! What was "it," a girl? A boy? She would have wanted a girl, a little Marian with deep lonely eyes, to hug up close to her and tell her she'd never be sad and lonely again. How could Marian have done it, then, knowing that she'd spend the rest of her life with those tiny accusing eyes upon her, asking, why, why?

Better to have raised the baby alone. Much better. Marian was strong, she was independent. She could have done it. My mother did, and it would have been so much easier in the seventies than in the fifties when public shame could still sear a scarlet letter in the flesh, and the fatherless baby at the breast might as well have been a millstone around the neck of the single mother. Now it was so different, so much more enlightened! What reason could there be not to raise the baby alone?

What if it was a boy? Well, why not? She could still do it. A boy can survive without a father. No big deal. There's always an Uncle Karl around somewhere, a part time substitute to fill in as needed at the Boy Scouts, at the jamboree, at the father-son hot dog roast around the campfire. That's all that's absolutely needed. You don't really need a father to teach you to swim in the deep water. You could manage if you had to. A few close calls, maybe, but you'd manage. Wouldn't you?

There'd always be unanswered questions, of course, about the third chair on the far side of the table. When the pudgy little boy with wide eyes asked why it was empty, when he looked up at his mother through long, uncombed bangs and asked who was supposed to fill that chair, what could she have said? How explained about the faceless man who had been no father to you but is still your father anyway, so that there's a gaping hole in your heart, so that you can't ever be complete and whole.

Giving up the baby for adoption would be even worse in a way. It doubles the ache. Even with one missing parent, there's always the insatiable hunger, the irresistible pressure to ferret out the truth, whatever it may be, whatever the cost, whatever the consequence. Because worst of all is not knowing. Your father? A derelict, was he? A baseball player, or psychotic, a cop or thief? You have to know because without knowing, you're left swaying precariously in the wind. You can't tell where you stand in the world. It's like floating weightless in space, in limbo. You don't know where you came from or where you're going.

But you're afraid you know. And that very fear drives you inexorably down the one and only highway you've spent your whole life trying to get off of, the road Roy Macklin took, the road I hated him for taking, the same road I nevertheless followed him down, just like the most mindlessly admiring, dutiful, despicable son. Ceaselessly duplicating the sins of the fathers—how do you stop? Where does it end, this insidious highway with no exit? Why can't you just make a sharp right turn, and veer off the scorched asphalt into long, fresh, sweet grasses and the buttercups of June?

I can imagine the reasons why Marian didn't want to be a single parent, didn't want that life for our baby. But I don't have to imagine them. My heart is overwritten with the scars left by my mother's choice.

Was Mom wrong then? Was Marian right? I do not have the insolence to judge them, when I have so much to answer for myself.

But I know that for Marian, too, the price of one moment was forever. Her decision must have ripped her up inside with a kind of pain that never went away. Not even after she married Mitchell. And then to find out he was brokering babies to fatten his wallet and bolster his limp ego! She wouldn't have needed the great doctor Simeon Landreau to tell her what to do.

There was nothing left for me at the clinic. No sense in prolonging my stay. I'd discovered what I'd prefer never to have known, and I'd learned none of what I'd come here to find out. Rising heartsick from the chair, I leaned wearily on the desk with its scratched plexiglas cover, its pile of yellowed file folders, and I knew at that very moment with the force of moral certainty that Marian's folder was among them.

It was on top.

Did Dr. Medaille simply forget to secure it away in her rush to find out what was happening outside? It's possible, but unlikely. She was used to keeping her head on straight in emergencies, and besides she'd already proved herself capable of twisting the knife in my gut. For Marian's sake. Medaille would reveal nothing herself, but she was not above giving me access to information without seeming to do it. She was not above taking the revenge that was within her power. There lay the poison, there for the taking.

I took. I read.

Two documents: the first, new, dated July 2, just a week before the murder. A fax request for a copy of Marian's Overdale file from Riverview Hospital, Medical Records Division, from the Director, Trevor Mitchell. Attached to it was the return-fax confirmation that the file had been sent to him. The second document was old. I didn't have to read the date. Authorization to Terminate a Pregnancy. Weeks since LMP: 24. Signed by the Patient, Marian Barclay, and the Attending Physician, Dr. Simeon Landreau, Riverview Hospital.

"Down! Put that down immediately! You've got no right to see the Barclay file." From across the room, Medaille's shrill voice rebounded off the bare walls as she entered the doorway. "Officer, I want that man arrested."

Queenie stood massively behind the petit Medaille, dwarfing her with his bulk. Badge on his coat lapel, Queenie's broad shoulders ominously filled the doorframe. He looked like he was about to explode and crush me in his wrath. One thing about Queenie I had noticed over the years:

the madder he got, the quieter he spoke, and now he was talking in meas-
ured, deliberate, and therefore very threatening tones.

"Evan, step away from the desk."

"Queenie, I…."

"Put it down and get away from the desk. Right now." His voice was
dead level.

"All right. No problem. Here's the file. No problem, see?" I dropped it
on top of the stack. Medaille ran around the desk, scooped up the files,
and scurried off with them.

"Up against the wall, Evan. You know the drill."

"Oh, come on!" I said in amazement. "You aren't going to arrest me! It's
not like I broke in here or something. I was just sitting here talking to Dr.
Medaille, when she rushed out and disappeared for half an hour. So I
looked at the file! So what? She wanted me to see it!"

"Now," he whispered.

I knew better than to prolong the conversation.

Gripping one of my wrists, Queenie cuffed my hands behind my back
and marched me out of the office. The harridan at the reception desk
looked up at me through shaggy gray eyebrows and hissed, "Hope they
hang you by the balls till you drop, asshole." Queenie ignored the woman.
I tried to.

Outside, surveyed by the slack-jawed remainder of the protesters, I
said, "What's the big deal, Queenie? Just for a lousy file? Isn't this sort of
overkill? Or maybe it's just a little police drama for the consumption of the
masses." He offered no response.

As we rounded the back corner of the clinic, I could see that a section
of the parking lot had already been cordoned off with yellow police tape.
Queenie marched me past the ambulance, its siren ominously silent, past
the uniforms who were standing around trying to look busy and important, past the coroner and photographer who stepped back to let us
through.

"There. That's the big deal," Queenie said patly.

In the center of all this official activity sat a gleaming green Z3 roadster, top down. Ben Drake was still at the wheel. His signature bowtie and braces, his car's sumptuous leather upholstery, soft as a baby's butt, were all bathed in blood. Eyes still wide open, more in surprise than terror, Ben's head lolled precariously on the driver's side door, exposing a gaping wound ripped across his neck from ear to ear.

"Do you own a green rayon jacket?" Queenie asked.

"You know I do! You've seen me in it enough times. What's the big deal?"

"Evan Wade," Queenie intoned, "you are under arrest for the murder of Ben Drake. You have the right to remain silent, you have the right to an attorney, you have the right, you have the right…."

"Oh, shut up, will you! I don't need any fucking rights. I haven't done anything," I exclaimed. "You've known me for years! How could you even think I would do something like this?"

"I thought I knew you, Evan," Queenie replied with a world of sadness in his voice. "But in my office, two weeks ago, I came to realize that you are a total stranger. I never knew you at all. But now I know you'll screw anybody to get a story. Anybody. Me, sure, I can handle it, but then Tricia, and now this? You **are** foul."

"Tricia? What are you talking about?"

"I'm talking about her getting the axe, booted not just out of her job, out of the profession! And her a single mom, with a daughter in and out of trouble. She'll never work in a M.E.'s office again, here or anywhere else, now that they found out she leaked the Barclay autopsy. To you, Evan! To you! She's lucky they didn't prosecute her! What did you do to extort it out of her? Blackmail?"

"No! Wait a minute. Even supposing Trish and I had a private conversation, how did they find out? I wouldn't betray her. I never told…"

"Never told anybody who couldn't pay you pretty damn well for telling?" he snarled. "Never told anybody who wouldn't try to sell your information to the next buyer? Never told anybody who was eager to repeat your words just where it would damage you the most? You told nobody but the scum bag reporter who stole your byline at the *S Trib*, the very one you wanted nothing more than to see with a permanent look of dumbfounded surprise on his face, behind the wheel of his pathetically ostentatious BMW roadster!"

"No, you've got it all wrong!" I protested. "I didn't even know he was here! What was he doing here, anyway?"

"You tell me!"

"How should I know? I did run across him once after I talked to you downtown. And I…" My voice trailed off, as I started to count up all our coincidental meetings starting with Marian's funeral up to the day before in the Radisson foyer, when he cornered me. I thought of all the information he had dug out about me and Marian from years back, and I knew it was no coincidence at all that Ben Drake had been shadowing me all the way to the Overdale parking lot that day.

"It's pretty obvious what he was doing," Queenie shot back. "But what were you doing here?"

"I knew you'd released Mitchell, and you'd been back here asking questions, starting over from square one."

"And who told you that?"

"Ok, it was Ben," I admitted, "but that doesn't mean…."

"So Drake dangled the bait in front of your nose, and he gambled you'd show up here sooner or later to do his work for him."

"It never occurred to me."

"Right," Queenie sneered. "You just thought he was passing along a little information because he was a good Samaritan, trying to help out a bosom buddy and respected fellow journalist!"

"No! But that doesn't prove I killed him!"

"Prove? You knew he was trying to beat you to the Barclay story and destroy you in the process. You knew he'd be here. Sounds like motive and opportunity to me. As for proof, we're two thirds of the way home, I'd say."

"This is idiotic. You've got not one shred of physical evidence."

"I'll tell you what's idiotic, Evan: a blood-soaked rayon jacket on the front seat of your car. And I'll wager that if the guys keep rooting around here long enough, we'll find your knife, too. You couldn't have had time to stash it very far."

"Jesus, Queenie, isn't it obvious that somebody's framing me? Why would I leave the jacket there?"

"Well, we'll see. Meantime, why don't we take a ride downtown where we can continue our conversation and you can meet my friends in Booking."

I continued my fruitless protests as he led me under the police tape to the unmarked car. There, outside the perimeter, stood Sherm and Nero and a couple of other reporters I knew, just as surprised to see me as I was to see them.

"Evan, what in the world?" Sherm said.

"It's a mistake, Sherm. All a mistake. I'll get it straightened out right away. But what are you doing here?"

"Jerry here heard the police call come in over the scanner and asked if I wanted to take a cab over with him to catch the action. But I had no idea. Ben Drake! And now you!"

"Yes," Nero chimed in. "I too came by taxi. Took a cab right from the hotel. But I had no idea, either!" he shouted after us, as Queenie dragged me away. "Murder at an abortion clinic! Who could have imagined it?"

Chapter 26

Sherm visited me in the Hennepin County jail a couple times. It was more than I deserved. After the MAPJ conference ended, he and Nero moved their things from the Radisson to a Super 8, so he could stick around for a few days. Not long, though, he said, since he'd have to get back to the *Sentinel*. I proclaimed my innocence, of course. I declared myself framed, and pretty crudely framed at that, but Sherm didn't know what to think, and so during his visits he would sometimes lapse into silence for minutes on end, neither interrogating nor comforting me. He just sat opposite me in the visitor's lounge, with the stench of fear and disinfectant swirling around us.

At least he was there. It was more than I deserved.

Once I said, "I suppose you'll have to write this up for the *Sentinel*."

"Nope," he said without looking up.

"I guess it would make the paper look pretty bad," I ventured. "*Sentinel* Reporter Accused of Murder!"

"Got nothing to do with it. That kind of stuff is for the *STrib*, or even the *Brainerd Dispatch*, but not for us. We see a pile of shit and we step around it, remember?"

"Sure."

"Well, however this turns out, you're in deep shit right now, and I'm not the kind of person that's going to savor it. I don't think my readers are, either."

"Thanks, Sherm."

"You've already got your share of publicity without my adding to it. Oh, yeah. In case you haven't noticed, the scandal sheets are having a field day. The reporter reported. Exorcising one of their own, the scapegoat, so that they can slide back into their comfortable self-righteousness. It's so easy to forget what it feels like to be on the other side of the byline. So easy to forget that the story is always about the reporter."

"Thanks."

"No thanks necessary." He went silent for a moment. I had to speak.

"Marian Barclay went to the Overdale clinic for an abortion, Sherm."

"Oh, Jesus, Evan." He sprang up and raised his arms in the air, as if invoking divine mercy, and then let them drop down again, as if in uncomprehending disgust. "She had an abortion just before she was murdered?"

"No. It was long ago, right after she and I split up."

"Oh, Jesus, you and Marian....?"

"That's what I found out at the clinic," I explained. "She had an abortion twenty years ago, and there's no point denying she was carrying my baby. I know how you and Nell feel about that kind of thing but, believe me, I didn't know!"

"You don't have to tell me any of this, Evan. I don't want to know. This is your private business, between you and your…conscience. I don't need to know any of it. Don't need to understand any of it. But what's this got to do with Drake?"

"I have no idea," I replied. "All I know is Drake was tailing me, and somebody killed him while I was inside talking to Medaille. He wasn't there when I first arrived. He was dead when Queenie dragged me back out."

"Right," he said noncommittally.

"You've got to believe me," I begged. "You're the only one I've got left, Sherm. Libby's gone. I'm sure Nell told you. I've got nobody."

"I know," he said blankly. I hoped he would put his hand on my shoulder. I needed some gesture of sympathy. Something by way of support. Anything. But Sherm seemed to be at his limit just being there.

"You're the only one now," I pleaded.

"There's nothing I can do to help you." He turned away and faced the door.

"You're already helping just by being here, Sherm. You deserve to know."

"I already know all I need to. It's like Nell said. You're obsessed. Can't keep your mind on your work. Can't treat your own mother like she's due. Can't keep the love of a good woman. When I think of what you've done to Libby! And to yourself! Here you sit in jail. It's like you're being dragged down, every day further and further down until the waters close over your head. You're in up to your eyeballs already."

"I know, Sherm," I said, bleakly.

"And who's pulling you down? It's you, Evan, just you. You're self-destructing. Everybody can see it."

"Don't you think I know? Don't you think I'd just like to put it all behind me? But I can't just walk away, Sherm, now more than ever—and I don't just mean because I happen to be in jail!"

"You've never been able to walk away. You're obsessed—or maybe possessed! Not in jail exactly, but you haven't been a free man ever since you moved back up north. Maybe it started even before that, for all I know."

"Yeah," I admitted. "Long before that."

"While you were still at the *STrib*?"

"Yes, before that. Even before I ever left the North Country to go to the Cities. Sometimes I think my story started before I was born. Written in the stars, it was. Like fate. So clear you could read it even if you had Nero's eyes. Remember those placards that Smit's people were carrying outside the clinic? 'Before thou camest out of the womb I knew thee!' Anybody who knew my mother's story knew my story too, so damn predictable it was."

"You can't blame your life on Roy Macklin."

"Who else should I blame my life on? I'm living because of him. Mine was no immaculate conception! Roy Macklin is my father!"

"You know what I mean, Evan. You are the master of your fate. Macklin didn't do anything to you."

"No, he didn't do anything to me. He did nothing but leave my mother, nothing but leave me. But that's not nothing, because I am my father's son. Evan Macklin, that's my name," I cried bitterly. "A chip off the old block, that Macklin boy is! Left his woman, left his baby. Yup, Macklin did it all. Which Macklin, though? Was it him? Was it me? Which is which? And now I too have that baby's lifeless eyes upon me, asking why? And what's the answer?" I shouted.

"I don't know," he conceded, putting his head between his hands.

"Isn't it Roy Macklin, Sherm? At least partly? Damn right, I blame him. I blame my mother, too. I blame Marian. I blame her father. I blame Landreau. I blame myself. There's plenty of blame to go around here. We could have a garage sale."

"Who's Landreau?" Sherm asked, but before I had a chance to answer, the guard came. He unlocked the visiting room door, and saying, "Time's up," ushered Sherm out. I watched him, head bowed, pad slowly down the pinkish purple, stench-ridden hall until he was out of sight and I was alone once more.

Sherm never returned to visit me, never had to. Queenie and his men found the knife, a common jack-knife wedged deep into a crack in the clinic's foundations. On it were two clear fingerprints. Much to Queenie's disappointment, they were not mine.

My release came the next day. I wasted no time in picking up the clothes I'd been wearing when arrested, along with the others they'd taken from Radisson. My second order of business was to retrieve the old Ford from the police impound lot. Thanks to a very thorough and highly professional inspection, all the McDonalds fries that I'd been storing for years in its various crevices were gone. Hope Queenie enjoyed them. He wasn't going to get anything else from me. Nor I from him. Landreau was my last hope, and not much of one at that. But I had to go.

In the jail lobby I called Sherm at the Super 8 to tell him I couldn't take him and Nero back after all. "I've got some loose ends to tie up down here before I can go home," I said.

"I know, Evan," he replied after a moment. "I already called Nell to come get us."

"She's a good woman, Sherm," I said. I thought of Libby, with hair the color of sunset. I thought of the empty cabin, and I almost wept as Sherm said, "She is, Evan, and it's a lucky man who married her. See you soon." But I was afraid it wouldn't be soon. I knew I wouldn't be heading north again until the corpses all were buried.

Landreau's practice was in Uptown and, without bothering to get a room or shower, I headed out to the professional building listed in the phone book. So many questions still unanswered, I thought as I drove. They seemed to be multiplying. The more I found out, the less I knew. What had brought Marian back to the clinic after so many years? Even if she wasn't a victim of Smit's bigots, did her murder still have something to do with her return? What did Trevor Mitchell want with Marian's Overdale records that he should send a request to fax them to Riverview? She'd told him she'd had a hysterectomy. How'd he find out about the abortion, then? And what about Ben Drake? He had made so many enemies over the years, it could have been anybody who killed him. Why would anyone want to hang it on me? Was it just coincidence that he bought it at the clinic?

Not likely. Not very damn likely, I thought, as I turned into a space in front of the Landreau's office building.

When it came to hiring receptionists, Medaille could have taken some lessons from Landreau. The perky young lady who greeted me—

"Natalie," her nametag read—managed to be warm and welcoming despite her aqua hair and nose ring, or maybe because of them.

I asked to see Landreau.

"Oh, I'm sorry," she said, sniffing the air, and looking behind her. "Dr. Landreau retired some time ago. Would you like to make an appointment with Dr. Helguson?"

It had to be Landreau, I told her.

"I see. Dr. Landreau still does treat some of his longtime patients here, but I'm afraid it's not very often. You might try him at home."

"Thanks. I'll do that," I said. She sniffed once more, gave me a quizzical look, then broke out in a big, knowing grin.

"You know, I really like your cologne," she said. "Is that musk or maybe one of these new pheromones?"

I wanted to say, "Glad you like it. It's a new scent called 'Jail Bait.'" But Natalie didn't deserve the sarcasm, and I wasn't much in the mood for joking just then. So I just said "No" and found my way out, no doubt leaving an aromatic trail of "Jail Bait" streaming behind me.

Chapter 27

Landreau's house stood out as a particularly offensive example of Kenwood's tract mansions and starter castles. When Bavarian King Ludwig II built Neuschwanstein, he designed it to look 500 years old and thus to assume the grandeur of the ages. Instead it just looked Disneyfied. When Simeon Landreau built his castle, it was intended to recall the majesty of Monticello, no doubt, but it looked more like Jefferson's doghouse.

But perhaps I am too severe. Doghouses do not generally have eight-tone Westminster chimes. He himself opened the door before the eighth tone sounded.

"You!" Landreau shouted in surprise and consternation. "What are you doing here? I thought you were in jail with the rest of the city's trash!"

"You can't believe everything you read in the papers."

"I have nothing to say to you. Go away." Before the old man could slam the door, I put my shoulder into it and knocked him back hard. Stumbling, he lost his footing and fell back on the gleaming hardwood floor.

"Get out," he screamed feebly, half in anger, half terror, as I stood menacingly over him. "Get out of my house this instant. Get out before I call Detective Cuene to throw you out!"

"Like you called him before?" I scoffed. "Much good it did you last time! But perhaps you'd like try your luck again, and give him a jingle just now? Wonderful idea. Why don't you get off the floor and do that?"

Landreau stood up and began hobbling around, looking for the phone.

"Yes," I taunted him, "you give Queenie a call, why don't you, and when he gets here, perhaps you won't mind explaining the sharing and caring sessions you had with your dearly departed confidante, Ben Drake. I'm sure Queenie wondered where the *STrib* got those juicy morsels on Trevor Mitchell's baby brokering scheme that proved so useful. What did it matter that they were irrelevant, completely irrelevant? Mitchell was tried, convicted, and hung in the papers before he ever got to court! I'll bet Mitchell's just aching to know who hung him, don't you think? Wonder what he'd pay to find out? By the way, he did get his Medical Records job back at Riverview, didn't he? Just curious. Or did you and your wizened cronies over there ensure that he embarked on a new profession?"

"He deserved everything he got," Landreau screamed, "and hasn't got half of what he deserves. Who do you think killed Marian? If I had my way he'd be hung for real, not just out of a job. I handed him over to them on a silver platter. But they are incompetent idiots. That's all, just idiots." Landreau's voice was savage, animal-like in its intensity.

"What do you mean 'handed him over'?" I asked.

"I told Detective Cuene that Mitchell had Marian's Overdale file faxed to him. That's what Dr. Medaille told Marian when she went to the clinic. A secretary or receptionist had received the request from Riverview, signed by the Director of Medical Records, on letterhead stationery, and she faxed back the material requested without thinking. Medaille, however, knew that the signator was Marian's husband. Estranged husband. I told Cuene that Marian had uncovered Mitchell's baby bartering scheme and was going to expose him. All that, and then they just release him! What more did they need? He was going to blackmail her into silence. Isn't it obvious? And when she wouldn't scare, he killed her, killed her in cold blood. She was so beautiful, so good. I loved her like she was my own."

Landreau was convulsed with grief and frustration, great sobs gushing out of him as he spoke. "I don't know what they need. I screamed at them, what more do you need!"

"What did they say?"

"They just said his alibi checked out," Landreau sobbed. "Mitchell was somewhere out of the office on the date and time printed on the fax. Idiots! Don't they know you can set those things for delayed transmission? Incompetents," Landreau shouted. "And now Marian's in her grave and her murderer is a free man! Now you're here trying to strong-arm me. What do you want? What do you want with me?" Landreau cried, as he plopped down despondently on the sofa.

"Well, even if Mitchell wasn't there, don't you think they checked his signature? And if it didn't match, that explains why Queenie's at a dead end. It's my turn. I want to know everything. I want the whole story, the truth about Marian."

"I'll tell you nothing." Landreau leaned forward and darted a bony finger into my chest. "You think you can pump me like you did that poor Medical Examiner? Mitchell deserved everything he got, and so do you. But can you say the same of that poor woman? Well, can you? Do you destroy every woman you touch?"

"Cut the crap, Landreau. I've read Marian's Overdale file, and I know she was pregnant. I know the baby was mine. I know you're the butcher who killed it!"

Landreau flopped back. He looked so old, so tired, that I thought I had him on the ropes until he said, "Well, you *are* scum, ignorant scum. Since when did you start wanting to know the truth about Marian, since you've spent your whole life trying not to know it. Now you find out she was pregnant with your child. Brilliant! You had to read it in the file. Investigative genius, that is."

"How was I supposed to know she was pregnant?"

"Didn't she ask you to marry her? Did you hear a single word she said? Anybody short of deaf, dumb, and blind would have known she was pregnant. But you didn't hear what she was saying because you didn't want to hear! You didn't want to know the truth about Marian, and never did, because you're a coward. Burton Barclay always suspected that about you, though he didn't know what you were afraid of. But I did, Mr. Evan Wade! I knew you for a bastard father hiding from his bastard son!"

I sprang up and hit him hard, splitting his lip and knocking him off the sofa onto the floor.

"Hit me again, you bastard," he cried as he lay there, a withered sack of bones. "Hit me again because you know I'm right. You want to know the truth, but you can't take the truth."

I stood over him, hands clenched, but the rage was draining out of me. I couldn't beat him. I was already ashamed. An old man, what was I thinking of? What did I hit him for? Because he had said the word that touched off the hair-trigger within me. The one word that seemed now to comprehend me more exactly than ever before, all of me, not just where I came from, which I could charge to others, but who I was, and what I had done. I hit him because he was right.

"You can't take it, can you, you bastard?" he screamed. "You don't want to know about Marian. You don't want to know about your own son."

"It was a boy, then?" I sat down and for the first time stared at the blood on my hands.

"Yes, it was a boy. You bastard," he hissed, as he crawled over to the sofa and pushed himself back upright. I tried to help the old man up, but he threw off my arm in contempt.

"I had a son?

"Yes, a bastard son."

"My son," I repeated quietly, trying to get used to the idea. But I had no image of fatherhood to summon up, no image of a son except a generic baby. Silent. Dead.

"I had a son, and you killed him, Landreau."

"I didn't kill anybody," he said matter of factly, dabbing his bloodied lip with a handkerchief.

"You aborted that baby," I shouted at him. "I betrayed Marian, but I'm no murderer. You killed my son. Oh, Jesus, I gave him life and you took it!"

"I've never killed anyone. I should have, though. Should have killed you! For twenty years, twenty long years I have wanted to kill you for what you did to Marian and that child! Dreamed about it at night, planned it in my waking hours, but I could not do it. She was like a daughter to me, you understand? The child I never had, but I'm no killer." Landreau had regained his composure, and that enraged me as much as anything.

"Oh, fuck you," I said. "I saw the paper. What are you denying it for, Landreau? I saw Marian's signature authorizing the abortion. And yours. Admit it! Admit the truth!"

"Haven't you had enough truth yet, Mr. Wade?" Landreau said, enjoying my pain and frustration. "Saw it written down in black and white, did you? And you tell *me* not to believe everything I read! I've never performed an abortion in my life."

"What are you taunting me for?"

"Because I don't have the courage to put a bullet in your head, you bastard," he said. His face was contorted in a malign smile. "Well, this will have to serve! By the time Marian came to me, she'd already been at two or three clinics. But she was too far advanced, they told her, too far along. She was desperate. She swore me to secrecy with Buddy, told me she wouldn't bring a fatherless child into the world. She wouldn't make a child go through what she did after her mother died. But I told her I didn't do that kind of work. Ever. My conscience wouldn't let me. But she begged me. I told her that the hysterotomy would make future pregnancy life-threatening. But she wept and begged me, as if she'd been my own daughter. And I couldn't deny her. Anybody else, but not her. Such was the love I bore that child. My whole life's commitment to the sanctity of life I was ready to sacrifice for her. So she signed the papers and I arranged it at Overdale."

"I knew it," I exclaimed in triumph.

"Shut up, Wade," he shouted. "You know nothing. Listen to me. I extracted the child from her abdomen, and as I was holding that tiny life in my hand, ready to cut the cord, it gasped for air, Wade, do you understand? It gasped for life! I was ready to dispose of it, and it breathed! The nurse and anesthetist saw it and looked at me. I saw it, and I knew at that moment that I couldn't do it."

"What?" I screamed. "Couldn't do what?"

"I couldn't let it die, Wade. Couldn't just stand there and let it die. I transferred it immediately to the Riverview neonate clinic. And the boy lived!"

"What?"

"You want the truth? The boy lived!"

"No," I moaned. "What are you saying?"

"Your bastard son is alive," Landreau said icily. "There's your truth, Wade! Deal with that, if you can!"

"No, you're lying! I don't believe you. Marian couldn't have abandoned our baby, our son!"

"You're right about that, at least. She couldn't have, if she had known. I told her nothing."

"Never told her! What kind of a man are you? She was like a daughter to you? And you never told her that her son was alive?"

"She pleaded with me for an abortion. Was I supposed to tell her I performed a live birth instead? I served the child, but I failed *her*! I couldn't tell her. Besides it's grounds for malpractice."

"Oh, you are a piece of shit, Landreau! You hid it from her so you wouldn't get sued! Is that what this is all about? Keeping this goddamn house in Kenwood?"

"Believe what you like, Wade!" he said dispassionately. "I couldn't care less. The fact remains I was there for Marian when you abandoned her and the baby, both. I saved your son's life. I sent him to Riverview. I filled out the birth certificate. I saw that he was placed with Social Services. I am more of a father to that boy than you ever were!"

"I've got to find him! Maybe it's not too late. Where is he now, Landreau!"

"What do you want, Wade? You think he cares about you?"

"I don't know, but I've got to find him. Where is he?"

"You think you can start being a father now? Or are you just trying to salve your conscience? You think you can make up for twenty years of nothing?"

"I can try."

"Idiot," he spat. "Leave it alone. What's done is done. Go back to Podunk and let it eat your heart out. Let it prey on you year after year, as it has me."

"Just tell me, Landreau. Tell me where to find my son," I pleaded.

"I've got no idea."

"You said you filled out the Social Services papers, and I'll bet you didn't just drop him there. I'll bet you followed him from a distance. Kept an eye on him over the years, just like you did me."

"I watched over him, yes. I wanted to see him adopted by a decent family. But he never was. Nobody would adopt him. Just one foster home after another."

"So where is he now?"

"I don't know. He came of age and left his last placement about eight months ago. I lost track of him then. I suppose I could have tried to locate him again, but I decided that he was an adult and didn't need me. He doesn't need you either, Wade. He needed you once. Where were you then?"

"I'm going to find him, Landreau. With or without your help, I'm going to find him. I'll do it if it kills me. What's his name?"

"Rowland, I called him. Ned Rowland. I hope it does kill you, Wade."

"Who were his last foster parents?

"The Schulters, north St. Paul somewhere, Seth and Verna. You go find him," he shouted after me. "I hope he puts a knife in your gut and sends you straight to hell!"

Before Landreau finished, I was well on my way.

Chapter 28

The Schulters had apparently converted their modest Roseville home into something of a shelter for homeless children of all shapes and sizes. I saw bassinets and guitars, bikes and building blocks filling neatly stacked nooks and crannies. In the living room, a diapered baby of indeterminate sex stood in a playpen, chewing contentedly on the upper rail. A likewise androgynous teenager with earphones slouched on the sofa before a silent big screen television. It was almost suppertime, and the house smelled faintly of roast beef and onions.

"Not much privacy to be had around this house, Mr. Wait. This'll have to do," said Schulter, as he did a 180 in his wheelchair and pointed to an overstuffed chair beside the sofa. I glanced apprehensively at the teenager. "Oh, don't mind Cheryl Anne," he said. "She can't hear nothin' with her Discman playing." It was then I noticed that the earphones were not attached to the TV, and since I surmised that Cheryl Anne had successfully isolated herself in an electronic bubble, I opened up my business to the man before me.

"As I mentioned, I'm looking for Ned and was hoping you folks could point me in the right direction."

"Ned, huh! Looking for Ned." Schulter shifted his weight by pushing down hard on the wheelchair arms and swiveling slightly to the side. "He in trouble?" the man asked, craning his neck insinuatingly.

"No, no, nothing like that," I reassured him. "I just need to talk to him."

"Talk to him, you say."

"Yes, that's all. If you wouldn't mind telling me where he might be found these days."

"Talk about what? He come in for one of those surprise inheritances like they do on TV? Because we're still Ned's legal guardians, you know, me and Verna. It's all legal." Schulter peered at me through narrow, suspicious eyes.

"I'm afraid not," I commiserated. "Not as far as I know. But I'll let you know if anything like that comes up."

"Yes. Best you do that, Mr. Wait, when you catch up with him. Ned was with us four years, you know. The second placement we ever had, me and Verna. Right after my accident."

"Is that right," I said, trying to seem interested and sympathetic.

"Yes, almost four years, and then he just left, like it was nothin'. Nothin' at all. It was not nothin' to me and Verna, I tell you. We can hardly make ends meet."

"Ned paid you rent, did he?"

"No," he scoffed, like I was a total idiot. "Family Services. Got more for him than the rest of these kids. Twice as much as for that baby there." I glanced over at the playpen. The baby was still trying to gnaw its way out, undeterred by its meager value. I thought I'd try again.

"Where is Ned now?"

"No idea. You get to depend on that money, you know, when you can't get work." He looked down in disgust at his useless legs and once more performed his lifting and shifting maneuver in the wheelchair.

"Did you try to find Ned, then, after he left?"

"Damn right, we did. Don't you hear what I'm telling you? We filed Missing Persons, but the cops said he's probably just run away again. We called Ms. Simperson at Family Services. See if they could bring him back. She knew where he was all right, but would she help us? No, says she,

Ned's a legal adult now. Legal! I said. What about us? What's the law going to do for us, me and Verna? You get to depend on that money, you know."

"I'm sure that's true," I added, fully convinced. What a father this one must have been, I thought. "Raising Children for Fun and Profit." A real turd, I thought to myself. But then what does that make me?

"Well," he went on, "we got an empty bed and they're working on another placement, I guess. Better hurry up about it too."

"Been a while since Ned left?" I asked.

"Months," he said. "A few months. I sorta lost track, though, exactly how many. Every day's the same when you're in one of these things."

The man whacked his hand on the chair wheel, then suddenly yelled, "Verna!" The baby was startled, but Cheryl Anne, isolated on her electronic island, didn't move a muscle. Again, at the top of his lungs, he shouted, "Verna!"

"Coming, dear," she answered from the kitchen. Replacing fugitive gray hairs in her bun, Mrs. Schulter entered the living room with a pleasant smile for her husband and me. "Yes, dear?"

"Wade here...is it Wait or Wade?"

"Wade."

"Wade here wants to know when Ned run off."

"Why, that would have been July. Yes, July, that's when it was." Mrs. Schulter wore a kindly if harried look about her eyes and mouth. There was a touch of grace and gentility about the woman, as if her smile bore the traces of some past life, some happier time that could not be wholly erased by the reduced circumstances of the present.

As she spoke, Mrs. Schulter caught up her apron and wiped her hands on it. That simple womanly gesture seized my heart. I had seen it a thousand, thousand times at home, every time Mom emerged from the kitchen through the living room door. It spoke at once of hard work and genteel graciousness, chopping onions and company manners, all the maternal care and courtesy that I remembered, all that I loved at Sacred Heart.

Mother, I called out inwardly, *Mother*, and I had to look away from the scene before me.

"Yes, I remember it was not too long after the 4th," Mrs. Schulter mused, "We had a picnic, Seth and me and the kids. I made Mars bar brownies with vanilla ice cream, Ned's favorite. My, didn't he love those brownies! But then he was gone, you know."

"Without so much as a thank you present," Mr. Schulter complained.

"Maybe he'll come back," I offered hopefully.

"Maybe he will," she said wistfully. "Like he did last year. I could tell he was restless. Like last February. He missed his mother so, especially in February, around his birthday. Did you know he could remember her from when he was just a little tyke?"

"Are you sure?" I asked doubtfully.

"It was amazing, but Ned could remember everything about her, from before he was in foster homes. Before he lost her. He would tell me stories when he first came to us, about how she loved him, about holding her hand and walking along a creek in a park. Beautiful stories, they were, just like out of a book. He would pick dandelions and put them in her hair as she lay in the tall grass beside the creek—a brook, he called it—and she would thank him with hugs and kisses. She led him beside still waters, he said. It was so poetic. He missed her so. He didn't have a lot of friends, so he stayed in his room a lot and read and remembered those stories. When he first came to us, that was. Later, not so much, not much at all. You know, you see a child that lonely and your heart goes out to them, but you can try and try, but finally what can you do?"

"I'm sure you did a great deal, Mrs. Schulter," I said, and meant it.

"I know I tried," she said. "We even tried to help him find his mother."

"Not a smart move, if you ask me," her husband interjected, unasked. "'What do you want to find her for?' I said to him. 'You spose there's no reason she didn't come looking for you? She's probably dead, anyway, or at least got another life.' He got everything he needed around here. And more! 'Maybe we're not good enough for you!' I said, but he was bull-headed, that kid. Wouldn't leave it alone."

"Oh, Seth," his wife said, "you can understand, can't you? One night, last year, Ned asked me to see his birth certificate. Well, I didn't have any birth certificate. Ms. Simperson had it, I said, if anybody did. Ned didn't mention the matter again, but I doubt he let it go."

"You can bet the farm on it," Mr. Schulter hissed. "Bull-headed as he was. Pretty dumb move, if you ask me."

"Well, I don't know, but he was a smart boy, Mr. Wade."

"Did well in school, did he?"

"Sure did," Mrs. Schulter said, "though I never saw him study much. Understood anything he put his mind to, could read any book. Poetry, history, everything! They were too much for me, I told him. Way above my head. But that boy would just stick to them and read and read, just like he would eat and eat those brownies. A real smart boy. He could have been a doctor or something. We thought he was headed in that direction after high school."

"Did he major in premed, then? Could I find him at the U, maybe?" I asked.

"Oh, no, no. He didn't want to go to college, but he did get an internship at that hospital near the University, across the river."

"Riverview?"

"That's right. Family Services placed him there. At Riverview. Ms. Simperson was real helpful."

"So Ned was a Candystriper then?"

"Well, no, not exactly." Mrs. Shulter shook her head. "Ned wasn't a real social person. Polite, very polite, yes. You know, whenever I came into the living room, he would stand up?" Mrs. Schulter sent the briefest glance at the comatose Cheryl Anne. "But, I don't know, something about him that could put off people. I didn't mind. I know he didn't mean it, but some people thought he was…well, secretive. You could never tell what he was thinking, and he thought a lot. You couldn't quite put your finger on it.

But he wasn't very social. He could type, though. He could type, and so he offered to type out forms. He asked if he could type out forms for them at the hospital. Wasn't that nice? Yes, they put him in the forms office."

"The Records office?"

"That's right, Records. It was Records, wasn't it, Seth?"

"Yeah, but they didn't pay him a dime. He had to take a bus down there. I sure as hell couldn't take him. Type all day, and half the night, and then they didn't even pay him nothin'."

An anxious, sinking feeling descended over me. The fax request from Riverview for Marian's records. Sent at night, with a forged signature. But it couldn't be. No need for panic. Ned had the birth certificate maybe, but there's no way Marian's name would be listed on it. I had a place to start looking for him anyway.

"Maybe I can find him at the Records Office, then."

"Well, they might have an address or something, but he left there same time he left here, you know. It was in the middle of July. Yes, I remember now. He took the Number 25 downtown, just like he always did. But the 56 came back without him. Never saw him again. We miss him, don't we, Seth?"

"Sure. We miss him all right. Can't hardly get along anymore," her husband groused. She paid no attention. Neither did I, for the scene before my eyes was fading swiftly away, and I had the feeling of sinking down into a great and terrifying darkness; it flowed murky and thick about me, but I glimpsed something fearful there. In the darkness I was beginning to see, really see for the very first time.

"Mrs. Schulter, I'm going to ask you a very important question." I leaned close to her, trembling as I spoke. "Would you promise me to be very sure before you answer?"

"Certainly, Mr. Wade, I'll try."

"Was Ned's last night, when he never returned, the night of July 17?"

"Why, I don't recall for sure."

"That would have been a Wednesday," I cautioned.

"It could have been," she hesitated, "but I'm just...."

"Woman, of course it was Wednesday," her husband broke in. "The day before the bimonthly checks come. Remember? Always the first Thursday and the third. We were waiting on the check, and when it come that Thursday morning, he was gone."

"No!" I wailed, for the blackness was closing in and I could see too much. In the inky darkness was visible a shadowy figure, a young man, faceless and shapeless but malign, hunched, clutching a gleaming knife in his fist, a scalpel. Oh God! Marian, your child, your killer at the door! Did you welcome him in? Did he smile and say, You don't know me. I am Ned Rowland. Did he say, I am your son, returned from the dead? Or did he strike wordlessly and without warning, strike again, and again, and again? Did you clutch at your stomach in terror and pain as the blood drained from you? Clutch your womb—oh, God!—as the life you gave took life from you? Killed by your own son! And mine! Oh, Marian, forgive me!

"Mr. Wade, are you all right?" Verna was asking. "Can I get you some water? What do you mean, 'no'? Isn't that what you were asking? I think it was the 17th like Seth says. That's what you wanted to know, isn't it?"

They were both peering at me, as at a madman.

"Yes, Mrs. Schulter, that's what I had to know."

"I'm sorry we can't be of more help," she ventured.

"I understand," I said, trying to pull myself out of the darkness, while sinking deeper and deeper. "But now it's more urgent than ever that I locate Ned. I must find him immediately. Do you have a photo, perhaps, a recent photo I could take along?"

"Don't think so, Wade," Seth said. "Wouldn't mind giving you one, but we don't do albums for these kids like we do for our own."

"Well, we might have one there, with the pictures of our Jamie," Verna said, as she scurried out to look for the family albums.

"Doubt it, but doesn't matter, Wade. You'll be able to recognize him easy, without any picture. The kid is fat."

"He was just stocky, Seth!" his wife objected from a far room.

"Oh, Verna, the kid ate us out of house and home," her husband hollered back. "He ate up most of our money all by himself. He was a pig. You know what they used to call him at school, Wade? Floyd, his nickname was. Floyd of Rosedale. A real porker."

"Children can be so cruel," she said, returning with a snapshot in her hands. "I'm afraid this is the best I can do, Mr. Wade. Ned and our Jamie. You're welcome to it. That's Ned on the right. Can't make him out very well, though, what with the sun glaring off those terrible glasses of his."

She held out the photo, but I couldn't see Ned. It wasn't the glare. I couldn't see the picture at all. For the darkness had closed over me completely, and from out of the depths I could see one thing clearly: the face and form of Marian's killer, the savage, innocent, flaccidly pathetic face of my own Shadow.

Chapter 29

On the way back north from the Cities, I felt empty, eviscerated. Steering into the darkness somewhere in the open reaches between Pierz and Brainerd, I recalled a Minnesota history book I'd read a long time back. A particularly vivid passage depicted an Indian method of torture. They'd rip open the victim's stomach, tie one end of his intestines to a sapling and make him run around it, watching his guts spin out of him till he was empty. Then he died.

That's the way I felt, like my life kept emptying out of me. I kept running round and round, but I did not die.

Everything was dark when I turned into the cabin driveway. No light shone hopefully out the front window, no light anywhere, and I left it dark when I got inside. I knew if I turned on the lights, the whole place would shout that Libby was gone, beginning another life, making a new start. I could not abide the light. I could already see too clearly.

In the darkness, the graves were giving up their corpses. Over and over, I replayed Marian's death in my imagination. Whether I sat silently in the dark living room or, down below, on the dock shrouded in the damp September night air, I saw Marian falling motionless on the carpeted floor, her own flesh and blood standing over her, the scalpel glistening in his clenched fist. Marian's open but unseeing eyes glared at me accusingly.

Time passed. I must have begun to doze while sitting on the dock bench, because as I fixated on the nightmarish scene, unable to turn it off, the characters started merging, changing roles and identities in meaningless confusion. Marian lay lifeless on the floor, but over the body it was me standing there. Me, scalpel in hand, begging forgiveness and trying to help her up. But her limp body would not rise again. Later, Marian stood on the dock, armed. As Ned began to climb up out of the water, gasping for air, she shrieked in pain and stabbed him. He begged for his life, but she stabbed him again, sobbing, and he fell backwards into the water, causing its green to flash red. Yet again, Nero grasped Marian's doorknob with crimson hands and fled laughing out into the darkness. But it was me who lay motionless on Marian's floor, my face contorted in surprised disbelief, my throat sliced from ear to ear.

Then I awoke, trembling.

There was no reason for me to go on searching for my son. He had discovered me months ago. How he managed it, I did not know, did not care. The fact was he had found me out. No need to look for him any more, I thought to myself. He had been following me all along. He would be looking for me now. He knew, no doubt, that I'd checked out of the Radisson hotel and the Hennepin County Jail. All I had to do was wait.

I didn't have to wait long. Sometime in the early morning darkness, heavy feet descended the seventy two stairs behind me. Deceptively tranquil and inviting, the open expanse of Woman Lake held my gaze until he reached the dock and shuffled up behind me. Then I had time only to stand and say, "Hello, son," before he felled me with one blow.

How long I remained unconscious I cannot say, but the first rays of morning were not yet visible when I awoke, head throbbing. I remember only finding myself tied down with heavy rope. Bound from hand to foot, my helpless body was wrapped as if I were dead and mummified. Inexpertly knotted but effective nonetheless, the rope looped, coiled its way about me, snake-like, rendering all resistance pointless. For good measure a single strand ran from my feet up behind to my neck.

"Hogtied," Ned chuckled, as he saw my groggy head begin to loll. "Hogtied, like the swine you are."

"Ned, please," I implored him.

"I AM NERO," he thundered, brandishing a club above his head.

At his feet lay two concrete blocks fastened together with a steel chain. I recognized what had been the makeshift anchor for our swim raft, and I was terrified. At that moment, not a gun or a knife could have frightened me as much as those two concrete blocks. For I imagined myself following them, feet first, down into the black water, my life's breath bubbling up as I plummeted down into the cold.

"Nero, don't do this, please!"

"Yes, I am Nero. The only true name is the one you give yourself! And what is your name, my prodigal father? What shall we write on your byline, on your headstone? Shall it be Dr. Frankenstein, creator of the monster that killed him? Or perhaps, it should be Laius, slain at the crossroads by the son he abandoned? Tell me your real name! Perhaps you don't know it! But the Shadow knows! I am Nero, not Ned Rowland. Never was. The arrogance of the man, thinking he could name me."

"You're not making sense, Nero. Who are you talking about? Simeon Landreau? He was only trying to help you!"

"Help? He helped me all right." Nero glared at me, his dark eyes blazing in scorn. "I never wouldn't have found her—or you!—if he hadn't been so helpful as to use his own name on my birth certificate."

"His own?"

"Landreau. Rowland. Landreau. Rowland. Just because he gave me life, he thought he had the right to give me his name. Give? I despise his gifts. He is not my father, the arrogant son of a bitch! But he led me to Marian Barclay."

"What do you mean?" I asked, struggling against the rope without effect. It seemed only to be tightening around me, constricting my breathing.

"It was all so easy," Nero said with a touch of smugness. "The Riverview medical records are very complete, very thorough. Landreau had no patients named Rowland. He had only four maternity patients that year, none due in February. Nothing special occurred that month but an office visit from one Marian Barclay. There was nothing but an unnamable 'procedure' performed at Overdale. Nothing but an unfortunate 'complication' abandoned at Riverview that very day, no questions asked. What was it that was left there? An unfinished death? An incomplete birth? A double abortee, that's what I am: an aborted abortion!" Nero laughed long and bitterly.

"Untie me!" I gasped. "Landreau told me what happened. He saved your life!"

"Saved?" Nero scoffed. "He damned me, condemned me to life, and I curse him for it." Nero was pacing, ranting. "'Cursed be the day wherein I was born: let not the day wherein my mother bare me be blessed. Cursed be the man who brought tidings to my father, saying, A manchild is born unto thee. And let him hear the cry in the morning, and the shouting at noontide; because he slew me not from the womb; nor let my mother be my grave and her womb be always great with me. Wherefore came I forth out of the womb that my days should be consumed with sorrow?' Why is that, I want to know?"

Tears of rage and sorrow streamed from under Nero's coke-bottle glasses and flowed down the fatty ridges of his cheeks. He took off the glasses and ran a loose sleeve across his face. Then, as he glared at me, I could see into his eyes: wide, fearsomely deep eyes, bottomless eyes, the color of the lake on moonless nights.

They were Marian's eyes.

"Why couldn't Landreau just let it alone?" he sobbed. "Was it cowardice? Was it courage? No matter now. Either way, I am. Makes no difference whatever, for it is left to me to finish what Simeon Landreau did not. Tonight is the end for me, Mr. Wade. A sword pierced her heart also."

"You killed her! How could you have stabbed your own mother?"

"Marian Barclay, my mother? No! My mother loved me! I remember every day so clearly, every moment, every detail, just the two of us. She held me close when the lightning flashed at night and we counted seconds waiting for the thunder to crack above our heads, and I felt safe in her arms. **That** was my mother, not this woman. Marian Barclay, who was she? I never knew her. I never murdered her. She tried to kill me. It was self-defense!"

"You killed her!" I shouted.

"I did not kill her," he replied, quite self-composed. "Her death was suicide, pure and simple! Didn't she know that when you kill your own flesh and blood, you kill yourself?"

"What are you saying?" I demanded. "I don't understand your riddles!"

"Then, listen! I christened myself Nero, for I too have been twice washed in the blood. Do you know what Nero's mother said as she was about to die? She tore open her tunic and screamed, 'Strike me here, in the womb that bore the monster.'"

"Who? Marian? Marian said that?" I asked, confused.

"Her name is Agrippina, the breeder of monsters," Nero said, distracted. "She welcomed the knife. Invited it. 'Strike me here!' she said. Don't you understand? Agrippina died of her own will, by her own hand, when her son killed her. Nero's mother plunged the blade into herself, in trying to slay the monster. The woman died by the scalpel that was to kill me."

"Oh, Marian! " I cried out. "Marian!"

"No, no, leave her alone! Never summon back the dead," Nero exclaimed. "Let them rest in peace. At the cemetery I longed to crawl back into her warm grave, where I belong. I should have stayed there and never come out. But I heard an old man shouting, 'You poor blind idiot! Marian didn't LIKE you.' It's a wise son who knows his father. I heard the old man's bitter accusations, Mr. Wade, and I knew you for my sire and her killer!"

"Killer? You're insane! I loved her!"

"Did you love her when you abandoned us?"

"I didn't abandon you!" I exclaimed in protest.

"Did you love her when you forsook us and put the scalpel in the hand that ripped her belly open? Landreau's hand, her hand, mine, and, yes, it was your hand too that held the knife!"

"No! I didn't know! I knew nothing about it!"

"Ah, you didn't know!" Nero sat down on the dock bench, whispering in my ear with mocking, taunting sympathy. "All innocence, are you? And what was it that you didn't know, Mr. Evan Wade? You didn't know you were fucking her? You didn't know whether you were wearing a condom? You didn't know where monsters come from? What was it exactly that you didn't know?"

"I didn't know that you...existed," I said, searching desperately for the word. "I didn't know you were alive!"

"I am a dead man," Nero contemptuously replied. "I have neither father nor mother, and I was never born. I was exhumed. Better that her womb had remained my grave than that I should have come back to kill my own flesh and blood. The corpse should never have risen, but tonight is the night that will undo what should have been left undone. And you!"

"What do you want of me?" I pleaded.

"Why, Mr. Wade, I want to be sure you never again say, 'I didn't know.'" Nero turned away and began pulling the concrete blocks across the dock, tugging on the chain that held them together. The blocks rasped across the dock boards, cutting a white scar in the cedar. The chain glistened silver in the moonlight.

"What are you going to do, Nero? Please don't do this!" I struggled frantically against everything that was tying me down. To no avail. Somehow, the more I struggled against the ropes, the more securely they bound me.

"Did you ever just want to start all over, Mr. Wade," Nero asked reflectively, "simply erase it all and start over from the very beginning? That's all I want. Just to begin once more with a clean slate, undo all the tears and all the blood. Have you ever wanted that, Mr. Wade, just to return to your mother's womb and be born again?"

"Don't kill me, please, Nero! I don't want to die!"

"Of course you don't, Mr. Wade. But you will. Or maybe that's something else you didn't know, didn't realize twenty years ago, didn't remember even in the cemetery? Is that why you abandoned us? No legacy, no progeny required, because you didn't know you were going to die? After tonight, I promise you, you will never forget."

"Don't kill me!" I screamed, and screamed again, hoping to attract attention. But no boat motor came to life, no light came on in the cabins nearby.

"I considered that possibility," Nero replied with a kind of savage tranquility in his voice. "But I will not kill you. I don't need to. Instead, I have detained you here to watch the corpse return to the grave where it was conceived. You are privileged—or is it condemned?—to witness the blessed event, so you will never forget it."

I didn't have to ask what Nero was talking about, for he had begun tying the cement blocks to his own ankles, testing the chain, making sure it was fast. And I cried out, "No, Nero! You don't have to do it! Don't do this!"

"What I do tonight, Mr. Wade, is of no great moment to me," he said, "whatever it may be for you. My death is already accomplished. I am a dead man, a walking shadow, for killing your mother is like killing yourself. Can you understand that? The wench is dead, and in stabbing her, I stabbed myself. It was over long ago."

"No, Nero, we can make a new start, together. Together, Nero! Think of it, a new life, even now!"

Nero removed his glasses and placed them on the bench. He picked up the heavy blocks in his arms, and turning to me slowly, asked, "Is there new life for a dead man?"

I shouted "No!" meaning "Don't jump!" but before I could explain, a look of great sadness came into his eyes and he heaved himself off the dock.

The water was not deep there, just deep enough, and it was over quickly. There was no thrashing, no struggle for life. The waves gently covered him over, receiving him back into themselves. He floated quietly there, just below the surface, arms extended, seeming to stand on an underwater island, his hair waving gently in the currents of the moonlit lake.

So I watched my son die, as he intended. I tried to close my eyes, but as I sat there waiting hour after hour, I could not help but look on his body swaying there, arms outstretched just under the water's surface, as if beckoning me. And as I found myself capable of looking upon him more steadfastly, I saw myself underwater, too, embracing my son, pleading for another chance, begging his forgiveness and his mother's for what I had done and left undone. But in reply I heard only the whisper of waves breaking softly against the long lakeshore.

Epilogue

The sun rose slowly after that seemingly endless night, now long ago. I remember wishing dawn would never come. I remember dreading the light that would make us a spectacle for all the gawking world, with all their prying questions, their interrogations and recriminations. I wanted to stay sheltered in the darkness. But in the early morning grayness, just as the unwelcome sun peeked above the tree-lined eastern shore, old Werner Omdahl, trolling silently down the dock line, came upon a scene he little expected.

I was glad it was him. Werner never talked much anyway. That morning he said even less. Using his filet knife, he cut the rope that bound me, and with great effort we pulled Nero up out of the water onto the bank, dragging the blocks behind him. Werner glanced over at me, wondering, but silent.

"Better call the cops," I suggested.

"Yep," he said, and ambled off in the direction of the cabin, leaving me alone with Nero.

The silver chain around his ankles glistened with watery diamonds in the sunlight. It seemed indecent to me that he should lie there shackled. I wanted to free him from the blocks that still lay submerged just under the surface of the water. Fetching the bolt cutter from the shed, I knelt beside him. But then looking down at the knotted chains, I hesitated. He had bound himself by his own hand, after all. Who was I to say he was not free already, as free as he could ever be, more free with the chain than he could have ever been without it? So I left Nero lying there on the shore, staring open-eyed into the blazing autumn sun, still bound by the chains that freed him.

The local cops arrived first, sirens screaming; Queenie and the others from the Cities came more quietly that afternoon. I got no apology from Queenie, nor did I expect any. He took my statement and his people combed the property, finding little but a pair of useless coke-bottle glasses lying on the dock bench. I told them to check Nero's prints against the knife that killed Ben Drake. Both of them had left the conference and followed me to the Overdale clinic, no doubt, each for their own reasons. Where one was born, the other died.

It's been years now, since that time, but Nero was right. I never again said I didn't know, because I never forgot anything about the whole story. On warm July evenings like this one, I stand leaning on the deck rail of the cabin, watching the breeze ripple the surface of the lake, and I see Marian's long, olive-tan limbs flashing in the gleaming water, and flailing in her dark red blood. I see her eyes, fearsomely deep eyes, dark as drowning pools, and suddenly they become Nero's eyes, weeping, raging, accusing me inescapably of killing her. And him. I see my son standing chained under the water, arms outstretched, beckoning me to embrace him, and I am terrified.

These scenes were indelibly seared into my memory because it was my own death that I saw during that long night. For as I embraced him beneath the waves, Nero put his arms around me, and now, years later, he has not released me yet. I cannot get free of him. I do not want to.

I don't want to get free of Libby either, for in the weeks and months that followed, I came to realize that I couldn't live without the sunlight in her wayward hair, without the song in her heart. Even tonight, drawn away from the dark lake by Libby and the Beach Boys filling the brightly lit cabin behind me, I feel infused with her vitality, enlivened by the big-hearted joy of life that streams from her throat.

If you should ever leave me,
Though life would still go on, believe me,
The world could show nothing to me.
So what good would living do me?
God only knows what I'd be without you.

After she left me at the Radisson, I had no right to believe that anything remained of the fragile bond between us. She was independent, she was country strong, but whether she needed me or not, God knows I needed her, I loved her, and I said so. She knew I didn't say it lightly.

From the *STrib* and *Dispatch* she had learned most of what had happened to Nero. I told her the rest. What I didn't tell her, didn't have to tell her, I guess, was what happened to me. Libby understood without explanation that sometimes things can happen to people that change them utterly. A death, a birth, and suddenly you are transformed. Which of these had happened to me, then? I cannot say. And it doesn't matter, for I now know that their effect is the same.

In the little Currier and Ives church nestled among old-growth Norway pines, the Evan Wade who obligated himself to Libby Farina from that day forward merely looked like the man who had been dragged there months before. Why Libby married me I will not try to explain, except to say that, somehow, during that long night in which I came to embrace my son, something happened to me. I don't mean I became somebody different; rather, as Libby had once put it, I became the man she had loved all along, the one capable of loving her in return.

"Come on in, Evan," Libby calls out. "Dinner's on and we're just about ready."

The old lion's paw table needed an extra leaf to accommodate all the place settings round the steaming roast corn from the Farinas' garden and the fresh walleye that old Mr. Omdahl brought over for us.

"Mom and Dad," Libby says to her parents, pointing to the chairs on the end, "you're down there next to Mrs. Wade."

We fetch my Mom from Sacred Heart on most Sundays, always when we invite Libby's folks over. Mom's lucid intervals are growing fewer, but I don't dread them as I once did. They become more precious as more rare. But even on bad days, like today, when she sits quietly in her favorite rocker at the hearth, seeing little, saying less, she does not stare vacantly out the window, down the road that never brought Roy Macklin back. Now, almost involuntarily, her eyes follow the pudgy infant darting about on unsteady legs, running from the safety of the aromatic old couch toward his grandmother's thin but steady knees.

"Evan?" she asks, looking uncertainly at the boy, as Libby picks the child up and hugs him to her.

"Ned. It's Ned, Mom," I say. His name is Nathan, Nathan Charles Wade, son of Evan and Libby Wade. We call him Ned.

"Of course," Mom says, her gray eyes smiling against the gathering darkness. "It's Ned!"

And so it is.

So may it ever be. A family begins anew in the old family home on the dark lakeshore, making a fresh start amid ancient white pines and stately red oaks that bow and wave to successive generations in the brisk night wind.

THE END

0-595-19956-9

92450380R00147

Made in the USA
Lexington, KY
04 July 2018